UNMASKED

UNMASKED

HOWARD K. POLLACK

STONESONG
DIGITAL

This is a work of fiction. All of the characters, organizations, and events portrayed in this novel are either products of the author's imagination or are used fictitiously.

Stonesong Digital LLC
Cover design by Erica Simone

epub ISBN: 978-1-7362059-9-0
paperback ISBN: 979-8-9862718-0-4

First Edition: 2022

10 9 8 7 6 5 4 3 2 1

Prologue

WHEN SHE ARRANGED TO meet her old friend and attorney, Xander Van Buren, Layni Bingham had no idea that this would be her last day alive. She was looking forward to seeing him for a little comfort and chatting with someone she trusted, someone who truly cared for her. Beyond that, she wasn't thinking about life and death.

Tourist season was in full swing in downtown St. Petersburg. All the shops were open and buzzing with customers, and the tables at the street cafés along Beach Drive were filled with people. Xander Van Buren arrived at The Birchwood Restaurant and took a table outside to enjoy the lunch scene. He hadn't seen Layni Bingham in quite some time, and he truly looked forward to seeing her.

He watched her as she walked up the street. She had aged well but was no longer the prom queen and spunky cheerleader he had fallen in love with so many years ago. He couldn't help himself, but he still saw her with his schoolboy eyes from close to twenty-five years back. To him she still looked like the gorgeous girl he fell in love with, but that was all in the past. He waved when she got close. "Layni, over here." He pulled the chair out for her. "Please, sit down. How are you?"

"Thank you. I'm doing fine, just feeling a bit apprehensive these days and I had this urge to give you a call and see you. It's been too long."

"Yes, it has been, and you know, it's always great to see you and catch up."

"Agreed."

The two spent some time exchanging pleasantries and bringing each other up to date about their lives. Then, after a time, Layni fell silent and began staring off into the distance. Xander gave her a few moments before speaking.

"Layni, is something else on your mind? You seem distracted."

"Well . . ." She hesitated and took a breath, "I've been wrestling with something for a while, and at first, I really didn't want to burden you with this, but after much thought I decided that you were the only one I could trust. But at the same time, I didn't want to get you too involved, so before I begin, I need reassurance from you that if I give you something to hold for me, that you will not tell anyone about it, no matter what. And you must give it back to me, and only me, not to anyone else."

"This sounds very mysterious. What is it that you want me to hold on to?"

"It's a thumb drive," Layni whispered. "It's password protected and encrypted, so you won't be able to open it up, but it contains very valuable information."

"I see. Well, as your attorney, anything you do, say, or give to me is confidential, so you needn't worry about secrecy. It's what I do." He sat back in his chair. "Does your husband know about this?"

"No, Doug would literally kill me if I told anyone about this, let alone you. He's away on business, and I have no intention of telling him about our meeting today."

"Layni, perhaps you should tell me a bit more about this. It's starting to sound serious. If you do, I'll be in a better position to help you."

"No, that's okay, the less you know the better. The most important thing is to make sure the thumb drive doesn't get in the wrong hands, and since no one will know you have it, it will make me feel much better. And when things blow over, I will come back and get it."

PART ONE

PART ONE

Chapter 1

AWAKENED BY THE FAINT vibration beneath his pillow, Detective Lance Dornhuber rolled over, slipped his hand underneath the pillow, and pulled out his cell phone. Looking at the time, he shook the grog from his head and sat up. *Nine-thirty, shit, overslept again. Mental note, stop drinking.*

"Dorny here. What's up captain?" He climbed out of bed and walked towards the bathroom.

"We've got bodies and one of the vics is from a very prominent family. I need you to investigate ASAP." Captain Kroger cleared his throat. "And you need to keep it quiet. This one can't get out, at least not yet."

"Sure thing," Dorny said, "You got any details?"

"Murder scene is over on Snell Isle, Brightwaters Boulevard. Big mansion on the water. Wife of some real rich dude killed in her bed sometime last night. I'll text you the address. Eddie is over there now."

"Gimme fifteen, I'll be on my way."

Sporting a two-day beard, Dorny soaped and wiped his pits and sprayed a fog of deodorant under each, dabbed cologne behind his ears, pulled his underwear out at the top and fogged his crotch.

That'll work. Another day, another spray. He smiled into the mirror, then frowned at the lines on his forehead that seemed to grow deeper every day. *Mental note, take a shower tonight.*

Ten minutes later, Dorny was headed down 22nd Avenue North towards Snell Isle in his '05 Toyota Camry. When he came to the waterfront, he shook his head. He never could get used to seeing how the other half lived. Coffee Pot Bayou and the houses all around it were gorgeous. This part of St. Petersburg was home to the very wealthy. Sports figures, celebrities, doctors, and lawyers all owned houses there. The properties by the bridge, while beautiful, didn't hold a candle to the mansions on Tampa Bay.

Once he crossed over the small overpass onto the Isle, he breezed past the statues of panthers, lions, and griffins that adorned Snell Isle Boulevard. He headed towards the Renaissance Vinoy Golf Course, a private club that catered to the ultrarich. Following the GPS on his phone, Dorny turned on to a side street and found his way to Brightwaters Boulevard. His eyes practically popped out of their sockets as he drove along the Boulevard. Sprawling mansions surrounded by finely manicured lawns stood majestically behind tall palms that swayed in the breeze. "How do you get to be this fucking rich?" he asked himself out loud.

Pulling up to the gate, he saw Detective Eddie Rumson, a short, portly fellow with a receding hairline standing in the drive talking to a gray-bearded old man in a paint-stained cap, a white T-shirt and shorts. Dorny hopped out of the car.

"Come on up, Dorny," Eddie said, waving his hand. The old man gave him a quick nod of the head as he approached.

"Who's this?" Dorny asked, thumbing at the old man.

"Jimmy Jenkins." The old man said.

Eddie cut him off and pointed. "He was working across the street, in the little park over there."

"Yeah, I was cleaning and painting the panther statue a little ways over, and I look up and the maid comes a runnin' out the house, screaming and cryin'." Jenkins recounted eagerly. "I trot over and she tells me the Missus is dead in her bed, along with someone else. So, I follow her into the house, and she takes me up to the bedroom and shows me. Shit, I ain't never seen a dead body before, let alone two in one place. Holes right in the middle of their foreheads, dead as can be."

"You been here long?" Dorny asked.

"About forty years or so."

"No, uh, I mean here, working on the statue."

"Oh, shit, sorry, I thought you meant . . ."

Dorny interrupted, "It's ok. When did you get here today?"

"I started working about an hour ago."

"You see anyone go in or out of the house since you've been here?" Dorny asked.

"Not a one, other than the maid. Like I said."

"Okay, I'm gonna ask you not to speak to anyone about anything that you've seen or heard. You're now a material witness to a serious crime, and we can't have you talking to the press, or anyone else. It may put you in danger. You understand?"

"Gotcha, boss." Jenkins nodded his head rapidly.

"And we're gonna have some more questions for you, so give me your contact info and don't disappear." Dorny turned to Eddie, "All right, where's the maid?"

"Carter's got her inside. She's real broken up. I wanted to call an ambulance for her, but the captain said we needed to keep it quiet, so I figured I'd wait for you."

Dorny said, "Anyone else here?"

"Not yet. CSI is on the way. There is a butler, but he was off last night, and the maid said he didn't come home, as far as she knew."

"Okay, let's go inside. I want to see the scene and get some first impressions, before the CSI crew get here."

The two men walked through massive wooden double doors that Dorny thought looked like they came from a castle somewhere in England. The entryway was grand, the ceilings at least 30 feet high, with two winding staircases, one on each side, leading up to a balcony. Straight ahead, through another set of French doors, sunshine glittering off the water shone through floor to ceiling windows.

"A little small for my taste," Dorny said, gazing up at the chandelier hanging between the two staircases.

Eddie smiled, "Ya think?"

The bedroom where the bodies had been found was upstairs, tucked far away down a long corridor. It too was huge, with high ceilings, a complete sitting room off to the left, and to the right, off in the distance, another set of open double doors exposing a closet larger than Dorny's apartment. Against the far wall, flanked by two floor to ceiling windows was an oversized bed. Propped up on pillows, looking almost alive except for the holes in their heads, sat two women.

Dorny and Eddie put on latex gloves and approached the bed, careful not to touch anything or otherwise compromise the scene. "Were they found like that, Eddie? Sitting up so prim and proper, naked breasts exposed?"

"Yup, posed. Maid said she found them in the bed there but didn't realize they had been shot until she got close."

"Ok, who is who?"

"Layni Bingham is the one on the right."

"Any idea who the other one is?"

"Maid hadn't seen her before, and I haven't had a chance to look around for ID or personal effects."

"Ok, do that," Dorny said as he examined the wound on Mrs. Bingham. "Small caliber, probably a .22, almost no blood." He gently raised the covers to reveal the rest of the body. "Naked all the way down, Eddie."

Eddie nodded and continued searching the room. Dorny walked around the bed and lifted the covers again. "She's naked too. Wonder if we've got a jealous husband thing going on here. This one looks personal. Other than that, this place is clean as a whistle. No sign of a struggle. They musta been surprised as they slept. Any idea where the man of the house is?"

"Maid said he's away on business—been gone since Monday. Oh, and check out the closet, there's a safe inside. No sign of forced entry. Looks like it must have been opened with the combination. The safe was ripped apart inside, and all the contents that are left are spilled out on the floor. You gotta see this safe man, it's like 5 feet tall and looks like it would withstand an explosion."

Dorny looked inside from the doorway. "Hard to believe the motive was robbery with two bodies positioned like that?"

"Seems like it. If it was a robbery there would be no reason to kill them, let alone to prop them up like that."

Dorny said, "Who knows, maybe the perp is an opportunist, two naked women in bed gets him going, so he kills one, because he can't handle two and have his way, then rapes the other, kills her and puts them both in a pose, for entertainment value, while he raids the safe."

"Could be," Eddie said, "but how'd he open the safe?"

"Good question. Maybe he coaxed the combination out of Bingham before he shot her? Probably told her he wouldn't kill her if she gave it up, then he shot her anyway."

"Real nice guy, huh."

"Well, this one has scandal written all over it," Dorny said, "but we'll have to see what CSI comes up with. Let's go talk to the maid."

The two men walked down the stairs and all the way across the house, which seemed like a five-minute walk, exited to the back from a breezeway past the kitchen, and made their way to the maid's quarters.

Inside, Carter was still consoling the maid, who sat on her bed, stoop-shouldered, hands covering each other in her lap. Her face looked drawn and pale, and her eyes were red from crying. Behind it all, she was still a striking girl, not more than twenty-seven years old and gorgeous. She had long dark hair, soft brown eyes, and a matching tan.

Dorny approached silently, looked at Carter and nodded. Eddie stood behind and a few feet away. "So, Carter, what has she told you so far?"

"Not much, Dorny. She's really beside herself, and in shock. Basically, she says she made her way upstairs just after nine, as she does every day, and the door to the bedroom was already open. She saw the two vics in bed and at first didn't realize they were dead, so she was very embarrassed. She called out but got no response. As she got closer, she saw what she thought was a mark on their foreheads and called out again. When she didn't get any answer, she went to the bed, and that's when she realized it was bullet holes. She screamed and ran out of the house and was met by the old guy out front."

"Okay, I'll take over from here. Thanks, Carter. Please go out front and when CSI gets here bring them upstairs, and we'll meet you up there when we're done." Dorny turned to the maid and said softly, "I'm so sorry for your loss." He took her hand in his. "But I'm going to need to ask you a few questions. Will that be all right?"

She nodded and sniffled.

Dorny released her hand. "First, what is your name?"

In accented English, she said, "Yolanda Estevez, but please, call me Yoli."

"All right, Yoli. How long have you worked here?"

"It will be two years this summer."

"Do you know who the second woman was in the bed?"

"I never see her before."

"Okay, can you tell me who lives here in the house?"

"Mr. B and Missy B. That's what I call them."

"Anyone else?"

Yoli said, "Well, in the main house, Miss Ashley come around sometimes, but only when Mr. B is home. And Mr. Darryl, he lives in the other room down the hall from me. He works here too, but not yesterday."

"What does he do?"

"He cooks, make food, and serves. I clean house and do laundry."

"Okay, and why wasn't Mr. Darryl here yesterday?"

"He had day off since Mr. B away, and Missy B no want to be bothered or have dinner."

"And who is Miss Ashley?"

"She Mr. B's daughter, not Missy B's. But she not come around for at least a month."

"I see, and so where were you last night?"

"In here. Missy B no let me in house after nine at night, until nine in morning."

"Is that normal?" Dorny asked.

"Yes, always like that. They want privacy and we no allow in house after nine o'clock at night."

"So, they were very strict?"

"*Sí*—uh, yes. Mr. B very important man. He no want me in same room with them, so if they in kitchen, I leave. If they in den, I leave."

"Do you like working here?"

"*Sí*—uh, so sorry, yes. My English not so good, sometimes I forget. I do like work here. Nice place, clean and big, very beautiful. I come from Cuba, and we very poor there, so this very nice here."

"Good, okay. Did you hear any noises, maybe even gunshots?"

"No, I don't hear anything in house from here. Very quiet."

"Well, do you know when the other woman came to the house?"

"I leave house just before nine at night and Missy B was all alone."

"Does she ever have company when Mr. B is not home?"

"Sometimes lady friends come at night, drink wine and play music, but then I leave house earlier on days like that."

"Does Mr. B go away often?"

"He important man, he go away a lot."

"Do you know what he does?"

"Oh no, he very private."

"I see, so tell me what happened this morning from the time you woke up."

"Every morning is same. I wake up, shower, dress, and go in house at nine in the morning to make bed and clean room, then I clean house and do laundry."

"You clean every day?"

"Very big house, I clean some rooms some day and other rooms other days, take me five days to clean house. I no work on weekend."

"So, you went upstairs at nine today. Then what happened?"

"I see door to bedroom open, usual not open, so I call out for Missy B and she no answer."

"Go on."

"*Sí*, so I walk in and see Missy B and other lady in bed. I call out, no answer. I come close and see hole in head. I scream and run outside." She started crying again and wiped her eyes with the cleaning cloth that hung from the waist of her maid's uniform.

"I'm sorry, just a few more questions—and this may be difficult, but I need to know—did you touch anything in the room when you came in?"

"No'"

"Did you see or clean any blood?"

"No, no clean blood."

"Okay, now I guess you know there is a safe in the closet?" Dorny asked.

"*Sí*, big safe."

"Do you know if it is often left open?"

"No, safe always closed. I usual go in and straighten closet and put away clothes after laundry."

"I see. Well, do you have any relatives who live nearby?"

"No, I all alone, my family lives in Cuba, I send them money."

"What about friends? Any friends that you can stay with?"

"No, no friends—just Mr. Darryl. He nice man."

"Just one more question—do you ever leave the premises?"

"Sometimes on weekend I go downtown."

"How do you get there?"

"I have bicycle, and sometimes Mr. Darryl take me, he has car, or I walk to bus over bridge and go."

"I see, last thing, do you have Mr. B's phone number to reach him?"

"*Sí*—it in kitchen in drawer by fridgerator." Yoli looked lost and confused. "What going to happen now?"

"We will call him and tell him what has happened."

"So what I do now?"

"Just stay here in your room until he arrives. Are you okay with that?"

"I think so. *Gracias*, uh, thank you."

Dorny offered an awkward smile, then turned to Eddie who had been quietly taking notes of the entire conversation. "Let's head out front and start digging."

Eddie turned and the two went back into the main house. "Well, what do you think Dorny?" Eddie asked.

"Hard to say, and while she doesn't seem to be hiding anything, I have to wonder why our vic would hire a hot-looking, young Latina to clean house. Makes you wonder who really did the hiring."

"I see your point."

"Yeah, and I also want to check out their security, see if there's any cameras and how the lock works on the gate. Maybe we'll get lucky and find some video footage of someone approaching the house."

"Good idea," Eddie said, "I did notice that the gate was closed but not locked when I got here. All I had to do was press the green button on the keypad and it opened."

"Weak security for a mansion like this, don't you think?"

"Now that you mention it."

Once outside, the men saw the CSI truck parked in the drive. Dorny said, "We didn't even hear them pull up or come into the house. I can see how Yoli didn't hear anything from her quarters."

"Makes sense."

Dorny perused the front entranceway and spotted a camera up high on a corner facing down at the doorway and another at the gate focused on the area where the keypad was located. "There you go Eddie," Dorny pointed, "now let's find out where the footage is stored?"

"Don't you want to wait for Mr. Bingham? Shouldn't we call him first?"

"Absolutely not. Until we know for sure he isn't involved, I'd like to do my own reconnaissance. C'mon, you know when a spouse is found dead, the first suspect is always the other spouse."

"But he wasn't around."

"And you based that on what? A story from a hot Latina maid."

"You've got a dirty mind; do you know that Dorny? Just because she looks good doesn't make Mr. Bingham a fiend."

"Yeah well, I've been at this for way too long to let anything slip by me, so between us, until we can fully confirm his alibi, he remains a suspect."

"Understood."

Once back inside, Eddie located a closet near the front entrance, opened the door and found a cache of electronics, a computer with blinking lights and a flat screen. "Check this out, Dorny— looks like a sophisticated set up, and it's definitely operational. We should get our tech person in here to figure it all out—it looks kinda complicated, and I wouldn't want to mess it up and accidentally erase anything."

"Copy that. See if one of our crew working upstairs can come down and figure this out. I'll go in the kitchen and get that phone number."

✳ ✳ ✳

The CSI team was already hard at work collecting evidence when Eddie walked into the bedroom. The bodies looked eerily calm sitting up in bed. They actually looked like they were watching the television, but for the holes in their heads. The crew worked around them. Ken Taylor, the senior CSI had just finished dusting the mahogany headboard.

"Looks like we've got a clear set of prints near vic one," Taylor said. "Full palm and all five fingers of a right hand." He looked over to his assistant, Jake Dalton, who was examining the carpet around the bed. "Jake, do me a favor and take prints of this vic's right hand so we can match or eliminate."

Dalton went over to his kit and pulled out the necessary equipment while Taylor continued examining the headboard.

"Sorry to interrupt, people," Eddie said. "But we need one of you to help with reviewing the security tapes from the cameras out front. We found a closet with a computer and hardware that looks to be up and running."

Taylor called out to Jenny Jones, who was in the closet examining the safe, "Jenny, you're our tech guru—go see what you can do for these guys."

"On it, boss," Jenny said and followed Eddie out the door.

Officer Carter, a tall, dark-haired cop, still bucking for detective status, had been standing by silently and followed behind, feeling a bit useless at the crime scene. His skill set was of better use on the street, canvassing for witnesses and interviewing them.

❋ ❋ ❋

Jenny had the recorder up and running in short order and rewound it to the day before. The video showed the mailman deliver mail at 2:15 P.M. and a FedEx delivery at 3:10 P.M. At 3:15 P.M., Layni Bingham arrived home, took in the mail and the FedEx package. At 9:20 P.M. the unknown woman approaches the house, the door opens, and she walks right in. No one else came or left for the rest of the night until the next morning at 9:15 A.M. when Yoli is seen running from the house and Jenkins meets her just past the gate, The two speak for a few seconds and then head back inside in a hurry.

"Well that rules out any entry from the front of the house," Dorny said. "Can you tell if there's a camera that covers the rear of the house by the water?"

Jenny continued scrolling. "I've got another one labeled 'waterfront' but it looks like that camera is either off or broken, no footage is available."

"Figures," said Dorny, "Let's go take a look at the backyard area and see if we can find anything there—thanks, Jenny, you can get back to doing your thing upstairs. We'll handle this."

Five minutes later, Dorny, Eddie, and Carter found themselves in a palatial setting overlooking Tampa Bay. A gigantic free-form pool with a walkway over the center of it took up half the yard. On one side was a large hot tub, on the other side there was a grotto with a waterfall spilling down over it. Nearby was a sunken bar with four swim up stools sitting in the water. An eighty-foot yacht was anchored at the dock. The three men stood speechless for a beat as they took in the scenery.

"Holy shit, man!" Carter said. "This place is sweeter than anything I've ever seen."

"Keep saving, son," Dorny said, "Maybe in your second lifetime, you'll be able to afford this kinda luxury."

"What a spread!" Eddie said, as he took in the view. "I mean, come on, there's just one couple living here."

"Don't forget the maid and butler," Dorny said.

"Yeah, right," Carter said, "and I bet they aren't even allowed in the pool."

"Okay guys, put your eyes back in their sockets and your tongues back in your mouths and find the security cameras. I'll head over to the waterfront."

The three men separated and scoured the area. Carter took the left side of the yard and Eddie took the right, while Dorny made his way over to the water and began examining the yacht. He climbed aboard and put his latex gloves on again, checked the sliding glass door leading into the salon. It was unlocked, so he went inside. The fridge was stocked with food, beer, and soda; the bar was stocked with top shelf liquor; and the pantry was full of cans, boxes of food, bags of chips, and all manner of goodies. Under the sink he found a trash pail and rummaged through it, found a bag from McDonald's with the remnants of a Big Mac, fries, and a Coke. Dorny smelled the contents, observing *Still a fresh odor, this food must have been eaten within the past twelve hours, or less. A Big Mac, on a yacht? There's something wrong with this picture.*

He walked further into the ship and opened the door to the main suite. The bed was unmade, and a towel lay on the floor at the foot of the bed. *Someone's been sleeping in my bed, said Papa bear, and using the shower too. Forensics, here we come.*

Dorny looked out the starboard-side window, not a porthole but a full-size window. He could see the faint line of Tampa across the bay. It was quite bright out and the sun's rays bounced brightly across the calm water. He then turned to the port-side window, which had a clear view up to the bedroom windows of the crime scene. He spent another five minutes inside the ship, then exited and strolled around the dock looking for more clues. Finally, he returned to the pool area to rejoin Eddie and Carter.

"Well, boys, I think we have another crime scene on the boat. Gonna need CSI to take a look."

"What'dya find there?" asked Eddie.

"Looks like someone stayed on that yacht last night, maybe waiting for our vics to settle in. But the other crime is the fast-food bag from McDonald's. I mean, who stays on a yacht and eats that crap anyway? He should be arrested for that alone. Me, I'd be having champagne and caviar."

"That may say something about the person who was on board," said Carter. "Probably not a well-bred rich fuck."

Grinning, Dorny said, "Good point, son. That'll narrow the suspect list."

"On another note," Eddie interjected and pointed, "there's a security camera up in the corner. Looks like it may at one time have been focused on the main doorway leading into the house, now it's pointed down directly at the ground—no good visual angle there at all."

"More lax security out back," Dorny said. "It makes no sense. I mean, you got all this wealth exposed right out on the water and no real security to speak of. I'd have had a goddam electric fence, a sharpshooter posted on the roof, and a couple of guard dogs."

"That's because you're paranoid, Dorny," Eddie said, "and being a cop for twenty years will do that to ya."

"I guess . . . but anyway, I'm thinking that whoever stayed on this boat may be our killer. Perfect set up. He hangs out on the yacht, eats his Big Mac, and watches through the window until the lights go out and our vics are asleep, then he sneaks in and kills them, cleans out the safe and leaves the way he came."

"So, you're saying this guy came by boat?" Carter asked.

"Probably," Dorny said. "Best guess, he comes with a rowboat, no engine, nice and quiet; then he ties up beside the yacht where no one can see it. He enjoys the rich life for a few hours, takes care of business, and he's gone like the wind."

Eddie nodded his head. "Hey, Dorny, you think the perp knew there were two women up there?"

"Good question. Maybe that's what surprised him, and why he had to kill them. We're still at square one. Let's gets the CSI crew in here too and see if our perp left us any presents."

※ ※ ※

Dorny sent Carter out to locate the closest McDonald's to see if they had any security footage from last night and if anyone who worked there could recall anyone odd or out of place. Not that it would be easy to pick out a guy who ordered a Big Mac meal from a crowd of Big Mac fans, but it *was* a lead.

Back in the bedroom, the crew were still working away at the crime scene when Dorny and Eddie returned.

"Find anything interesting, Taylor?" Dorny asked.

"Still digging, but one thing for sure, the fingerprints on the headboard are neither of our vics', and from the shape and size, I think we're looking at a female. I understand we've got a maid who found the body. We need to get her fingerprints."

"Okay," said Dorny, "Eddie can take one of you down to her apartment and print her. Just go easy on her, she's been through a lot."

Taylor looked at Jake. "Why don't you do that while we finish up here."

Dorny asked, "When is the ME going to arrive? We need the bodies examined ASAP."

"ME should be here momentarily."

"Good, because we've got another crime scene you guys need to look at."

"Another one, where?" said Taylor.

"Yacht out back, looks like the perp may have spent some time in the master suite dining in style. May have even taken a shower. Should be some good forensics in there."

"Okay, we'll get to it once we finish up here."

Jenny finished up in the closet and came back into the bedroom. "Check this out, when I opened the top drawer in the night table beside the bed, this piece of paper fell out from underneath the drawer. It's the combination to the safe. I just tried it and it works. Looks like it was taped to the underside of the drawer, and maybe the perp found it, used it, and tried to tape it back up, but he didn't do a good job of it."

"Nice find, Jen," Dorny said. "Keep digging and let me know if you find anything on the yacht. Eddie, I need you to take a ride over to the marina on Snell Isle Boulevard and talk to the guys that work there. Maybe you can get a line on that rowboat. In this neighborhood, it would seem that a lone rowboat on the water at night might be noticed. Get a list of everyone at that marina who owns one."

"Roger, Dorny."

"And while you're doing that, I'll call Mr. Bingham."

"You gonna tell him about the other woman?"

"Not right away. I think I'll spring that on him when we meet in person."

** ** **

Dorny made his way back to the pool area, sat down on a lounge chair under a foxtail palm, took a deep breath of ocean air, and punched in the number for Douglas Bingham.

Three rings later a cheery voice answered, "You've got Doug, who's this?"

"Detective Lance Dornhuber, St. Petersburg Police."

"Excuse me, did you say 'detective'?" Bingham's voice suddenly lost its bright tone.

"Yes sir, I did, and I am very sorry to have to report to you that there's been a murder at your home."

Now panicked and standing at the foot of the bed in his hotel room, Bingham looked over at the sleeping body that lay beneath the covers. "Uh, what, a murder? Who, when, how did this happen?"

"I'm very sorry, Mr. Bingham, it's your wife."

"That can't be, I just spoke to her last night, she was fine. This is a joke, right?"

"No sir, I don't joke about murders."

Bingham sat down on the bed and let out a heavy sigh. "Mr. Bingham, are you still there?"

"Uh . . . yes, just hold on, I need a minute."

"I understand. Please try to stay calm, take it easy, I'll stay right with you." Dorny could make out the faint sound of a man crying, then a few deep breaths. "Are you still with me, sir?"

A few more seconds of silence, then, his voice choking up, Bingham said, "I'm still here detective. Can you tell me what happened?"

"We're going to need you to come home right away."

"Of course, but please, what happened?"

"Sir, we're still in the beginning stages of the investigation, but preliminarily, she was found in the bedroom with a bullet wound to her head."

Alarmed and in a high-pitched voice, he shouted into the phone, "She was shot? When? No! This can't be true." The body beneath the covers began to move and a young girl poked her head out and looked up. Bingham put his index finger to his lips and shook his head from side to side.

"I'm sorry, but it is. I promise you we will figure this out. It happened sometime last night, or early this morning. Until the medical examiner can do his job, we won't be able to narrow down the time frame beyond that."

Even more distraught, "Medical examiner? Nooo, this can't be happening, there must be some kind of mistake. Are you sure its Layni?"

"We are sir. She was in bed and your maid identified her."

"In bed!" Bingham shouted. "She was shot in bed? This is insane."

"I know this is difficult, and I wish I could have told you in person, but I wanted you to know as soon as possible. Now, how soon do you think you can get back home? We are going to have a lot of questions, and we will need your help trying to piece this all together."

Bingham was shaking his head. "I'll be there as soon as I can. I've got a jet at the local airport; I just need to call and get my crew on it."

"Very good, and please come directly to the station. Do not go back to your home right now. It's a crime scene, and until CSI is done with it, you can't go there."

Visibly perturbed, Bingham shouted into the phone. "What! My own home, I can't go to my own home? I need to go there! I need to see Layni! This is wrong, very wrong."

"Sir, by the time you arrive, she will have been taken to the coroner's office for further examination."

"Look, you probably don't know who I am! So, I suggest you contact Mayor Sandoval. He'll vouch for me. I don't want anyone touching my wife's body until I see her! Do you understand me?"

"I hear you sir. We will do what we can under the law, but please understand that the longer we wait to examine her, the more difficult it will be to determine exactly what happened?"

"I thought you said she was shot?"

"Yes, but most important is time of death. It will help us to narrow things down."

"Whatever, just don't touch her till I get there." Bingham clicked off the phone and placed it on the bed. He paced around the room for a few minutes then headed into the bathroom and took a shower.

Dorny wondered whether this was a truly heart-stricken husband who said all the right things and sounded shocked and upset, or an Oscar-worthy performance. The phone, though, was not the best way to gauge a person's guilt or innocence. He really needed to meet Bingham in person, so he could ask him the tough questions and see his reactions face to face. That would have to wait until he returned to St. Petersburg. *A jet, huh? Must be nice.*

Dorny sat in the shade of the palm making notes and taking pictures with his phone. He wasn't sure if the pictures were for the case or for his own personal torture. He knew he'd never be rich, nor would he ever own a yacht, let alone a rowboat, but it wouldn't stop him from dreaming of the good life. *Mental note, buy some lottery tickets.*

Chapter 2

BINGHAM ARRIVED AT THE airport an hour after the call from Dorny. His jet was fueled and ready for takeoff. He raced up the steps and ordered the pilot to take him back to Albert Whitted Airport in St. Petersburg as quickly as possible. It was a small airport used primarily for private planes and small jets. The runways were too short for commercial flights, and the place was not equipped with much in the way of security. It catered mostly to the leisure class and small businesses but was conveniently located just five minutes from downtown St. Petersburg.

Once in the air, Bingham punched in a number on his cell. "Mayor, it's Doug Bingham, I need your help."

"Hello Doug," came from the voice on the other end of the phone. "You sound stressed, what's up?"

"It's Layni, she's been killed—"

"What? For real? By who? When?"

"Slow down, yes, for real. I don't have all the details, I'm actually on my way home, but she was found dead, shot in bed."

"Oh no! That's horrible, I'm so sorry. If there's anything I can do to help—"

"Yeah, well, there is. Do you know a Detective Dornhuber over in St. Petersburg Police Department?

"Name sounds familiar, but I don't know him personally. Why?"

"Well, he's at my house now and they want to take Layni's body—shit, I can't believe I'm really saying that—'Layni's body'—it sounds so surreal, but he wants to take her to the coroner's office to examine her. I need you to intercede. I don't want them cutting her up and doing all kinds of tests on her."

"I don't know Doug, I'm not sure I have the power to do something like that, and even if I did, it doesn't sound right. I mean, why wouldn't you want her examined?"

"Look, they said she was shot, so they obviously know how she died. Why would they need to cut her open and defile her body? I won't allow it! You've got to do something!"

"Hey, I get it, but this is something that is out of my control, and if I were to even make the call, it wouldn't sound right and could be misconstrued. I can't afford to get in the middle of a murder and a police investigation right now—it's an election year."

"Screw your damn politics, Jason, I was there for you and helped you get elected the first time. Have you forgotten all the money I poured into your campaign and the two thousand dollar a plate dinner I threw for you at my home?"

"No, I haven't forgotten; but you got something out of it too, didn't you? So, let's not discuss this on the phone any longer. I feel terrible for your loss, just please don't bring this up again, and I'll forget we ever had this conversation."

"I won't forget this, Sandoval." Bingham clicked off the phone and tossed it on the table without saying goodbye. *Lousy politicians, only there for you when they need your money. Screw him, he can damn well forget re-election.*

He pushed the call button and a slender blonde emerged from the rear cabin. "Do me a favor Tara, pour me a Chivas, neat, make it a double, and bring me some water. I don't feel much like eating right now."

"Of course." Sweet smile. "Will there be anything else while I'm here?"

"As a matter of fact, I think I'd like a massage, can you change your outfit and bring me a robe as well?"

"Absolutely, let me get your drink first. I'll be right back."

❀ ❀ ❀

Two hours later, Bingham climbed into the seat of his recently acquired Aston Martin DB11 and raced to his home. *Did that detective really think I would just show up at the police station?* In ten minutes, he was through the gate and at his front door. Police caution tape covered the entrance and a sign read: CRIME SCENE, DO NOT ENTER. He pulled the tape off the door, inserted his key, and proceeded through the doorway. He bolted up the stairs and found another line of tape across the door to the bedroom. He ripped the tape and ran immediately to the closet safe, which was now closed. After a sigh of relief, he spun the combination and pulled it open. "Fuck!" He cursed aloud to himself. *The asshole detective didn't mention the safe was robbed.*

He began taking inventory but knew right away that it was gone. Blind rage. Shoes flying. More curses. After a ten-minute rant, he slammed the safe shut, turned, slid down and propped his back up against it and cried. Not tears for his wife, but rather tears for the contents of the safe.

After a time, Bingham's phone rang. No caller ID. "Hello, who is this?"

A deep, gravelly voice replied, "You have what we want, and if we don't get it immediately, there will be more fatalities."

"What are you talking about? Did you kill my wife?"

"No more games. We will be in touch." The line went dead.

Bingham was perplexed. *If they killed Layni then they also took the thumb drive from the safe. So why would they still be looking for it? This makes no sense. I need time to figure this out, but I have to get to the police first.*

✳ ✳ ✳

Bingham gathered himself up, made his way to police headquarters and entered looking for Detective Dornhuber. He was ushered into a small room with a large mirror. He'd seen these types of rooms on television before and knew the mirror was two-way. He sat for a few minutes, until the door opened.

"Mr. Bingham, I'm Detective Dornhuber. First off, I want to say I am very sorry for your loss."

"Thank you, Detective. Now what can you tell me so far?"

"At this time, I don't have a lot to tell you. Our crime scene team is evaluating the evidence collected at your home and hopefully that will lead to more concrete conclusions. All I can say right now is that it appears that the motive was robbery. Your safe was found open and apparently ransacked, but you'll need to give us a full inventory, so we can make a better evaluation. So, once we finish up here, I will escort you to your home and we can look inside so you can write me a list of missing contents."

"Look Detective, whatever may or may not be missing, I couldn't give a fuck about it." He raised his voice and made it quiver. "My wife is dead, and I can't even wrap my head around that yet, so give me a fucking break! Whatever money or jewelry was in that safe can be replaced. Layni can't. And I want to know who did this." His voice even higher now, "Do you get me?"

"Loud and clear, sir. My apologies again. Let's just try to calm down and work together here; perhaps you have information that you aren't aware could help us figure out who did this and why?"

"First, I want to see Layni. Can you take me to her?"

"I'm sorry but I can't do that right now. She is being examined."

"I thought I told you not to touch her!"

"Again, sir, it is not my call, and we need to get the bullet out. It could help to lead us to the killer."

"I'll have your badge, Detective!" shouted Bingham. "That's my wife you're cutting up, without my permission."

"Please try to calm down. I understand your anger, but you're not making this any easier. If you want to help us get to the bottom of this, I am going to need your cooperation."

Bingham stood and began pacing behind the table, looking up at the mirror every few seconds. After a time, he stopped, turned, and placed his hands on the back of the chair, leaning toward Dornhuber and speaking more calmly. "Okay, Detective, how can I help?"

"Thank you. So, I'm told you've been out of town since Monday. When exactly did you leave and where did you go?"

"Wait a second, I thought you wanted my help? What does where I went and when have to do with anything?"

"Look, these are routine questions I have to ask. We need to eliminate you as a suspect."

"A suspect? You think I'm a suspect?"

"No sir, I didn't say that. I said we need to eliminate you as a suspect."

"Well, for whatever it's worth, I don't appreciate this line of questioning, but I left Monday morning around ten. I took my jet to Texas for business and spent Monday and Tuesday there and returned today, after you called me."

"Ok, I'll need a copy of your pilot's flight plans. Now where did you stay?"

"The Ritz-Carlton in Dallas."

"Were you with anyone who can vouch for your whereabouts?"

"I'm sure people at the hotel should be able to."

"What about your business meetings, anyone from there who can verify?"

"Look, my business is private, and I am not going to provide you with that information. I don't need my business associates involved in my personal life. You can check with the hotel, I'm sure they will have records of me being there."

"Very well, sir, we will do that. Now you mentioned on the phone that you had spoken to your wife on Tuesday night. What time would that have been?"

"I would say probably around nine or so. She called me to check in and we spoke for a few minutes. I'm sure that information is logged in my phone."

"Fine, may I see it?"

"Not a chance. I will not allow you, or anyone else, to invade my privacy. I will look at it myself and tell you the exact time." Bingham took out his phone, thumbed his print and clicked on his recent calls. He scrolled down, casually erasing a few of the calls, until he reached the one from his wife. "Okay, it was a four-minute call that came in at nine fifteen in the evening. Does that help you detective?"

"Yes, thank you. At least now we have a time frame to work with. Tell me, how was your relationship with your wife?"

"My relationship? What are you getting at? Our relationship was fine. We loved each other. I still can't believe she's gone." He forced the chair forward and covered his eyes with his hands. "I need a minute," he said, more subdued. "I'm sorry, please excuse me. I need some water."

"Yes, certainly." Dornhuber rose, went over to the door, opened it and spoke to the officer standing guard. He sat back down and waited while Bingham quietly sobbed.

A minute or so later the door opened, and the officer handed Bingham a Zephyrhills bottle.

He twisted the cap, took a long swig, and placed the bottle on the table. "Are you okay to continue, Mr. Bingham?"

"Yes, thank you."

"Okay, now I'm going to tell you something I haven't mentioned before, but something you need to know."

"And what's that?"

Dorny pulled on his earlobe and winced, taking a breath. "There was another victim. We, uh, we found your wife in bed . . . with another woman."

"You what? She was with who? A *woman*—that's just not—that's not possible." Bingham deflated like a leaky balloon. "Who is she? Where did she come from? This makes no sense at all. My wife wasn't into other women."

"Well, they were both naked, but we are doing some tests, maybe there is an explanation. Let me ask you this, do you have any enemies?"

"That's an interesting question Detective. In my business I make some friends, but honestly, there are certainly people who don't like me very much."

"What type of business are you in?"

"International finance."

"I see, well of late, has anyone made any threats to you or your wife?"

"No, not at all."

"Okay, let me ask you about your security system. We accessed it and saw that only the cameras in front were recording; the ones out back were not even on. Also, your front gate didn't need a code to open it—all we had to do was push the button. Why so lax?"

"Actually, Detective, the gate is on a timer. It unlocks automatically in the morning at nine o'clock and locks again at dusk, which is programmed to change times as the seasons change. The neighborhood I live in is very safe. As I'm sure you saw, there is only one way in, and the street is basically a cul-de-sac with a pocket park in the middle, so only the few families who live there even come down the road. No one around us has had any robberies or intrusions of any kind in many years."

"What about the waterfront? That looks like very easy access."

"I wasn't aware that the cameras were not working in back. Frankly, I haven't checked the system in quite some time. I have always felt very safe in my home, so much so that we never even set the alarm."

"What about your yacht? Do you normally leave it unlocked?"

"No, why?"

"We found evidence that someone was on it last night. The bed was unmade, the shower was used, and there was fast food residue in the trash."

"You're kidding. Do you think whoever was on it did this?"

"It's a possibility. We're looking into it. Let's talk about your domestic worker. How well do you know Yolonda?"

"She's been with us for about two years, very loyal, keeps to herself, does a good job. How is she doing?"

"Understandably, she was very broken up about all this."

"I'll speak with her when I return to my home."

"That would be good. She tells me that she is not permitted in the house after nine at night and before nine in the morning."

"Yes, that's true, we enjoy our privacy and don't need servants in our home in the evenings. They do their work during the day and then have their evenings to themselves, as do we."

"So that goes for Darryl, as well."

"Yes."

"And were you aware that he wasn't home last night?"

"Yes, Layni told me when we spoke last night."

"What can you tell me about him?"

"He's been with us for about a year now, also loyal, great chef, comes from Hong Kong."

"Do you know where he might have gone last night? We need to speak with him."

"Well, he has a car, so he could have gone anywhere. I don't know much about his personal life, never paid much attention to it."

"I see, how about a cell number for him?"

"Nope, don't have that either, sorry. But he's pretty reliable, I imagine he'll be back by tomorrow. Layni gave him time off, but she would have told him to be back by tomorrow, since that was when I was supposed to return."

"Okay, can you tell me if and who might have known you were going away for a few days?"

"It wasn't a secret; not that I recall telling anyone, and I wouldn't know who Layni may have told."

"What about your office, maybe a secretary, someone on your staff?"

"I don't go into the office on a regular basis. My job is done on the outside, and I travel quite a bit, so at any given time, yes, they would know I was away, and certainly it's no secret. So, my staff could have told clients that I was away on business. However, they all know that I am always reachable on my cell phone." Growing impatient, Bingham started fidgeting his fingers. "Is there anything else Detective? I really would like to see Layni."

"I'll have to check with the ME on that. I would imagine after the exam is complete, which may be another few hours. Meanwhile, why don't we go to your home, so you can look at your safe and see if you can tell me what is missing."

"I can do that myself; I don't need you to tag along. I'll call you after I've looked."

"I'd rather accompany you. It's important we get this information right away, in case someone is trying to pawn anything."

"Look, Detective, I really need some time to process everything. I still can't believe this is happening. Just give me some space here, would you?"

"Very well." Dornhuber sighed, checked his watch, looked back at Bingham and could see he was visibly distressed. "As long as you do it today."

※ ※ ※

Dornhuber had been with the St. Petersburg Police Department for more than twenty years, the last five of which as a detective in homicide division. He had investigated several murders, some even grisly, and while this didn't qualify as grisly, it stood out. Initially, the motive appeared to be robbery; however, it seemed much more planned out than that. Robberies were usually sloppy, the home found ransacked, and if there was a shooting it normally would be the result of the burglar being surprised. Here, the shooting was more execution style. One shot to the head of each vic, clean, small caliber, minimal bloodshed, and rather than the burglar being surprised, it appeared that the vics were the ones who had been surprised. Also, nothing else in the home was even touched. The perp went only for the safe, so it had the feel of an inside job, someone who knew the layout of the home, knew, or thought he knew that only the wife would be there, knew there was a safe, and may have even known where the combination was hidden. Dornhuber began to suspect that the motive was murder, and that the robbery was simply a diversion. The scarcity of evidence convinced him even more that this was a planned, professional hit, and perhaps the perp was surprised by the second woman being there and had to kill her too.

He sat at his desk reviewing the preliminary CSI report. The fingerprints on the headboard did not match the maid's prints, and the initial run through AFIS, the state and federal criminal databases, turned up nothing. Dornhuber then expanded the search to include the civil database that covered government employees, civil servants, as well as certain licensees including (but not limited to) liquor store owners, insurance agents, real estate agents, and attorneys.

Within minutes the search returned a match: Candace Lansiquot, U.S. citizen, 34 years old, residing in St. Petersburg, Florida, profession: realtor. No priors.

Grabbing his cell off the desk, he bolted toward the door while punching in Eddie's number. First ring, Eddie picked up. "What's up Dorny?"

"I've got a lead. That print on the headboard, we've got a match. Where are you now?"

"I'm just pulling up to Headquarters. I finished up over at the marina."

"Okay, I'll meet you downstairs in the lot."

"I'll be there in five minutes."

※ ※ ※

Dorny's car was baking in the sun. The air conditioning barely worked, and the men had to open their windows to cool off. "You ever going to get this fixed, Dorny?"

"Fixed? The whole car needs to go. I'm planning on getting a new car, just waiting for the right time."

"Yeah sure, okay, when Hell freezes over. Anyway, don't leave me hanging, tell me about the girl."

"Right, so after I got the print match, I did a quick check on Facebook to see if she had a page. She does, and she's got quite a few public pictures out there. She's a real estate agent in St. Pete, she is quite pretty, and she looks great in a bikini."

"You're so predictable, Dorny. I know where you're going with this, and it only took me ten seconds."

"What are you saying? Am I that transparent?"

"You said it, not me."

"Okay, I won't jump to any conclusions, but how would you explain a full palm print on a headboard."

"If she wasn't hot, Dorny, would you have come to the same conclusion?"

"But she is, so that's a game changer."

"Remains to be seen."

"Oh, and one last thing before we talk to her, we're keeping it quiet about the other woman. I don't want that getting out in the press. Maybe we can use it to our advantage."

"Good thinking."

Twenty minutes later they arrived at her apartment, a condominium in St. Pete Beach, a water-view high-rise. They took the elevator to the sixth floor.

"Here it is Eddie, 614."

Three knocks, short delay, door opens, stunning woman appears in a tight spandex outfit, sweat dripping from her face.

"Can I help you gentlemen? I'm right in the middle of a video workout."

"Candace Lansiquot? Do I have that pronunciation correct?" Dorny asked.

"Very good, you can be proud of yourself. Did management send you up here? I told them I don't work from home, and if you're looking for an apartment, I can direct you to the website."

"No, ma'am. I'm Detective Lance Dornhuber and this is Detective Eddie Rumson." He handed her his card. "We'd like to ask you a few questions."

"Questions? About what? Did something happen here?"

"No, no, it's about Douglas Bingham. You know him, don't you?"

She hesitated for a moment and widened her eyes. "Uh, well, I know of him."

"Perhaps you can elaborate on that?" asked Dorny.

"I'm not sure what you mean by elaborate, Detective."

Dorny pursed his lips, "We think you know more than just *of* him."

"Why do you say that?"

"Well, have you ever been to his home?" asked Eddie.

"I uh, yes, as a matter of fact I have been. I was there last week. There was a fundraiser at his mansion."

"I see," said Dorny, "tell us a bit about this fundraiser."

"Habitat for Humanity, they build homes for low-income people. I'm a realtor, and I often go to these types of events to network for my business."

"Was this by invitation?"

"Well, sort of. You see, you buy a ticket, and it gets you into the fundraiser. Then throughout the evening, there are auctions, and people bid, and all proceeds go to Habitat."

"Did you have occasion to spend any time with Mr. Bingham?"

"I did speak with him for a short time. But I spoke to many people, I handed out my cards and had a few drinks. Now tell me, why all the questions? Is there a problem?"

"There may be," said Dorny, "and that will depend on how you answer my next few questions."

"Fine, ask away."

"Okay, can you tell me where in the house you were during this gathering?"

"There were a few rooms where the fundraiser took place. It is a very large mansion, and we all roamed around many of the open rooms on the main level."

"Did you go anywhere else, other than the main level?" asked Dorny.

"Not that I recall," Ms. Lansiquot said. "Why is this so important? I don't understand."

"Well, we were just wondering how your fingerprints wound up on a headboard in the master suite?"

"My fingerprints on a headboard. This is crazy. What are you suggesting?"

"I'm not suggesting anything, Ms. Lansiquot. I just need a straight answer, because Mrs. Bingham has been killed, and yours are the only fingerprints found near the body."

"What! Killed? How? When? I would never."

"Well do you mind explaining then how your fingerprints got there?"

"I, uh, I just . . . let me think. It was a busy night, everyone was drinking and having a good time. I remember talking with Mr. Bingham, and remarked how magnificent his home was, so he offered to show me around. We went upstairs, and I remember him showing me the master suite, and I do recall touching the headboard. It was made of a stunning mahogany wood, and I was taken by it. I suppose that was how my fingerprints got there."

"Very convenient," said Eddie, "so why didn't you just say so in the first place?"

"Look, that was last week. I walk through a lot of houses in my business. I just had to think back on it. But if you're suggesting that I'm involved in a murder, well that is absolutely ridiculous. And why would I want to kill Mrs. Bingham?"

"That's what we would like to know," said Dorny.

"You're making a big mistake, I swear, I had nothing to do with this."

"Can you tell us where you were last night between nine o'clock and say six in the morning?

"I was here, in my apartment, sleeping."

"Was anyone with you? Anyone who can vouch for your whereabouts?" asked Eddie.

"I, uh . . . I was alone. It was a Tuesday night. I'm always home Tuesday nights."

"Okay," said Dorny, "and if you're as innocent as you say, then I suppose you wouldn't mind if we came in and looked around your apartment?"

"I am innocent, but I'm also not a fool and have no intention of letting anyone in here without a search warrant. And I assume you don't have one, otherwise you would have shown it to me already. So, I suggest you take a step back, so I can close my door. I'm truly sorry to hear about Mrs. Bingham, but as I said, I had nothing to do with her murder." As she closed the door she said, "Good day, gentlemen."

Once back in the car, Eddie made some notes in his pad. "What do you think of her now, Dorny?"

"She's obviously hiding something. I'm not sure what, but I have some ideas."

"I figured as much, but we need more before we can get a search warrant, let alone an arrest warrant."

"Agreed, but I have an idea—perhaps a way we can push her to make a mistake. In the meantime, we need to put a tail on her and see what she does next. If she's our killer, and the gun is in her apartment, she's going to need to dispose of it. We also need to get her cell phone records and see who she's been speaking to. I'm willing to bet she's a lot closer to Douglas Bingham than she's letting on."

"There you go again," Eddie said. "With you it always comes back to sex."

"Well did you get a good look at her?"

"So, now you think he's banging her and that's the motive?"

Dorny rubbed the back of his head. "Just a theory, but here's how I see it: Bingham's a player, he's got money to burn, and an average looking wife who's getting old. Maybe he finds out she likes women too, who knows? A knockout like Lansiquot happens to come along. He's probably been seeing her for a while, maybe even had sex with her at that fundraiser last week, while his own cheating wife entertained the guests downstairs. They concoct a plan to kill the wife and make it look like a robbery. He tells Lansiquot where to find the combination to the safe, then he promises her that she will be the next Mrs. Bingham if she does the deed. Lansiquot shows up thinking only the wife is there. It messes up her plans, and she has no choice but to kill the other woman as well."

"That's a real stretch at this point, Dorny. Too many questions. Like, why not simply divorce her?"

"That's easy. Under the law, Mrs. Bingham would get a lot of the money and other assets like the mansion, the yacht, maybe the jet. Who knows? But I will tell you this: I interviewed the guy and he's full of himself, loves his money, and would not want to be made a tabloid story, especially if it gets out that she goes both ways. Imagine what headlines about a scorned wife with a female lover who is trying to run her cheating husband through the mud would do to his business. He wouldn't risk all that. Easier to kill her; but he's not stupid enough to do it himself, so he plans a business trip and while he's away, the hot young mistress offs her."

"You've been reading too many detective novels, Dorny. The evidence is flimsy. We would need a helluva lot more than your speculation to make something like that stick."

"I know, but if we can put some pressure on Lansiquot to come clean, maybe offer her a deal if she gives up Bingham, perhaps we can solve this thing fast."

"You really like Bingham for this murder?"

"I do. The guy was smooth, both when I spoke to him on the phone and when he came down to the station. Almost rehearsed. He cried on cue, he got angry at the right times, and he demanded to see his wife's body."

"So now you think a guy is guilty because he acted the way an innocent person would act?"

"Well, when you put it that way," Dorny rubbed his chin, "I just have a hunch. Look, it's clear he's hiding something. She is too. So, without any other suspects, let's roll with this and see where it takes us."

"Ok, I'll get Carter over here to keep an eye on her."

Chapter 3

AFTER LEAVING THE POLICE station, Bingham stopped off at a phone store, purchased two burner phones with cash, and continued his way home. He had to figure things out. There weren't many people who knew about the thumb drive, but any one of them would have paid a fortune to either possess it or to have it destroyed. But none of them should have known that he had it, let alone where it was being stored, except Layni. None of this made sense.

Using one of the burner phones, he called Grant Perkins. Two rings and the call dropped. He punched in the number again. Another two rings and he answered. "Hello, who is this?"

"Grant, it's me, Doug."

"What's with the strange number? I thought you were a solicitor."

"It's a burner, my phone may be compromised. It's important that we meet and talk in person."

"Sounds serious, what going on?"

"Not over the phone."

"Okay, usual spot, say 7:30 tonight?"

"Perfect, see you then."

Back at home, Bingham went into the kitchen, pushed the call button on the wall, and buzzed Yolonda's quarters. "I'm home. Please come meet me in the den. We need to talk."

"On my way."

He walked into the den, made his way over to the bar, and poured himself a Chivas. Glass in hand, standing by the window, he looked out past his yacht and across the water to Tampa. At the sound of footsteps, he turned. "How are you, Yoli?"

"Scared. I still don't believe this happen."

"Yes, very scary, but we will get past this." He downed the Chivas and placed the glass on the bar. "I know you spoke to the police, but I need to hear it from you."

Yoli repeated what she had told the police.

"You didn't tell them anything else, did you?"

"No, that just between us."

"Good. Okay. I'd like you to take some time off now and go home to your family. I'll buy you a plane ticket and give you a month's vacation pay. You should be with your family right now."

"*Sí*, gracias, that is so kind of you."

"I'll make the arrangements for tomorrow morning, so please be ready."

"*Sí*, I will." Yoli hesitated, "Is there anything else you want to say to me, Doug?"

"Now isn't the time."

✳ ✳ ✳

Bingham arrived at the Vinoy Hotel at 7:15 that evening and turned his car over to the valet. He proceeded to Marchand's, the main restaurant inside the hotel. High ceilings, old world charm, and a massive, well-adorned bar in the center made this a must-visit locale for anyone who came to St. Petersburg. He was greeted by the maître d'.

"Nice to see you Mr. Bingham. Will you be dining with us tonight?"

"Not tonight, Antonio, I'll be going to the bar."

"Very well, sir. If there is anything else I can do for you, please let me know."

"Thank you."

The sounds of people eating, talking, and laughing rose and were absorbed into the thirty-foot ceilings. Bingham made his way to the bar, found a comfortable spot away from the other patrons, and ordered a double Chivas, rocks. On the flat-screen over the corner of the bar, the Lightning game was just starting. Bingham's financial adviser, Grant Perkins, a sharply dressed, trimly bearded young man, arrived and took the seat next to Bingham.

"Evening, Grant," Bingham said, nodding.

"Evening, Doug," Perkins said as he motioned for the bartender. "What can I get for you, sir?"

To the bartender, "Don Julio 1942, neat, please." To Bingham, "So what's going on Doug? Why the burner phone?"

"It's complicated, but first off, and I don't mean to shock you, Layni was killed last night. Shot in bed while I was away."

"What! That's insane." Perkins hesitated, at a loss for words. "I'm so sorry, Doug. Do you know who's responsible?"

"No idea, but the police are investigating, and they haven't ruled me out as a suspect."

"You? Why?"

"I don't know, I guess it's the husband thing. They always think it's the husband."

"This is terrible, I don't know what to say. Last I heard from you things were moving forward. Will this cause a problem?"

"That's why I called you down here, Grant. Whoever did this got into my safe and may have stolen the thumb drive."

"Oh no, that is not good, not good at all. That's all your leverage."

"I know, but the drive is password protected."

"You said 'may have stolen.' Is there something else you're not telling me?"

"I received a call from someone . . . I didn't recognize the voice, but he threatened me that if I didn't give it up, there would be more fatalities. Fatalities was the word he used."

"Is there a backup somewhere?"

"No backup. The drive is the only source of all that information in one place."

"So, you're screwed, all the leverage is gone."

"Not yet. No one else knows I no longer have it in my possession. And I have no control over progress—they cut me out of the loop when I disapproved of the new course of action. The thumb drive can't stop it. I just need it to protect myself."

"I really wish you would tell me more about what's going on, Doug."

"It's better you don't know. It'll only put you in danger, but I will tell you this, if things go as planned, this progressive administration that has been running the country for the last three years will be finished. All you need to do is just make my trades and leave it at that. I'll worry about the drive."

"Okay, but who else would have known that you had the drive in your safe?"

"Layni."

"Shit Doug, so they killed her for that?"

"It would seem so, and I can't let the police know, either. Which means they'll be wasting their time looking at me as a suspect."

"And you're sure this won't affect anything?"

"It won't. Just confirm that all my investments are in place. That's all I need you to do right now."

"We've been making the purchases as quickly and quietly as we can, so we don't arouse any suspicions with the regulators. I'll do a quick review, but I think we're fully invested."

Chapter 4

CANDACE LANSIQUOT WAS NERVOUS, to say the least. Being a suspect in a murder investigation was the last thing she needed right now. But she knew how the system worked and that they had to err on the side of caution. The cops would probably be back with a search warrant at some point, and she needed to retain a lawyer as quickly as possible.

She made a call to her good friend and boss, Amanda Simmons at Grandview Realty, for some advice on a top-notch attorney and was given the name Xander Van Buren, Esquire, a prominent St. Petersburg attorney who had been practicing criminal law locally for over twenty years.

First thing the next morning, she called for an appointment and arrived at his office in downtown St. Petersburg at eleven o'clock. The decor in the waiting room was quite impressive. Pictures of Van Buren with current and former mayors, former presidents Barack Obama and George Bush, and even a few celebrities, one of whom, while notorious, had been cleared of all charges, thanks to the venerable Xander Van Buren. There were wood paneled walls, oak floors, and floor to ceiling windows, all of which suggested high fees lurked behind the office doors. Candance would be OK with that; she had a substantial cache of available funds from her side endeavors, and there were several wealthy benefactors who could not refuse her.

A middle-aged secretary appeared at the door. "Please come with me, Ms. Lansiquot. Mr. Van Buren will see you now in the conference room."

Lansiquot followed her and was ushered into an even more lavish room with a twelve chairs around a handsome wooden conference table. Large windows afforded magnificent views of Tampa Bay. She sat down as a handsome, well-dressed man with steel blue eyes and jet-black hair entered.

✻ ✻ ✻

"Good morning Ms. Lansiquot, I'm Xander Van Buren." He reached out to shake her hand.

"Nice to meet you, Mr. Van Buren, and thank you for seeing me on such short notice."

"Not a problem. I understand you work with Amanda. She's a good friend."

"Yes, she speaks very highly of you."

"Okay, so tell me, what can I do for you?"

"Well, I may be getting ahead of myself here, since I haven't been arrested or anything, but two detectives came to see me yesterday afternoon and pretty much accused me of murdering someone. Of course that's crazy! I couldn't possibly kill anyone. But that didn't matter to them."

"Really, first off, who did they say you killed?"

"She's a wealthy socialite. Her name is Layni Bingham."

"What! Layni has been killed? Are you sure?"

"It's what they told me." She looked directly into his eyes. "So, you know her?"

"Yes. When did this happen?"

"They said Tuesday night."

"Oh my God, this is tragic! I knew her well. And frankly, if you had anything to do with this, I cannot represent you. She was a friend of mine."

"I swear, I had nothing to do with this. It's a huge mistake! The police have got it all wrong. I was home all night Tuesday. Please you have to help me."

"A few questions first. Who were the detectives?"

She reached into her purse, pulled out a card and handed it to him.

"Lance Dornhuber. Dorny. I know him well. Good cop, but he tends to have tunnel vision when he sets his sights on a suspect. Who was the other one?"

"Eddie, something or other. I didn't get his last name."

"Rumson, yeah, they're a team. He's a follower, not a leader. Okay, so tell me what they said to you, and more important, what did you say to them?"

"They asked me if I knew Doug Bingham. I said I did, but not well. They asked me if I had ever been to his mansion. I said I had been there last week. He sponsored a fundraiser and I attended to network for my real estate business. Then they asked me if I had ever been in his bedroom. At first, I said no, but then they told me my fingerprints were found on his headboard, near the body. I then recalled that Mr. Bingham showed me the primary bedroom suite, and I touched the mahogany headboard while remarking it was gorgeous."

"I see, and that's it?"

"Well, they wanted to come in and look around my apartment, but I refused and told them that without a search warrant, no one was coming in."

"That's it, nothing else?" Van Buren asked.

"Well, I told them it was ridiculous, and that I didn't kill her, but they looked like they didn't believe me, which is why I felt I should talk to a lawyer."

"Okay, I'm going to need to make some calls. Two things though. First, do not talk to anyone about this, and I mean anyone other than me. Second, I need to know everything about your relationship with Douglas and Layni Bingham. I don't like surprises, so tell me, how well did you really know them?"

"As I told you, I spent about ten or fifteen minutes with Mr. Bingham at the fundraiser. I recall seeing him at a few other events over the past year or so, and probably tried to speak to him at those. I knew he was very rich, and I wanted to network to help grow my business. As to Mrs. Bingham, I never met her, never talked to her, but I had seen her at the fundraiser, and at others. They are quite popular and visible people in St. Petersburg."

"Yes, I am aware."

"Is it going to be a problem that you were friends with Mrs. Bingham? I mean, I don't want you to think for a moment that I killed her."

"It won't be a problem. Believe me, I want to find out who did this to her. More than anything right now."

❋ ❋ ❋

After Candace Lansiquot had left his office, Van Buren allowed himself a few minutes to shed tears and absorb Layni Bingham's tragic murder. They had known each other since attending St. Petersburg High together, and he still had feelings for her.

He walked down the hall and into Griff's office. Griff was his law partner and his brother. There was no one else in the world Xander could trust like he trusted him.

Griff looked up from the file he was reading. "What's up Xan?"

"Hey Griff, I've got some bad news and a new case we need to discuss."

"Uh oh, you've got that look in your eyes. Sit down and spill it."

"This one's tough and very close to home."

"Go on."

"It's Layni Bingham. She was murdered Tuesday night. Apparently shot and killed while in her bed."

"Layni Bingham, formerly Elaine Kolter, your old high school sweetheart? I'm so sorry."

"Yes, and it's all very strange. She actually came to see me Tuesday afternoon and was stressed out. She gave me a thumb drive to hold on to because she was concerned someone might be after it."

"What's on the drive?"

"I don't know. She wouldn't tell me other than to say it had very valuable information."

"So, let's look at it."

"Can't. It's password protected, and she specifically asked me not to look at it."

"Well, if she's dead, and was killed for it, I think we need to find a way to unlock it. I would imagine whatever is on it will help lead us to who killed her."

"I realize that Griff, but there's more. I was just retained by a local realtor, Candace Lansiquot, who was questioned by our old pal Detective Dornhuber and his sidekick Eddie Rumson. They think she may be the killer."

"Bro, whoa, back up a sec! How can you be representing her when you were first retained by Layni?"

"I know. It's complicated. But the way I see it, and from what Lansiquot already told me, she had nothing to do with this."

"And what makes you so sure?"

"Dorny's got flimsy evidence. Apparently, they lifted her prints off the headboard in Layni's bedroom. She explained to me that last week there was a fundraiser at the Bingham estate, and she touched it while getting a tour of the mansion."

Bemused, Griff said, "And you believe her?"

"I do. I could tell by her demeanor that she was telling the truth. But aside from that, my representing her will allow me access to Dorny's file and all the CSI evidence, and no one will be able to question any of my digging. I'll get to interrogate 'Smug Doug' Bingham, and I'm fairly certain that he's involved with the thumb drive."

"Well, I know you've always had it in for Doug, ever since he stole Layni from you back in school."

"That's not it—you know I don't hold grudges like that. I just never liked the guy and never trusted him. I don't think he ever changed from back in high school, and that's almost thirty years ago."

"You're not going to tell him you have the drive, are you?"

"No, I can't. In fact, I can't even tell Dorny about it. Layni asked me not to tell anyone. The fact is, whatever is on that drive was worth killing for, so we can't let anyone know about it."

"You realize that if you don't tell Dorny about it, you're technically withholding evidence that may help the police determine who killed Layni."

"I am aware, but as far as I'm concerned, she was my client, and it's privileged."

"That's a stretch, but okay, all I can say is, here we go again."

"So, you're on board Griff?"

"Did you really need to ask?"

"Just making sure. All right, I'm going to head over to see Dorny and get my feet wet."

"I'll hold down the fort, Xan, just call me if you need me."

"Will do."

※ ※ ※

The day was a scorcher, and the humidity was typically high, so Van Buren drove to police headquarters instead of walking the few blocks. Once inside, the desk sergeant looked up from whatever he was reading, nodded his head and gave him a flat smile. "What can I do for you, Counselor?"

"I need to see Dorny. Is he available?"

The desk sergeant picked up the phone, punched in a few numbers and spoke quietly into it. Looking back down from his high counter he told Van Buren to have a seat, it'd be a few minutes. Van Buren stepped back and sat down on a bench that ran along the back wall of the precinct. A few minutes later, Dorny walked through the doors.

"Afternoon, Counselor," Dorny said, eyeing him up and down. "Nice suit. What's up? We've got no cases together that I'm aware of."

"That means we're due. How have you been?"

Dorny said, "I could complain, but no one would give a shit." Hands on hips. "So, what brings you here?"

"Candace Lansiquot. The name ring a bell?"

Dorny's eyes widened. "That was fast, we only interviewed her yesterday. How'd she come to you?"

"Not important. Just wanted to get an idea why you're so interested in her."

"Sorry, but I'm not at liberty to discuss it. It's an ongoing investigation."

"C'mon Detective, she's my client, and you're going to have to disclose anyway."

"That may be true, but she hasn't been arrested—yet, so you have no legal right to anything."

Van Buren said, "Look, I'm actually here to help, consider it a favor. From what she's already told me it sounds like you've got nothing on her; and frankly, after hearing her story and assessing her demeanor, I'm convinced she's got nothing to do with your homicide."

"And I'm just supposed to believe you and drop my investigation? I guess you win all your cases that way." Dorny smiled. "Just tell the cops your client didn't do it and we believe you. Case closed, right?"

"I wish, but no, I don't expect you to believe me, at least not right away. But you and I have been doing this dance for quite some time, and while things do get heated between us sometimes, we do have respect for each other and a common goal."

"Respect yes, Counselor, common goal, not exactly." Dorny reached into his pocket, pulled out a clip of bills and waved them at him. "Your goal is to make money. And you do, a lot more than I do, and a lot more than I ever will. My goal is to put the bad guys behind bars, and I do, and a lot more than you ever will. In fact, it's your job to keep them out of prison, and you do that quite well—usually without my assistance. So why do you suddenly want to help me?"

"All right, Dorny, enough with the pleasantries. I've known you long enough to know that you've got ethics, unlike some of your compatriots, and you wouldn't want to waste time prosecuting the wrong person, let alone put an innocent one behind bars."

"Thanks for the kudos, but you know I still can't give you any information until our initial investigation is complete, and we determine if the evidence is sufficient to indict your client." A beat. "And frankly, Lansiquot lawyered up pretty fast, which tells me something. I mean she hasn't even been arrested."

"Oh please, so only guilty people hire lawyers?"

"From where I sit."

"Okay, how about just answering a few questions for me then?"

"Depends on the questions."

"Fair enough; so, do you have any other suspects?"

"We do, but I can't tell you who they are."

"Any that you intend to arrest?"

"Possibly."

"How soon will you know?"

"We are still waiting on some forensics, and once we have had a chance to analyze what we've found, we'll be in a better position. Right now, we're just in the beginning stages."

"I see. By the way, Detective, I haven't seen anything in the paper about the homicide. How'd you manage that?"

"I have my ways, but out of respect for the prominent people involved, we are trying to keep this low profile. Of course, as you well know, that won't last much longer. I suspect the homicide will leak very soon, but we still intend to keep the details as quiet as we can."

"Can you do me a favor then? If the time comes that you decide to arrest my client, please let me know, and I will bring her down. That way you don't have to make a big show of it, and we can keep the press at bay."

"That I can do. Will that be all, Counselor?"

"For now, but just remember, Candace Lansiquot is my client, and you are directed not speak with her again without me there."

A broad smile. "I wouldn't think of it, Xander."

"Thanks, Dorny," Van Buren said. He turned to leave, then turned back. "One last thing, do you have a problem if I have a chat with Doug Bingham?"

"Frankly, I'd prefer you not speak with him just yet, but I can't stop you."

✳ ✳ ✳

Back in his car, Van Buren called the office. "Hey Griff, I just met with Dorny. He's sealed up tight, won't even give a preliminary since Candace hasn't been arrested yet."

"You had to know he would pull that."

"Yeah, I guess, but I had to try. He did say there were other suspects, and that they hadn't gotten forensics back. Which gives me an idea."

"Go on."

"If the usual forensics team is working this case, that means Jenny would be on it. I'm thinking I could give her a call and see if she's willing to spill something."

"You want to ask my girlfriend to compromise her position as a CSI tech?"

"Uh, yeah. She's helped us before."

"Only to right an injustice, Xander."

"Okay, well then, why don't you talk to her and see how she feels about this one. Maybe you can squeeze something relevant out of her."

Griff said. "I think it's too soon, and without an indictment she could get in real trouble."

"Look, I get it, make it confidential, see what she says. If she is totally against it, drop it, tell her it was me insisting, not you. I'll play the bad guy on this one."

"I'll give it a shot. What's your next move?"

"I'm thinking about paying a visit to Smug Doug."

"Really? That could be awkward. Do you intend to tell him who you're representing? That could be a mistake."

"I don't intend to tell him that I'm involved at this time. I'm simply going to go to offer my condolences, and while I'm there I'll play nice, but look for a tell. He never was a very good poker player."

"You're assuming he will even speak to you."

"I'll use my charm. Worst case, he refuses, and if Candace is arrested, I'll get a second chance."

❋ ❋ ❋

Van Buren pulled up the drive at the Bingham residence and pushed the call button. Short delay, then a gruff voice answered, "Who is it, and what do you want?"

"Doug, is that you? It's Xander Van Buren."

"Yeah, so, I'm in no mood for visitors. What do you want?"

"Listen, I heard about Layni. I'm so sorry. I simply wanted to see how you were doing."

"I'm handling it, just not in the mood for visitors right now, I'm sure you can understand."

"I do, but maybe talking about it will help. I'm here as a friend."

"Look Xander, we were never really friends. You and Layni were, but not me, and high school was a long time ago."

"I know, but when something traumatic happens, you have to brush all that aside."

"I appreciate that, but perhaps some other time." A beat. "Maybe I'll reach out to you in a few days." The mic went dead.

Strike two. This was not looking good for his batting average. He backed up from the gate, wheeled around and sped off to his office. *Time to do some computer research on Doug.*

❊ ❊ ❊

Griff found Van Buren in his office a few hours after he returned. "You ready to brainstorm yet, Xander?"

"Hey Griff, sure, c'mon in. But first, did you speak to Jenny yet?"

"No, I can't do that over the phone. I have to talk to her in person."

"Understood. Okay, so check this out. I've come up with quite a bit of information on Doug and three separate entities that he controls. Bingham International, Ltd., Synergy Properties, LLC, and Luxor Corp. Synergy and Luxor didn't seem too interesting, so I chose to weed them out for now and focus on Bingham International."

"What does that company do?"

"They're involved in international finance. From a simplistic standpoint, Bingham brokers international monetary transactions as well as brokering the purchase and sale of goods between organizations in various foreign countries. Layni told me the thumb drive contained valuable information, which it is now clear someone killed for. So, it wasn't a stretch to think it had to have something to do with Doug's company. Seems to me there's a lot of opportunities for corruption in international trade."

Griff said, "So now you think Doug's involved in some international conspiracy to affect worldwide trade?"

"Well, I wouldn't go that far, but it's not hard to believe he may be involved in something corrupt. You know as well as I that the U.S. has major trade imbalance issues with a number of countries. We're hitting them up with tariffs, and trade wars could be next. I mean, look what's going on with China. It's been in the news quite a bit. Maybe he got in bed with the wrong people?"

"It's a theory; a little out there, bro, if you want my opinion. So where do you go from here?"

"Stu Saxon, my buddy at the FBI. He has access to information we can't get on the web, and he owes me a favor. I'm going to pay him a visit and see if he can do some intel for me."

"And the point of all this is?"

"If Candace isn't the killer, and it seems clear she isn't, then we must find the real killer, because the police won't. They'll take the path of least resistance. And because they aren't privy to the thumb drive, they will have no reason to look any further, so we must do their job for them."

"Gotcha bro, but as I said before, I think we need to find a way to get into that drive. That seems to me to be the most direct way to figure this out."

"Agreed. But finding someone who is very tech savvy and who can be trusted is going to be a problem."

"Uh, excuse me, Xan, but are you forgetting something?"

"Forgetting what?"

"Jenny, my CSI girlfriend. She's not only beautiful and smart, but she's also a computer whiz. That's a big part of her job."

"That may be pushing it. We can't expect her to hold back that information from Dorny. And if she doesn't tell them about it, she could really get in trouble. At this point, I think we need to find someone totally independent."

Chapter 5

———✳———

DRIVING UP TO BOB'S Outdoor Adventure Store was a trip in and of itself. It was like driving through a campground nestled in the woods and surrounded by indigenous vegetation. Bobs carried everything one could imagine for the active outdoor enthusiast from scuba gear, kayaks and canoes, to backpacks, tents and camping attire, but most importantly, guns. Doug Bingham was there for guns and ammo only. He needed protection and could only rely on himself for it. As a former National Guardsman, he already had a carry permit but hadn't owned a gun in years. He wanted real firepower too, and Bob's was the place to go. He purchased two automatic rifles as well as two Springfield XD 40 caliber pistols with twelve-round magazines and the ammo to feed them. He even purchased a holster, so he could always carry a pistol with him.

Once back at home, he reset all his security cameras and made sure all his doors and windows were locked and that the alarm system was functioning properly. He placed a rifle in his bedroom under the bed and one pistol in the kitchen drawer by the refrigerator. The second rifle was left leaning against the wall by the French doors that led out to the yard. The second pistol was strapped to his side along with two additional preloaded magazines. He was now ready, and if anyone dared to invade his home, he would make sure they never left alive.

Returning to his den, he poured himself a double Chivas, neat, and downed it in one shot, then poured another and tossed in three cubes of ice. Sitting down on his sofa, he switched on the 100-inch flat screen and clicked the remote to his desired channel. By that time, it was seven o'clock and the local evening news was on. Amazingly, there was no mention of a homicide on Snell Isle, and that made him feel a little better.

After a time, he rose and wandered around the huge, empty house. The quiet was alarming, and all he could hear was the newscaster droning on about the local car show that was to take place at Vinoy Park the coming weekend. At any other time, Doug Bingham would have looked forward to the event, but tonight he had other things on his mind. He figured that whoever wanted the thumb drive would be coming after him, and he would have to be eliminated to tie up any loose ends. He made his way to the garage area that housed a dozen vehicles from sports cars and SUVs to a stretch limousine he never used. Satisfied that it was all quiet inside his home, he returned to the kitchen, lowered the lighting within and turned it on out back by the pool and dock. After eating a cold sandwich, he went back to the den and sat on the sofa watching the television, though not really paying attention. He was focused on survival. His instincts were good, and he knew someone would be coming for him tonight. It was just a matter of time.

Two more glasses of Chivas, and he dozed off, only to be awakened when the television went dark, and the lights went out. Someone had cut the power. Bingham dropped to the ground, crawled over to the French doors, and grabbed the rifle. He couldn't see well out back, although the half moon was shining over the water and providing some light. He reasoned that there had to be at least two attackers, one out front who cut the power by the street, the other coming in by water, where he was much more vulnerable.

Bingham decided his best option would be to take the fight to them. They wouldn't have expected it. He made his way through the kitchen, out the smaller doorway and into the backyard. Crouching low, he raced along the rear wall, and made his way to the sunken bar that served the pool. That kept him low and out of sight while still allowing him to see a good portion of the yard and dock area.

A sudden burst, the sound of breaking glass, then light and smoke filled the den inside. Good, that meant Bingham's attacker still believed he was in the house. He watched quietly as a figure dressed all in black emerged from the rear of the yacht and moved quickly towards the French doors that had been obliterated by the blast. Resting the rifle on the bar and sighting it, Bingham followed the figure until it slowed enough for a clear shot, then he pulled the trigger. The gun spit bullets from its muzzle and the figure dropped to the ground. Bingham wasn't sure if he had hit his mark and killed his target, or if he simply wounded them. Seconds later, the return fire forced him to duck down below the bar. Noise like that would surely alarm the neighbors, and the police would respond quickly.

An errant cloud moved in and covered the moonlight, allowing the figure to limp-run towards the waterfront. Bingham couldn't see well enough to shoot on target again, so he fired aimlessly in the direction of the yacht. A few seconds more passed, and the sound of a jet ski racing off behind the yacht could be heard.

Off in the distance, police sirens blared as cruisers raced down Brightwaters Boulevard toward the Bingham estate.

✳ ✳ ✳

Dorny arrived on the scene twenty minutes after the local police. Firemen had already secured the inside of the home and doused the small fire in the den. Another crew worked out back poolside looking for clues. The quiet of Brightwaters Boulevard had been seriously disturbed. Neighbors were out on the street in their nightclothes, but were held back by the police, who had used their cruisers to block off access and secure the scene out front.

Douglas Bingham stood in the entrance hallway watching as the police searched the premises, and the firemen contained the last of the fire.

Dorny approached Bingham, "Are you hurt?"

"No Detective, thankfully I'm okay."

"Can you tell me what happened?"

"I'm still trying to piece it all together. I was watching TV in the den and the power went out. I was worried that whoever killed Layni might be coming back for me, so I grabbed my rifle and went out back," hard swallow, "where I figured I'd have a better chance of fighting off whoever was coming for me. I made my way to the bar by the pool and hid. Suddenly something exploded through the French doors and the den lit up in flames. Right after that I saw a figure making its way from the dock over to the door, so I started firing my rifle. I think I wounded him, but he returned fire and ran back to the dock. Seconds later, I heard a jet ski take off behind my yacht."

"What makes you think you wounded the intruder?"

"It looked like he was limping as he ran off."

"All right, Douglas, no more games. This attack is a major escalation. You need to tell me what's really going on here."

"Honestly, I have no idea."

"Look, you can't expect me to believe that. You were carrying a rifle as well as a pistol on your hip, so you were obviously expecting an attack. That tells me that whoever killed your wife came back specifically for you. This was planned. Whoever did this knew how to cut the power to your home and came ready to engage with weapons. They mean business and this is not something you can handle on your own. You are clearly in danger and unless you tell me what you know, we won't be able to protect you."

"I really don't know what to tell you, Detective. I'm at a loss myself."

"So why the guns?"

"I got nervous after my wife was killed. Can you blame me?"

"C'mon Douglas, be straight with me, and I'll try to help."

"I don't know what else to tell you."

"You're making a mistake. It's clear you know a lot more than you're letting on."

"I'm sorry, but I really don't."

"Fine, if that's how you want to play this, I'll need to see your weapons—all of them, and your ammunition. We're going to have to compare it to whatever we find around here. I'm sure we'll come up with spent cartridges from both your gun and the intruder's."

"I only used the rifle. You can have that, but I'd like it back right away. As for the pistol, I have a carry permit, and there is no reason for me to give it up. I have every right to protect myself, and clearly, I need it."

Dorny said, "My suggestion, you need to lay low for a while. Do you have another place you can go to while we try to figure this out?"

"Frankly, Detective, I'm not letting anyone scare me out of my home. Once you're finished here, I intend to clean this place up and hire a couple of security guards. Do you have any recommendations?"

"Big mistake, but I'll see what I can do." A beat. "And while I'm here, did you have a chance to go through your safe and determine what is missing?"

"I did, and it is basically my wife's jewelry and about twenty thousand in cash. It's insured."

Dorny said, "Here's a thought: perhaps whoever is after you was looking for something else in the safe and couldn't find it, so they came back when you returned, to try again."

"I haven't a clue what that would be, Detective."

Handing a card, "Well, if you think of something, you know where to reach me." Dorny looked around at the damage to the den. "I'll leave an officer here for you until you can get your repairs done, and I'll make some calls to get you private security."

"Thank you, Detective. Am I still a suspect?"

"That remains to be seen."

"Really? After all this?"

"Frankly, it's up to you, Douglas. If you would be more forthcoming about your own suspicions, that might go a long way to clearing you."

"I'll take it under advisement."

Dorny said, "You do that." Then as an afterthought, "So where is Yoli?"

"I gave her a month's vacation and sent her back to Cuba. She needed a break."

"I see. And have you heard from Darryl?"

"Actually, no, he hasn't returned yet."

"Do you have a way to reach out to him?"

"I'll have to check around. I imagine Layni had his number here somewhere."

"Please do that, I would like to speak with him when he returns. Also, tomorrow I need you to come down and meet me at the coroner's office. You can see Layni now, and I also want you to look at the other woman and see if you can identify her."

"Okay, I appreciate that. Thank you."

※ ※ ※

Dorny returned to his car and called Carter. "Can you give me a status on Candace Lansiquot?"

Carter said, "I followed her this morning, and she went to the Van Buren law office. After that she made a stop at the office of Grandview Realty and lunched at Stillwaters Tavern on Beach Drive in downtown St. Petersburg. She returned to her apartment around three o'clock. I stayed until five and had Junior take the overnight." Looking at his watch, "It's after eleven, so he should still be there. You want to call him, or should I?"

"Do me a favor, give him a ring, make sure he's awake and can confirm that Lansiquot is still at home."

"Copy that. So, what's going on? Why the late call?"

"I'll fill you in tomorrow, but there was another incident at the Bingham estate. No fatalities, but a lot of fireworks. I just want to rule out Lansiquot."

"Okay let me see what Junior has to say, but I instructed him to call me if she went anywhere. He hasn't called, so most likely she's still at home."

"Fine, just confirm it."

※ ※ ※

Junior's phone buzzed, startling him awake. "Hey Sarge, what's up?"

Carter said, "You still on the job over at Lansiquot's place, Junior?"

"Sure am, why?"

"Can you verify that she's at home?"

"Give me a sec." He reached for his binoculars and focused on her apartment six flights up. "Faint light in the front window is all I can see."

"Is it possible she got out while you weren't looking?"

"I doubt it, but I can't say for sure. There's a few ways outta this complex, but I can see her door and front window clearly from here."

"Do me a favor, take a walk up there and make sure she's home. There's been an incident over at the Bingham estate and Dorny needs to rule her out. Knock on her door if you have to."

"But it's after eleven at night, Sarge."

"Just do it."

"And what do I tell her when she answers?"

Annoyed. "I don't know, tell her you're sorry, that you knocked on the wrong door. Just don't let her know you're a cop."

"Roger."

Junior made his way to the elevator and rode it to the sixth floor. The apartments were situated along an outside hallway, so all front doors and windows were visible from the parking lot. He rang the bell at apartment 614 and waited. No answer. He rang again, still nothing. Finally, he knocked, first softly, then louder. Still nothing. He moved over to the window, which opened into the kitchen. A dim light was on, allowing him to make out the kitchen and the den in the background. No other lights were on beyond that.

He pulled out his cell. "Hey Sarge, I'm at her apartment, and she hasn't answered the door. I'm looking into the kitchen, and I don't see any activity. I don't know how she could have gotten past me, but it don't look like she's here."

More annoyed. "Fucking great. Nice job, Junior. Do you think you can pick the lock and get inside without drawing attention?"

"I could try, but you sure you want me to do that? I mean, we got no warrant."

"I think Lansiquot may be injured inside, and you need to check to make sure she's all right."

"Gotcha, Sarge, I'm on it."

Junior pulled out his little tool kit, found what he needed, and picked the lock. He pulled his Glock, entered, and sidled along the wall until he reached the den. The dim light from the kitchen allowed him to see into the den. He made his way to the open door leading into the bedroom, flicked on the light, again, clear. He cleared the closet and the bathroom. Same. No one was home.

He called Carter. "Sarge, I'm inside, she's not here. I got no idea how she managed it, but she's gone."

"Okay, get your ass outta there, leave it like you found it and stick around outside to see if she shows up. If she does, call me, don't approach."

"Copy that."

Carter speed dialed another number.

"Dorny here, whatya got for me Carter?"

"Looks like Junior lost her. She ain't home."

"You're sure?"

"Yeah, I had him go in and check the place out. She's not home."

"Shit!"

"I know. I told him to get out of there, but stick around outside and call me if she returns."

"All right, keep me posted."

Dorny called a morning meeting. Eddie and Carter sat at one side of the table, chewing on bagels, Ken Taylor, Jake Dalton, and Jenny Jones from CSI sat across the table, and Dorny stood at the front of the room by the whiteboard.

Dorny said, "Ken, bring us up to date."

"Okay, as you know, the fingerprints were identified as belonging to one Candace Lansiquot. We also found a few long dark strands of hair that belong to a woman. We've ruled out the two vics, and based on the description of Lansiquot, we believe them to be hers. They were found in the bed beneath one of the pillows. We also found a faint set of prints to the left of the first set, spread out about 2 feet. These were from a left hand and are probably Lansiquot's as well, but we don't have that info yet either."

Jake Dalton chimed in, "Best guess, Lansiquot was positioned on the bed kneeling on top of someone and holding herself steady with her palms pressed against the headboard."

Eddie said, "You mean, like she was having sex with someone, and was on top?"

"Apparently," said Jake Dalton.

Carter said, "Kinky. Three women all going at it, and one decides to kill the others."

"Let's not jump to conclusions," Dorny said. "Did the rape kits come back yet?"

Jenny Jones jumped in, "Yes, no sign of forceable penetration on either vic, no sperm, no evidence of prophylactic use, and no bodily fluids associated with sex found on the sheets either."

"From the staging it appears that the perp wanted it to look like a sex scene, even though it wasn't," said Dorny.

"That's what I'm thinking," said Jake Dalton. "The bed was clean, barely even looked slept in. We also found both vics' clothes in the hamper in the bathroom."

Eddie said, "So someone tidied up a bit, probably after the shootings."

"Meaning, whoever it was felt comfortable that they could take their time," said Dorny.

Ken Taylor added, "The entire room was immaculate, like it was barely even lived in."

"Chalk that up to the maid," Dorny said. "She told us she cleaned the room every day."

"Well that begs the question, how long could those prints have been there?" Taylor asked. "I mean, if she cleaned every day does that mean the prints had to have been left there that night?"

Dorny interjected. "Depends on how thorough her cleaning was. I have a different theory. The maid said she goes through the house and cleans the house all week long, and looking at the size of that house, she couldn't do more than three or so rooms a day. Maybe she only straightened up the bedroom and didn't always dust the headboard. Those prints could have been there from the prior weekend when they had a fundraiser at the estate. I bet that Lansiquot was sort of telling the truth, and that Bingham was showing her around the house. She just didn't tell us how special the tour really was. Looks like the two of them had a quicky that night with her on top. Her claim that she just touched the headboard to admire it was a nice touch, but with two sets of prints, it's obvious what really went down."

Taylor said, "And that would coincide with finding her hair under the pillow."

"That still doesn't rule her out as a suspect," said Dorny. "In fact, it may very well implicate her, along with Bingham."

"How so," asked Carter.

"Oldest motive in the book, son. Sex and money. Bingham gets Lansiquot to off his wife with the promise of becoming the next Mrs. Bingham."

"Yeah, but what about last night then?" Eddie asked. "Why would she, or anyone, come back to the house and shoot it up?"

Dorny said, "Bingham's a smart dude. Maybe he sets up the whole thing last night as another diversion, same as robbing the safe after the homicides. The only thing that messed up the plan was she wasn't expecting there to be another woman in the house, so Lansiquot improvises and sets up a phony sex scene for another diversion. And even the damage in the den wasn't so bad.

The gunfire could be a set up too, a few shots from two different directions, and that's all he needs. He even asked me last night if he was still a suspect. On top of that, Lansiquot wasn't home last night and never came back. Somehow, she slipped out and Junior never saw her leave. We're still trying to track her down."

"Wild theory, Dorny," said Ken Taylor. "Very hard to prove all that. No D.A. would touch it without more."

"Agreed, so let's move on," said Dorny, "Just keep it in the back of your heads."

Jenny Jones said, "The safe was ransacked, contents strewn all over the floor in the closet. Looks like the perp was looking for something in particular."

"Well, Bingham told me only money and jewelry were stolen, and he didn't seem too upset," said Dorny. "Twenty thousand cash and the guy doesn't even flinch. Jeez."

"Anyway," said Jenny Jones, "No prints or other forensics in the closet, or on the safe, or its contents, so that's a dead end."

"What about the yacht?" asked Dorny. "Did you find anything there?"

Jake Dalton said, "We found some prints in the head, in the galley, and in the master suite. Most are duplicates of each other and probably Bingham. We eliminated our vic's prints, but there were a few others that looked large enough to be male, so we ran them all through AFIS and got no hits. No prints that matched Lansiquot either. Mostly a dead end on the ship."

"I went to the McDonald's on Fourth Street," said Carter. "When I asked about patrons who purchased Big Mac meals any time after seven o'clock P.M. that night, they actually laughed at me. No camera footage available either inside or at the drive through. Complete waste of time."

Eddie said, "Yeah, and I went to the marina on Snell Isle Boulevard and asked about rowboats. Apparently, there are a few that come in and out. Usually, it's kids that fish on the bay. Nothing out of the ordinary that day, and no one was working that night either. Also, no video cameras, and the gas dock is closed after dark. Another dead end."

"Autopsies come back?" asked Dorny.

"Yeah, I have the report here," Jake Dalton said, holding up a set of papers. "Nothing remarkable. Confirms the deaths were by gunshot wounds to the head, both sometime between ten o'clock P.M. and four o'clock A.M. Some wine in both of their systems, no drugs, prescription or otherwise. Looks like they also ate some cheese, crackers, and dip. Not a lot of real food in their systems, just the junk."

Eddie said, "Do we have an ID on the other vic?"

"Still nothing," said Ken Taylor. "We found no ID or purse of any kind at the house, and her prints are not in the system. Also, no one has filed a missing person report. It's weird."

Dorny said, "Does seem strange, but I have Bingham coming to meet me later today to view his wife's body, and I'm hoping he can ID the other vic. So, until we have more info, that will have to wait. Okay people, let's focus on where we go from here. And, while I like the murder/sex angle, we still need to investigate other possibilities. That means we can't ignore the fact that Bingham is rich and involved in international trade. I find him evasive—among other things—but we need to look into business deals of his and his contacts too. Start digging into that while I see if we can get a warrant on Lansiquot, so we can get her phone records."

Taylor said, "So Bingham is our prime suspect now and Lansiquot is number two, but we arrest her and see if she flips on him?"

"That's the plan since we've got no one else right now, and it's clear they're both hiding something. Let's dig in and see what's mixed in with the dirt."

Chapter 6

V AN BUREN DIDN'T WANT his brother Griff to think he was
insensitive to his relationship with Jenny, or that he would
compromise it for a case, but he truly believed she would be willing
to help. He knew how much she cared for Griff, and while she had
a strong sense of duty, she could also temper her enthusiasm when
it came to real life situations.

Griff was meeting her for coffee immediately following her
briefing with her team and promised Van Buren he'd come right
back to the office with whatever details she was willing to provide.
In the meantime, he continued going through the information he
had found on Doug Bingham's business dealings, then placed a call
to his old frat buddy and teammate, Stu Saxon, over at the FBI.
They were best friends and teammates in college and always kept
in touch. Reliable and discreet, Van Buren could always count on
Special Agent Stu Saxon. He speed dialed him.

"Stu, how goes it?"

"What's up Xan? Always good to hear from you buddy."

"I'm missing our basketball scrimmages, starting to get out of
shape, and need to get some exercise. You up for some one-on-one
this afternoon?"

Laughing. "I'm over in Tampa today, but I'm not too busy. I could meet you later, say around four, over at the outdoor courts at St. Pete High."

"I'll be there, better bring your A game, Stu."

"Count on it."

Griff walked in, almost on cue. The smile across his two-day stubble told Van Buren he had some news.

He said, "What's with the shit eating grin, bro?"

"Xander, if you're going to use a cliché, you should know that eating shit doesn't make anyone grin."

He waved him off. "Ahh, whatever—just tell me what you found out."

"Okay, so Jenny's on board to a certain extent. She wouldn't tell me everything, but she did give me a few tidbits of information."

"Like?"

"Like, there's more than one vic. Apparently, Layni was found in bed with another woman, both shot in the head, both naked."

"Layni with another woman? Not possible. She never went that way in all the years I've known her. Who was the other woman?"

"Still no ID on her, and they also aren't sure if the two were having a sexual dalliance. The bodies were in staged positions, both sitting upright against pillows, as if watching TV, their breasts exposed. There was no physical evidence of sexual relations, but no final determination has been made."

"Suggesting that it was a scene designed to misdirect."

"Correct. Anyway, Jenny also told me that there was a second set of prints on the headboard, also belonging to Candace Lansiquot. And that based on the positioning, it appears she was straddling someone in the bed. That someone being Doug. Seems that there was a fundraiser at the estate the prior Saturday night, and they suspect that when he was showing Candace around the mansion, she did a bit more than just look around."

"That's not what Candace led me to believe. She told me they barely knew each other and had met only briefly in the past."

"Well, the evidence suggests otherwise. Not only that, but they also found some of what they believe is her hair underneath a pillow, so it sounds like she's not telling you everything."

"What do you mean 'believe is her hair'?"

"They don't have her DNA, or any hair from her head to compare it to, but the color and length seem to match." Griff took a breath and brushed the hair off his forehead. "They'll confirm it once they get a sample."

"Which means they are going to have to arrest her."

"Seems that way . . . but there's more."

"What else?"

"I'm surprised you haven't seen the news. There was an incident last night over at the Bingham estate. A small explosion in the den and some gunfire outside. No one was hurt, and there are no suspects. Apparently, Doug had a weapon and fired back, thwarting the attack. Whoever it was took off on a jet ski before the cops arrived."

"Well, that would put a damper on the sex and murder motive, Griff, wouldn't you think?"

"Not the way Jenny tells it. Dorny thinks that was staged to throw them off track."

"Really? That seems a bit of a stretch, even for Doug."

"I agree, and so does Jenny, but she's just following Dorny's orders at this point. Are you going to confront Candace Lansiquot about this?"

"Not right away. I want to follow up on Doug first. I'm playing hoops with Stu this afternoon, and I'm going to get him to investigate Doug's businesses, courtesy of FBI resources."

❈ ❈ ❈

St. Petersburg High School was located off Fifth Avenue North not too far from downtown St. Petersburg. It was an old building that still possessed some of the charm associated with the decor of a bygone era. Van Buren hadn't been inside in a very long time, and he didn't have the desire to enter. The basketball court outside was perfectly fine, although he would have preferred to go up against Stu on a court with a wood floor and a glass backboard. Saxon had the upper hand in terms of height, but Van Buren was much quicker, so the games were always a fair contest of skill and could get a bit physical, despite their ages. The weather was cooperative, and the sun rested coolly behind some afternoon clouds. The smell of freshly cut grass reminded him of his days running track there. He took a deep breath and reminisced as he walked to the court. He arrived before Saxon and took some shots from behind the foul line. He also made sure to stretch a bit.

Ten minutes later, Stu called out from the parking lot, "I see you're taking this one seriously, Xan. Too bad you weren't as dedicated back in college. Maybe then we could have won the championship."

"I was fouled, the ref didn't call it, and that's what took us down. I'd have made that shot if it wasn't for that."

"You should have passed it to me—I would have taken it inside and dunked over that guy. He was 6 inches shorter than me."

"Past history, Stu. Let's see if you still got game."

They played hard for about thirty minutes, until both were almost out of breath. The score was tied ten to ten on a game to eleven, and Van Buren had the ball. He dribbled left, palmed a crossover dribble to his right, stopped short, and took a jump shot from the right corner of the foul line. The ball soared just out of reach of Saxon's hand and swished through the hoop.

"Game over, Stu!"

"No way Xan, you have to win by two, or have you forgotten the rules?"

"Oh, that's right." He passed Van Buren the ball and lined up for the next play. Van Buren faked right, drove left, and zipped right past him with a layup that won the game.

Stu said, "Since when have you learned to go left? That was what was missing from your game in college."

"Something I learned in the Marines." He tossed him a water bottle and twisted one open for himself. They sat down on the bench and laughed.

"Good game, Stu. You still have it, sort of. We should do this more often."

"I agree. We can't let ourselves get old before our time." He chugged his water. "So, what else is going on? I know you didn't bring me here just to play hoops."

"Very astute of you. Guess I can chalk that up to your FBI training."

"Something like that." He pushed Van Buren's right shoulder in jest.

"I've got a case, and I need you to use your resources to look into someone's business dealings. I don't have the technological resources that you have, and this one is very important."

"As long as it's not part of an ongoing FBI matter, I should be able to help."

"Great." Van Buren gave him all the details, brought him back to his car, and gave him copies of what he had already downloaded from the internet.

"Give me a couple of days, and I'll get back to you with what I've found."

Chapter 7

꘎

DOUG BINGHAM ARRIVED AT the coroner's office in time to meet Dorny in the lobby. They took the elevator down to the basement where bodies were stored until examined, then claimed or held for disposal. A cold, antiseptic odor overpowered the men as they exited the elevator. Cinder block walls lined the hallway. As they walked the empty corridor, their footsteps echoed off the cement floors. Inside the lab, one wall was lined with large, metal pull out drawers that housed the bodies.

"Douglas, I want you to be prepared before I show you your wife's remains. She won't look anything like she did when she was alive, but the medical examiner did do the best he could under the circumstances."

"Thank you, Detective, I've been preparing myself for this. Please just open the drawer."

Dorny pulled the drawer out and exposed Layni's body. Bingham looked for a moment, then stepped back, drew a deep breath, and began to cry. He covered his mouth and gagged. "Excuse me, but this is harder than I thought. I can't breathe. Please close the drawer."

Dorny closed the drawer while focusing on Bingham's reaction, thinking to himself that it was sincere. He was truly upset and not feigning the emotional response.

"Take your time, Douglas, I know this isn't easy. I also need you to look at the other woman's remains to see if you can identify her."

"Okay, just give me a minute. I need to sit down." He stepped further back.

Dorny pulled a chair over for him to sit and handed him a bottle of water. "Drink this and relax for a minute. When you're ready, we can move on and then get out of here."

Bingham sipped the water and stared up at the ceiling for a few minutes before he spoke. "Okay, I'm ready. Let's get this over with."

Dorny steered him over to another drawer and pulled it out. "Do you recognize her?"

He looked quickly and stepped back, bringing his hand to his mouth again. "My god, that's Suzie Bloom. She's an old friend of Layni's. I haven't seen her in a couple of years. She and Layni were good friends in college. She must have come in from out of town. Last I knew she was living in New York."

"We couldn't locate her ID or her cell phone, and we need to contact her family. Would you know how to get in touch with them?"

"Layni probably has her contact info in her cell phone. I can check when I get home."

"That would be very helpful. To be clear, you didn't know that Layni was having her visit while you were gone?"

"I had no idea at all, and she didn't tell me when we spoke on the phone that night either."

"I see." Dorny hesitated, "Would you like to go now?"

"Yes, please, I think I've seen enough." Bingham's eyes clouded over. "I'm not sure what I'm supposed to do right now. My mind isn't processing all this. Should I be making arrangements for the funeral?"

"Yes, that would be appropriate."

Without another word, Dorny led Bingham out of the lab and down the hall to the elevators. Once inside, Dorny said, "Here are the names and numbers of a few security guards I would recommend." He handed him a slip of paper.

Bingham looked at it briefly, folded it, and placed it in his pocket. "Thank you, Detective."

※ ※ ※

Dorny started his car, opened the windows, cranked the air conditioning, and speed dialed Eddie. "I just left the coroner's. You in the mood for dinner?"

"Sure, where do you want to meet?"

"Lure, over on Central."

"I know the place, gimme fifteen minutes."

Dorny found a parking space a few blocks away and walked up Central Avenue where he passed several bars and restaurants with outdoor seating. Most were buzzing with tourists and locals enjoying another warm, humid evening in St. Petersburg. He stepped inside of Lure, which had seating in the front and a semicircular bar at the back. The hostess led him to a small table off in the corner, where he still had visibility to the street. He wanted to know who was coming and going and never sat with his back to the door.

Eddie arrived as the waitress brought two glasses of water and menus.

"I hope you're hungry, Eddie, I haven't eaten all day."

"I can always eat, Dorny." He patted his burgeoning belly, smiled, sat down, and hoisted a menu. Within minutes, meals were ordered. Burgers, fries, and cokes. Fare of the day. "So, how'd it go with Bingham?"

"He reacted appropriately when he viewed his wife's remains. He also identified the other vic. Apparently an old college friend of hers. He's going to check his wife's phone for contact info so we can wrap up that end of it."

"Sounds good. What next?"

"Still waiting on the warrant for Lansiquot. Once that comes in, I promised Van Buren we'd let him bring her in."

"Let's hope he has an easier time locating her. I spoke to Carter before I left. He's over at her apartment building with Junior, and she hasn't returned. I'm wondering if she skipped town when she realized we were on to her."

"Frankly, Eddie, I suspect that she was the one who attacked the estate last night and is now in hiding."

"But Bingham said he thinks he wounded the assailant. Why would he shoot her?"

"That's his account, and I don't believe any of it. I think he set the whole thing up with her and they're playing us."

They stopped talking as the waitress arrived with their meals. She set them down and smiled. Dorny said, "Thank you," and smiled back.

Eddie watched her walk off and said, "I don't know, Dorny, with all due respect, this entire scenario of yours is really out there. You know that I'm not one to second guess you, you're usually on the money, but this one really has me scratching my head."

"I'm playing a hunch. And if I'm right, it all comes back to Douglas Bingham, whether Lansiquot is involved or not. Either way, the two were doing the nasty and that gives us leverage. So we use it as best we can and see where it leads us."

"Far be it from me to question you, boss."

Dorny pointed and said, "Eat your burger," just as his phone began playing AC/DC's *Dirty Deeds Done Dirt Cheap*.

Eddie laughed, "When did you change your ring tone?"

"Just did this morning. Apropos ain't it?" Smiling as he answered, "Dorny here, who's this?"

"Hilary White, DA's office. Your warrant is in."

"Thank you, be there shortly."

Chewing, Eddie said, "Warrant?"

"Yessir, time to call Van Buren to round her up." Dorny punched in the number, two rings and Xander Van Buren answered.

"Xander, it's Dorny, we've got an arrest warrant for your client. Consider this a courtesy call. How soon can you bring her down to the station?"

"Give me 'til tomorrow, and I'll call you back and coordinate."

"Okay, but if we don't have her in by nine o'clock tomorrow morning, all bets are off and we go after her."

"Understood."

Chapter 8

ᴀ⁀—❋—⁀

AFTER HANGING UP WITH Dorny, Van Buren placed a call to
Candace Lansiquot's cell phone. She didn't pick up, so he
left a message of urgency and then called her at Grandview Realty.
They advised him that she hadn't come in for two days, and they
too had not been able to reach her. Even though he was still sweaty
from the one-on-one match with Stu, he decided to take a drive to
her apartment to see if she was okay. She lived on the other side
of St. Petersburg, near the Gulf of Mexico, so it took him twenty
minutes to reach her place.

He rode the elevator to the sixth floor, found her apartment and
rang the bell. No answer. He knocked hard on the door and looked
in the window. No response, and no movement inside. He called
her cell again; it went to voice mail. Not good. He had no other
way to reach her. He rang the bell at the apartment next door. An
elderly man who walked with a cane answered the door and said he
hadn't seen Candace in a couple of days. He tried the apartment on
the other side, but no one was home.

He called Griff on his cell. "Hey bro, we've got a problem.
Dorny's got the warrant on Candace, and I haven't been able to

track her down. She isn't answering her phone, and I'm over at her apartment, and she's not home."

"That's not good. How much time did Dorny give you to bring her in?"

"Tomorrow at 9:00 A.M., then he's going after her."

"You think she skipped?"

"Makes no sense. Why would she have come to me if she had no intention of sticking around?"

"True, but maybe she got cold feet, or . . . and I hate to even say this, maybe something happened to her. Do you think Doug could be behind this?"

"Unless she contacted him, there would have been no way he even knew she was involved."

Griff said, "We need her phone records. I bet your basketball buddy Stu Saxon can help with that."

"Good idea. Talk to you later." He hung up and called Stu.

Laughing, "Hey, Xander, did you call to rub in the win?"

"No, I actually need another favor, and this one as fast as you can."

"What's the deal?"

"I've got a client I need to locate, and I'm hoping you can access her cell phone records to see who she's spoken to. She's disappeared, and I'm worried about her."

"I can do you one better. If you've got her number, I can track down her location, as long as her phone is on."

"That would be great, I'll text you her contact info. I need this real fast, so call me back when you've got some info."

"Will do."

Van Buren headed downstairs to the management office. After hours and closed. He took down the phone number posted on the door and went home to shower.

✱ ✱ ✱

The next morning, Van Buren made a courtesy call to Dorny at nine o'clock to tell him that he could not locate Candace Lansiquot. Dorny reminded him that the warrant permitted him to enter her apartment and look for anything that would implicate her in the homicides and/or lead him to her whereabouts. Van Buren told Dorny to keep him informed. Just as he hung up, Stu called him.

"Xander, I've got the info you need and can email you her phone records. As to her whereabouts, we've tracked her to Tampa. That's the last place she used her phone. I don't have an exact location, but she has been moving around."

"So, her phone is active, and she's just not picking up my calls."

"Apparently. Is she in some kind of trouble?"

"You could say that. There's a warrant for her arrest, and I was supposed to bring her in, so she's officially a fugitive."

"You gonna go after her?"

"No, I'll leave that up to the local police. I'm not really keen on aiding them in an arrest. But definitely email me her phone records, that may help me with my case, assuming she gets caught."

"Okay, and I've got someone working on your other request too. I'll get that to you when it's done."

"Did I say I owe you big time, Stu?"

"One day I will collect on that, you can be sure."

PART TWO

PART TWO

Chapter 9

Two months earlier . . .

MAI LING WAS A brilliant virologist. She was also a spy. She had been working as a lab technician at the Institute of Virology in China for more than a year and had become very familiar with the rigorous safety precautions that had to be taken when working in the fields of research undertaken there. Her field was the etiology and epidemiology of emerging infectious diseases. These diseases are some of the greatest threats to public health around the world, and Ling was placed there specifically for that reason.

The plan was in the works from the day she started at the institute, and everything was in place. No one suspected her; she had maintained a low-key presence throughout the entire term of her employment, acting deferential and subservient the way a first-year tech was supposed to act.

Her mission, for which she would be handsomely rewarded, was to release a pathogen into the population to create chaos in the world, but most importantly in the United States. She had been cautioned to avoid making it look intentional, so she needed to select an existing pathogen that was highly contagious and could be easily transmitted from animals to humans.

Going about her daily routine, she had access to many deadly viruses, which gave her a several choices. In the end she isolated the strain she wanted, and secretly began working on a cure. After much research and experimentation, she was successful, but she also knew that there was no way she could just walk out with the virus, because safety concerns required constant monitoring. Everyone who worked there had to undress and pass-through cleansing stations when leaving the premises, and nothing was permitted to be removed from the lab. That meant she would need to infect someone inside the lab and have that person unwittingly introduce it to the outside world.

Over the course of her tenure, Ling monitored the daily routines of a few technicians at the lab. One, a Chinese American, Dr. Daniel Xinghuan, whom they called Dr. X, was on loan from a lab in the United States for nine months, so she set her sights on him and planned to infect him a few days before he was to return to the States. She watched him and learned that he had lunch at precisely one o'clock every day. He brought his lunch with him and kept it in a plastic container in the refrigerator.

When it was finally time to implement, Ling was ready with the virus. She planned to spray it on the table and counter surfaces as well as the refrigerator door handle in the break room just to make sure it would spread. However, there was only a short window during which the virus would remain active, so timing was critical.

As was her usual routine, Ling entered the break room at ten minutes to one. She had the spray in her lab coat. A rectangular table stood in the center of the room with six chairs surrounding it. No one was in the break room. Lined against the far wall were a row of cabinets solidified by a granite countertop that also housed an electric stove. A cork board with various notes, cards and solicitations occupied a side wall. A large refrigerator rested up against the third wall.

Most everyone, including Ling, brought their own lunch and left it in the refrigerator labeled with their names, so picking out Dr. X's lunch was easy. She sprayed it on the lid of his container, on his sandwich, on the refrigerator door handle, and on all the surfaces in the room. She then sat down with her lunch.

Minutes later, Dr. X entered the break room, took his lunch and sat down to eat. A few more technicians also entered and took their lunches. Collateral damage. Ling waited until Dr. X ate most of his sandwich, then she excused herself. Her mission accomplished, she left, with no intention of ever returning.

❋ ❋ ❋

Mai Ling's escape and departure from China was immediate. Half of the money she was to be paid had already been wired to an untraceable overseas account in the name of Maria Chen. She returned to her apartment, opened her safe, retrieved her American passport and plane ticket with the same name and adopted her new identity. She cut and dyed her hair to match the picture on the passport, checked her appearance in the mirror and smiled. She was thirty-four, slender, stood 5 feet 4 inches tall, and was extraordinarily attractive. However, by the time she finished prepping herself, she looked plain and unappealing, with poorly applied makeup and short, curly brown hair. Satisfied with her new look, and leaving nothing behind, she took a taxi to the airport.

Passing through security was easy, as was customs when she arrived in New York. Her destination, Chinatown. Since she had already inoculated herself with the vaccine, hiding in plain sight was her best option. She also enjoyed the game of cat and mouse, though she felt she had covered her tracks well. Groomed as a spy since her teens, Maria Chen was accustomed to being a chameleon and could change her appearance in a flash. She was supposed to lay low until she had been paid, but she already anticipated that the second half of her fee was going to be held up. The only leverage she had was that she could synthesize the vaccine, and that would be worth millions more when the time came.

Upon arrival at John F. Kennedy International Airport, she retrieved her luggage and took an Uber to the apartment she had rented months before. Having previously lived in Chinatown, she had no trouble getting around. She unpacked and headed out to the market to stock up on food and other essentials. For Maria Chen it should have only been a waiting game, but she had other plans.

Chapter 10

‿━✳━‿

Present day . . .

SPECIAL AGENT SAXON CALLED Van Buren on his cell. He had gathered information on Doug Bingham. They agreed to meet at Van Buren's office that Saturday morning. When he arrived, Saxon was already waiting for him in the lobby. They rode the elevator up and went into the conference room. He opened his briefcase and laid out a thin set of papers on the table.

Saxon said, "We've come up with some info on your guy."

Van Buren picked up the stack and fanned it with his thumb. "Sum it up for me and I'll go through the paperwork later."

"Sure. So, Bingham is heavily connected to a certain political party that is trying to regain the White House—at any cost. He has major interests overseas and in China especially. He conducts that business through his main entity, Bingham International, Ltd. The company is solid, no financial problems, no bankruptcies or lawsuits pending. He is the major shareholder, owning 70 percent of the stock, and while the company is private, there are at least a dozen other shareholders. Everything looks legit on the surface, but we are still digging. However, he uses his other entities, Synergy Properties, LLC, and Luxor Corp. as investment vehicles. Synergy owns some commercial properties, but also owns a number of overseas entities that are heavily invested in the financial markets. We found significant short positions in select publicly traded companies. Same with Luxor Corp."

Van Buren said, "By 'short positions' you mean he is betting that the underlying stocks will go down at some point."

"Correct. He's loaded up on put options as well as direct short positions on some stocks. He is also holding large positions in a few stocks that I suspect he feels will increase in value."

"So, what's so strange about all that?"

"Well, first of all, it's the timing of the purchases. Most have been done over the last two months. The other thing is the grouping of companies he is shorting. We are running algorithms to find the common denominator, but from the looks of it, he seems to be anticipating a major recession. It's as if he knows something no one else does. When we compare his positions to the positions of most seasoned investment companies and large trading firms, he is completely at odds with just about everyone else."

"Interesting. What types of companies are you talking about?"

"He is betting against oil, steel, copper, and other commodities. He is also loading up on companies that do a lot of online business such as Amazon."

"I find it hard to believe this is all about insider trading, Stu."

"I don't think it is either, Xander, but there is something going on. I mean we aren't talking about chump change here. He has countless millions, probably more than 20 million dollars, all invested in the last two months. And all of it in overseas accounts. Who does that? It's as if he is so sure of the outcome, he has no reason to worry about risk."

"Which means he either knows something no one else does, or he's involved in a plot to cause it to happen."

"Do you really think this guy is capable of doing something that would upset world markets to such an extent?"

"I don't know, Stu. I find it hard to believe any one person could have that much influence."

"Agreed, and at this point he has done nothing wrong or illegal. So, we have no basis for a warrant or anything for that matter. But there is something very suspicious here, and we need to keep digging."

"Yes, we do. So, tell me about this algorithm you mentioned before. How does that work?"

Stu sucked in a breath, puffed his cheeks, and blew out. "Some of that is beyond my technological understanding. But we have tech people that can create programs with algorithms that assimilate the data and come up with scenarios that where areas of the economy would suffer if certain events were to occur. I don't know exactly how any of that is done, I just leave it up to the back-office geeks and nerds."

"I see, yeah it's above my pay grade, too."

Chapter 11

DORNY AND EDDIE SHOWED up at the Bingham estate Saturday afternoon. They had more questions for Doug Bingham and needed to follow up. They pulled up to the gate and pressed the green access button. The gate did not open.

Dorny said, "I guess Douglas decided to tighten up security." He pushed the call button.

A grainy voice answered, "Who's there?"

"Detectives Dornhuber and Rumson. We need to talk."

The gate slid open, and Dorny rolled through and pulled up the drive. A minute later, Bingham opened the front door. The two detectives exited the car and made their way to the house.

"May we come in," asked Dorny.

Bingham opened the door wider. "Follow me." Bingham ushered the detectives into the library on the other side of the house, as the den was still being repaired. The library was a comfortable room with books lining shelves floor to ceiling on two walls. A comfortable, deep maroon leather couch stood up against a third oak paneled wall. A large desk occupied the space across from it, and a large glass coffee table rested on a Persian rug filling the gap in between. The room had a warm cozy feel.

Gesturing to the couch, Bingham said, "Please sit down." He then proceeded to sit at his desk across from them. "So, what can I do for you?"

Eddie said, "We have some more questions."

"I didn't think cops worked on weekends."

Dorny cleared his throat and said, "We're always working." He pulled out his pad and pen and flipped through the pages. "We were hoping that you had located Suzie Bloom's contact information."

"I have. Would you like me to get that for you?"

"In a minute, let's just get through all of this first. We were also wondering about your butler, Darryl. We never got his last name. Did he ever return?"

"Yao, and oddly, no. I hadn't quite thought about it with everything else going on."

"Do you think you can find his contact information?" asked Eddie.

"I would guess it's in Layni's phone. I can check that too."

Dorny wrote the name Yao on his pad. "Thank you. Please get those for us now."

Bingham opened the desk drawer, pulled out his late wife's phone, punched in the code and scrolled until he found what he was looking for. He took out a pen and paper and wrote down both of their names, addresses and phone numbers, walked out from behind the desk and handed it to Dorny. "Will that be all, Detectives?" He walked back behind his desk and sat down.

"Not just yet," Dorny said. "Can you tell me anything about Candace Lansiquot?"

A quizzical look played across Bingham's face. "Who?"

"Candace Lansiquot. She's a realtor here in St. Petersburg. It's not a common name, so we're sure you'd remember it."

"Sorry, doesn't ring a bell."

Eddie said, "That's odd, seeing as she told us she had been to your home, and in fact she was here last Saturday night at your fundraiser."

Flat smile. "You must be kidding me. We had over one hundred guests here that night. You can't expect me to remember every single one of them."

"She was very memorable," Dorny said. "Mid-thirties, strikingly pretty, slender figure, long, dark hair. You couldn't miss her; she makes quite an impression."

"No, sorry, I was very busy entertaining and must have missed her. There were a few attractive women here that night."

Dorny stood up, walked over to the desk, and dropped a photo in front of Bingham. "Take a closer look. Any bells?"

Bingham shook his head. "I've already said no. Where are you going with this?"

Dorny put his pad on the coffee table and sat back down. He waited a few seconds, turned, and looked at Eddie, then refocused his gaze on Bingham, folded his fingers through each other and said, "We have reason to believe you're not being truthful, Doug."

"Meaning?"

"Meaning, she not only told us that she attended the fundraiser, but that you took the time to show her around your home. In fact, she claims you showed her your bedroom."

"That's a lie!"

Eddie said, "Look Doug, we wouldn't be pressing you on this if it were as simple as that. In fact, our forensics team uncovered her fingerprints on your headboard, as well as hairs that belong to her in your bed."

"What are you suggesting, Detective?"

"We aren't suggesting anything, but it seems clear, from the positioning of the fingerprints—and there were two sets, positioned in such a way that she was on the bed apparently straddling you with her palms pressed against the headboard."

The color left Bingham's face. "Perhaps there's some other explanation."

Dorny said, "Well, if you have one, we'd like to hear it."

"I think I've said enough. This conversation is over. I'd like you gentlemen to leave now."

"Look Doug, you can either answer us here, or at some point you'll be brought in for further questioning, because as of now, we believe you have lied to us about this, and if you've lied to us about this, it suggests to me that you're probably lying to us about other things."

"Are you saying I need a lawyer?"

Eddie said, "We're not saying anything, but usually we find that it's the guilty people who ask for lawyers."

Bingham squirmed uncomfortably in his chair. "You've got this all wrong. This has nothing to do with you, or the investigation."

"How so, Doug?" asked Dorny.

"Okay, so if I answer you, can you assure me to keep this between us?"

Dorny said, "As long as it has nothing to do with our investigation, sure, no problem."

"All right, so I know how this looks, which is why I didn't say anything before, but yeah, I do know her, and yeah, we were together in bed that night. We had both been drinking heavily, and she came on to me. She's very hot, and I just couldn't refuse her—but that was it, one night stand."

"With your wife right downstairs?" Eddie said. "Pretty ballsy and really nasty, wouldn't you say?"

"Hey, I don't need you to judge me. So, I made a mistake. I'm sure you're not perfect either, but I swear, this had nothing to do with Layni's murder. I mean, how could it?"

"Well, for starters, with her prints as the only ones that came up, she becomes a prime suspect," said Dorny. "Add to that there's a warrant out for her arrest, we searched her apartment, and she has disappeared. That makes all this very suspicious. Cheating husband, dead wife, missing girlfriend. You tell me Doug."

"You see? That's why I didn't want to say anything!" declared Doug. "I knew you would think that, but it's just not the case. I had a lapse in judgment, but you're making much more of this than there is."

Eddie said, "Remains to be seen. In the meantime, don't leave town."

"Fine, but now I think it's time for you to leave."

The two detectives got up and Bingham showed them to the door. As they were leaving, Dorny said, "One more thing. When was the last time you spoke to Candace Lansiquot?"

"That would be last Saturday night, at the party." He closed the door behind them.

Dorny and Eddie left the estate and headed back down Brightwaters Boulevard, leaving the wealthy suburb in the rearview mirror.

Dorny said, "What do you make of his story now?"

"The guy's a slime, and now I'm thinking that your initial suspicions may have some validity after all."

"Money, sex and murder, oldest trio in the book." Dorny turned left on Snell Isle Boulevard and accelerated. "I need you to make the delicate call to the other vic's family and break the news to them. I'm going to track down the butler, Darryl Yao. Maybe he can shed some light on dear ole' Doug's extramarital activities. We also need to get Bingham's cell phone records. Let's see who he's been talking to."

❋ ❋ ❋

Doug Bingham took his second burner phone from the safe and punched in Candace Lansiquot's phone number. After five rings it went to voice mail. He didn't leave a message.

Chapter 12

DOUG BINGHAM'S REGULAR CELL phone rang. He had never heard the voice before, but it was female and with a slight Asian accent. The call came in on an untraceable line with no caller ID. Bingham said, "Who is this?"

"Who I am doesn't matter. I am going to make this simple. We want the thumb drive. And if you ever want to see your daughter alive again, you will produce it."

"The thumb drive? I don't have it. It was taken the night my wife was murdered."

"We know for a fact that it was not retrieved at that time. It was not in your safe."

"Wait a second, how do you know about the safe? Did you have something to do with her murder?"

"You have forty-eight hours." Click.

"Hello, hello—" He looked at his phone. Disconnected.

Panicked, he called Ashley. Five rings, voice mail. He left an urgent message and called his pilot, "Carl, it's Doug, get my jet ready, we're flying to New York immediately. How soon can you get me in the air?"

"Give me an hour, boss. The jet is all fueled up, so it'll be quick."

"I'll be there in forty-five minutes."

Bingham packed a small bag, took both of his pistols, four extra magazines, all fully loaded, and another box of hollow point ammo, and headed for Albert Whitted Airport in downtown St. Petersburg. Since it was a private jet, there would be no security, and no one to prevent him from bringing a firearm on board.

✳ ✳ ✳

True to his word, Captain Carl had Doug Bingham wheels up in less than an hour. Doug was frantic—he knew he had to reach Ashley as quickly as possible. Her life was in danger, and she'd have no clue what was going on. He had intentionally kept her out of all his business dealings, so that if anything ever went wrong, she would have plausible deniability. He stared out the window, almost willing the jet to fly faster. In his mind's eye he saw the little girl he loved more than anything in the world, sitting on his stomach giggling while he bounced her up and down. His mind then flashed to her on stage as a young teen dancing a solo in a statewide competition. Tears filled his eyes as he remembered her bounding towards him grinning gleefully, her arm held high waving the first-place trophy she'd won for her performance. His mind then cut to the shooting range where he taught her how to load, handle, and fire a pistol. She did well and managed some impressive target groupings her very first time. Then he visualized her as he sat in the front row during her college graduation. She accepted her diploma as they announced her graduating with honors. She finished top ten in her class.

Then it struck him. He hadn't even called her to tell her about Layni. Not that it would have mattered much, the two never liked each other anyway. Ashley always felt that Layni stepped into her dad's life, under suspicious circumstances, right after her mother died. Layni was his ex-girlfriend from high school, and Ashley had convinced herself early on that Layni was only interested in her dad's money.

Still looking out the window, as his mind continued playing out milestones from Ashley's life, he saw the Freedom tower off in the distance. He took out his phone and made another call to her. Two rings and she answered.

"Hi Dad, how are you?"

"Never mind me, how are you, baby?"

"All good, what's up."

"First, tell me where you are."

"Right now, I'm having lunch in the city. You sound strange, is everything ok?"

"No, it's not, which is why I'm calling you. A lot has happened over the last week, and it's important that you listen closely. You are in danger, and you need to get some place safe, until I can get to you."

"What? What's going on?"

"For starters, Layni is dead, she's been murdered."

"What! Oh, no, who would do something like that?"

"I'm not sure yet, but what I do know is that whoever it is, is also after you."

"Why? I don't understand. This sounds crazy."

"It is, and I don't have time to explain right now, but I will when I see you."

"So, what am I supposed to do?"

"First, make sure you aren't being followed. But do not, under any circumstances, go back to your apartment. Go to the nearest police station, and tell them you think someone is stalking you, and you want to file a report. Then just wait there for me to come get you. I should be landing at Republic Airport on Long Island shortly, so figure I will meet you in less than two hours."

Ashley was already looking around at everyone in the cafe. "I'm scared Dad, I don't know where there's a police station close by, and what if they get to me before I can find one? Maybe I should just stay in plain sight?"

"Where exactly are you now, Ash?"

"Midtown, not too far from Penn Station."

"Ok, good, then get to Penn, there are always cops, as well as armed soldiers patrolling. Find one, preferably a soldier, and approach him and tell him you are scared that you are being followed. I'll get there as soon as I can, just be careful. It might be an Asian woman coming for you, but it could be anyone, or more than one. So don't trust a soul."

"Okay Dad, please hurry."

"I will. I love you, Ash. Call me when you can."

Beads of sweat began to form on her face. She slowly rose from her seat, picked up the package she was carrying from her Times Square shopping spree, placed seventy-five dollars on the table and walked out the door. It was a crisp, sixty-degree spring day, still March but the sun was out with little cloud cover. As she walked where the sun came through between the buildings, it felt warm. Ashley shivered.

Walking down Times Square towards 34th Street, Ashley constantly looked behind as she moved. As a precaution, when she turned down 34th Street she made her way into the corner office building, looked at the directory, then proceeded to a bank of elevators. When one arrived, she waited to see who entered the elevator, avoiding everyone until no one was left in the lobby. She wanted to ascend alone. As she stood there, she noticed a woman standing outside the entrance to the building looking at her through the large plate glass window. An uneasy feeling crept over her, and when their eyes met, the woman quickly averted her gaze and walked off.

Ashley took the next elevator to the tenth floor, found a suite of attorneys, entered, and asked for a key to the lady's room. The receptionist obliged her. She walked down the hall, located the bathroom, and went in. Taking a stall, she opened her shopping bag and removed a pair of jeans, a black top, and the running sneakers she had bought, took off her skirt and blouse and placed them in the bag, threw her heels, the bag, and the rest of its contents into the garbage and left. She didn't bother to return the key and simply tossed it in the sink. She then pulled a hair band from her purse, pulled her hair up into a ponytail and secured it with the band. Hoping she looked sufficiently different, she took the elevator to the second floor, found a stairwell, and walked down the last flight. She figured she would leave the building from the other side, which worked out perfectly because one exit was not visible from the other. She exited the stairwell and strolled casually to the revolving door and passed through. She then walked up 33rd Street and headed to 7th Avenue and Penn Station.

Maria Chen wasn't fooled. She maintained her distance and continued following Ashley as she made her way to Penn.

Ashley had gotten close to 7th Avenue when she turned and recognized the woman who was looking at her through the window earlier. The woman was still half a block away but moving more quickly and closing in. Ashley ducked into an electronics store and positioned herself between the aisles to avoid being seen. A skinny, twenty-something boy, wearing clothes two sizes too large for his emaciated frame approached her. He had a greasy, pimpled face, ear buds and a man bun. "May I help you find something?"

Ashley scanned him from head to toe. At any other time, her first instinct would have been to wave him off in disgust, but she needed help. She eyed his name tag. "Thank you, Marcus, I do need your help, but not with a purchase." She smiled. "You see, I'm trying to avoid someone who is following me. Do you happen to have a back door where I could leave without being seen?"

"We're not supposed to let customers in the back alone, and I'm the only one on the floor right now, so I can't take you back there. I could get canned."

Ashley pulled out a twenty-dollar bill from her purse. "Look Marcus, I'm really scared. My life could be in danger. Just point me in the direction of the back door and I'll go right out. I promise. And perhaps, some other time, when I'm safe, I'll come back here, and we can do some business." Ashley offered a big smile as she placed her hand on his chest. "You seem like a nice guy, and you'd really be helping me out." She looked him right in the eyes. "I'd really owe you one."

Marcus practically wet his pants, gave her a goofy grin, and walked her to the back of the store. "Through that door, go to your right past the stacks of boxes, you'll find a steel door. Just make sure it's closed tightly behind you."

Ashley said, "Thank you, and if a woman dressed in a black leather jacket and blue jeans comes in here, please don't tell her you saw me."

"No prob."

Heart racing, Ashley hurried through the stock room, pushed open the door and exited into an alleyway behind the building. Instinctively, she knew where she was and to head west, but there was no street access in that direction. She began trying the doors along the alley, pulling at each, one after another. All were locked. Finally, a door swung open up ahead. An old man wearing a Yankees cap, a cigarette dangling from his lip, pushed a hand cart loaded with crates into the alley. She ran up to him, passed by without a second glance, and went through the door. Crates and boxes were lined up in narrow rows forming their own aisles. She made her way to the front and into the main area of the novelty store. A middle-aged woman wearing a flowery blouse and spectacles that hung from a lanyard over her ample, sagging breasts, came out from behind the counter and approached her. "Who are you and what are you doing in my storeroom?"

"I'm sorry, I got lost in the alley and yours was the only door that was open. I meant no harm, I just had to get out of that alley."

"Well, you don't belong back there!" She crowed, "Either buy something, or get the hell out of my shop."

Ashley looked around and asked, "Do you carry mace or pepper spray by any chance?" Big grin. "Course we do honey, you havin' problems with your man?"

"Something like that."

"Well follow me then, let me show you what we've got." She led her to a cabinet on the wall that contained various items for self-defense including small pepper spray canisters that fit in the palm of your hand. Hanging alongside were sets of brass knuckles, nun chucks, throwing stars, and other related products. "Anything here interest you?"

Ashley smiled, selected two pepper spray canisters and a set of brass knuckles, paid, and left through the front entrance. She opened the bag, removed the brass knuckles, and put them on her right hand, took a pepper spray canister in her left, placed the other canister in her purse and discarded the bag. She looked left and right, did not see the woman, and continued towards Penn Station. Minutes later she stood at the intersection of 7th Avenue and 33rd Street waiting for the light to change. Maria Chen hid across the street behind a Souvlaki cart vendor that was positioned at the corner near the entrance to Madison Square Garden. Chen had a syringe filled with sodium pentothal that she intended to use on Ashley to knock her out. Timing was critical though. Chen couldn't act until Darryl Yao showed up with his car, and he was still two blocks away, stuck in traffic. As an added precaution, Chen also had a taser gun hidden in the small of her back. Either way, she was taking a big risk trying to pull off an abduction in broad daylight in front of Penn Station. Fortunately, although cops were nearby, there were none in the immediate vicinity.

When the light changed, Ashley proceeded through the intersection, still glancing behind her. She didn't think there was any way Chen would be waiting up ahead. Still, she had pepper spray and punching power ready to use, if necessary. Ashley had always been resourceful. She learned early on how to defend herself, taking kickboxing lessons for almost seven years while growing up. She also knew how to use a handgun and had been to the shooting range many times with her dad years ago. But that was before Layni made him get rid of his pistols.

Thinking back to her days of training—and how she whined to her dad about how silly it was for her to be taking martial arts—she now hoped that her training wouldn't fail her. She remembered her trainer, Keith, a big guy with an easy disposition. He showed her how to punch, kick, block, and evade. And, after a time, the moves became instinctive. Keith even praised her for being a fast learner. Dad always told her how much it helped that she was a dancer and very athletic.

When Ashley passed by the Souvlaki cart, she heard a screeching sound as a car came to an abrupt stop in the street behind her. Simultaneously, Maria Chen came out from around the cart and grabbed Ashley by the right arm. With her free hand she brought the syringe up. Ashley hesitated momentarily, then raised her left hand and pushed the pepper spray nozzle as she aimed at Chen's face. Chen wasn't prepared. She released Ashley, dropped the syringe, and reached for her eyes just as Ashley pulled away. Using the brass knuckles, Ashley threw an off-balance punch at Chen connecting at her jaw. She screamed for help and began to run. Bystanders looked on, but no one came to her aid. Chen's eyes stinging, she regrouped and gave chase. Yao slowly moved the car forward to keep pace, but Ashley managed to reach the stairs leading down into the station. She descended quickly, saw a cop up ahead, and ran towards him. Chen stopped on the landing halfway down the stairs, turned and disappeared, quickly making her way to Yao's car.

Chapter 13

⌐—✺—⌐

DORNY HAD BEEN TRYING to reach the butler, Darryl Yao, through his cell phone, but the number had been disconnected. He was able to reach the cell phone provider and was advised that the account had been closed by the customer. The address connected to the phone was the Bingham address. However, the address provided by Bingham for Yao was in New York. More specifically, a section of Chinatown in lower Manhattan. He ran the name through DMV and came up with a hit—the problem, Yao used the Bingham address for his license. He ran the name through the criminal database, again nothing. All Dorny had was a DMV picture and license. His car was also registered at the Bingham address, so he did have a license plate number. With his suspicions mounting, Dorny didn't have much of a choice. He couldn't take a trip to New York at this point, so he would have to rely on the NYPD and ask them if they could check out the address and locate Yao. Normally he would request assistance when looking for a criminal or a fugitive, but Yao was neither, and his failure to return to the Bingham estate and having his phone account closed did not amount to criminal activity. At best, he had a missing person case. Dorny decided to put a BOLO out for Yao's car, a 2010 Honda Accord. Silver, of course, is the most common color for that make and model vehicle.

Chapter 14

───❈───

ASHLEY BINGHAM REPORTED THE incident to the police at Penn Station and gave a description of her attacker. Black leather jacket, blue jeans, short curly hair and Asian features. The woman never spoke but could have a bruise on the left side of her chin from the brass knuckles, and her eyes might be red from pepper spray. When asked why she was carrying pepper spray and brass knuckles, she answered the police honestly and told them that she was being followed and purchased those items as a safety precaution. The police were impressed with how she handled herself but advised her that it was highly unlikely that they would be able to find her assailant.

She remained in their field of view and called her father.

He answered on the first ring, the urgency in his voice apparent. "Ashley, what's happening, where are you, are you all right?"

"I'm fine Dad, but you were right, I was attacked before I got to Penn Station, but I fought her off, and I'm safe with the police right now."

"Thank God. Did they catch her?"

"No, she ran off."

"Did you get a good look at her?"

"It happened so fast, I really only got a glimpse of her and what she was wearing. But you were right, she was Asian."

"Well, I'm glad you're safe. I should be in Manhattan in a half hour, I'm already on the road from the airport. Stay where you are, and I'll pick you up on 7th Avenue in front of the Garden near the taxi lines. Just stay with the police until I call you."

"Okay, but when are you going to tell me what's going on? I'm really worried."

"We'll talk when I see you. Until then, be careful . . . love you."

"Love you too, Dad."

✳ ✳ ✳

A half hour later, Doug Bingham arrived at the entrance to Penn Station and Madison Square Garden on 7th Avenue and called Ashley. She asked the police officer to accompany her to the car and he obliged. Bingham thanked him for looking out for his daughter, she got in the rented Land Rover, and they left the city.

"So, tell me Ashley, what happened back there?"

Ashley was still pumped up from the encounter. "Dad, you won't believe it. I realized I was being followed, tried to lose her by going through some stores and an alley, ended up in a shop that sold pepper spray and brass knuckles, so I bought them, and had them ready. I thought that I had lost her, but she showed up and surprised me right on the street. I sprayed her with the pepper spray and punched her with the knuckles and ran off. She chased me, but I got away and ran to the police. That's when she took off. It was unreal, I can't believe I did that."

"Wow, I'm proud of you, I always knew you could take care of yourself—and you're ok, you didn't get hurt?"

"No, not at all. Now you better tell me, what the hell is going on? Are you in some kind of trouble? What happened to Layni?"

109

Doug remained quiet for a time as he drove. He kept looking through the rearview mirror, wondering if they were being followed. He took a few extra turns and when he was sure they were safe, he headed for the Midtown tunnel and began traveling under the East River toward Long Island. The muffled sound of tires racing along the pavement echoed inside as Bingham began to speak. "I'm not sure where to start, Ash. They killed Layni while I was away and ransacked the safe. At first, I thought it was just a burglary gone bad, but it's not, it's something a lot more serious. And I know you aren't going to like what you hear, so please try to understand, and don't judge me just yet."

"You're scaring me, Dad. Just tell me already, and don't hold back. I'm not a kid anymore."

"I know, but this is very bad, so be prepared."

"Like I haven't been prepared so far."

"Ok, well, I got involved with some influential politicians in Congress and brokered a transaction with some oligarchs in China. It started out innocently enough. The goal was to find a way to oust the president and ruin his reputation so that our party could take over at the next election."

"You didn't do anything illegal, did you?" Ashley interrupted.

"Just listen. When I first made the introductions, to protect myself I recorded everything. I also secured documentation and had photographs taken of meetings. All the information and evidence was downloaded onto a thumb drive, which I kept secret. Only Layni knew about it . . . or so I thought."

"So, what were they planning to do to hurt the president?"

"At first, it was simply going to be a trade war with China, but apparently that wasn't enough. As time went on, it was decided that something needed to be done to create chaos in the world economy."

"Whose idea was that?"

"Difficult to say, it came up during back-and-forth negotiations, some of which are recorded and on the drive."

"And you have the drive?"

"I did, but it was stolen from the safe that night, or at least I thought it was, but when that Asian woman phoned me, she demanded that I turn it over to her or they'd kill you."

"I see, so you don't know where it is then?"

"No."

"Okay, go on. So, what was the plan?"

"Here's where it gets murky. Someone suggested releasing a contagion that could be spread and unleash a panic that would stifle the world economy for a time."

"You mean like germ warfare? Are they crazy?"

"Not exactly germ warfare, Ashley, more a super virus that would spread quickly and force countries to seal their borders to prevent further transmission. That, in and of itself would slow the global economy, and since this progressive administration has made a big deal about opening our borders and easing immigration restrictions, along with their other far-left policies, their supporters would lose confidence and they wouldn't get re-elected."

"But what about all the people that would get sick."

"Collateral damage as far as they're concerned. You have to understand that they don't think the same way in China. All they care about is defeating us, and they hate the president, so anything they can do to get him out of office is fair game."

"And our politicians, they're okay with this?"

"When it comes to this president, apparently so."

"So where are they with this plan now."

"They cut me out of the loop a while ago. The last thing I heard was that a super virus had been developed, but it was far more potent than expected and has the capacity to kill hundreds of thousands, if not millions of people, if not contained."

"Is there a cure?"

"That I don't know."

"Has it been released into the public yet?"

"About a month ago, so it may already be spreading. We'll know soon enough."

"And so, they're after you because you have the proof as to who is behind all this."

"Yes."

"Oh my God, this is awful. You're actually tied into something that not only can destroy the economy but something that will kill people! What have you done? Why would you do this?"

"It's not as simple as that. I didn't get into this with those intentions. These people went off the deep end, and I just tried to protect myself."

"Well, you need to tell someone! Go to the FBI or something. People have to know about this, and fast!"

"I can't. If I do that, I'll either end up dead, or in jail for the rest of my life."

"There has to be a way to stop this."

"I wish there were, and I've been trying to come up with something, I just need some time."

"Honestly Dad, it doesn't sound like you have much time, and I don't want your legacy to be that of an evil madman."

"I won't let that happen; I promise. Right now, I need to find that thumb drive. If it wasn't stolen the night Layni was killed, it's either still in the house or it can be tracked down. Layni was the only other person who knew where it was. Maybe she did something with it before she was killed."

Chapter 15

ONE DAY HAD PASSED since Dorny and Eddie completed their search of Candace Lansiquot's apartment. They found nothing consequential that would implicate her in the homicides, other than the fact that she apparently fled the jurisdiction. However, they did manage to find a cell phone bill and were able to obtain her number. Dorny sat in his office going through her cell phone records and found numerous calls to and from Doug Bingham. He was still waiting on copies of text messages, which would better indicate the extent of their relationship, but it was clear that they had been communicating for some time, and that Doug had lied when he said they simply had a one-night stand.

Eddie barged into Dorny's office. "We've got a lead on Lansiquot's location, or at least where her cell phone is. Tech was able to pinpoint her by using the cell towers to triangulate."

"Where is she?"

"The Hard Rock Hotel and Casino in Tampa."

Dorny closed the file, jumped up, and said, "That's about a forty-minute drive, let's go."

Taking Dorny's car, they headed north on I-275 to the Howard Frankland Bridge. They drove through Tampa and hit some construction traffic, which slowed them down. Once they passed through the city of Tampa, the Hard Rock was fifteen minutes further ahead and could be seen from the highway.

As they approached, Eddie said, "It's a big place. How are we going to find her?"

"If she's there, we'll locate her. You know how security is at these casinos. Cameras everywhere."

They pulled up to the valet station, left the car, and went inside the hotel. As they walked towards the entrance to the casino, the sounds of bells, chimes and musical chords could be heard above the roar of the crowd. The thick smell of cigarette smoke engulfed them. The best efforts of the vents and filters did little to mitigate the offensive odor. Dorny pinched his nose. Eddie coughed. They proceeded inside, located a security guard, and approached him.

Dorny pulled out his badge. "Good afternoon, I'm Detective Dornhuber, this is my partner, Detective Rumson. We need to speak to the head of security. It's an urgent matter."

"That would be Bill Grace. He's probably upstairs in the viewing center. If you tell me what this is about, I can call him."

Dorny said, "We believe there is a fugitive inside the hotel. We have an arrest warrant, and we'd like to keep it quiet and see if we can track her down and apprehend her without incident."

"Yes, that would be our preference too." The guard took out his phone and made a call. "Boss, it's Wayne Lomax. I'm at my post. I have two detectives down here; they need to speak with you. They've got an arrest warrant for someone who may be staying here."

Grace said, "Give me a few minutes, I'll be right down."

Eddie scanned the casino, shaking his head. "I don't know, Dorny, places like this always amaze me. I mean, how do people do this when they know they're probably going to lose their money? The odds are against them, but they just keep coming back."

"I hear ya. I wouldn't be caught dead in a place like this, but people do win sometimes and when there's even a slight possibility of hitting it big, that'll draw a crowd." An elated screech rose above the din. "There ya go, Eddie, see that, another lucky patron."

Eddie laughed as a burly, middle-aged man dressed in a blue sport jacket, jeans and an open collared shirt made his way towards them. His stride was that of a confident, seasoned pro who had probably been in law enforcement before taking on a more glamorous title.

He extended his hand to Dorny. "Bill Grace, how can I be of assistance, gentlemen?" Dorny shook his hand, "Detective Lance Dornhuber, and this is my partner, Detective Eddie Rumson. We're with the St. Petersburg Police Department, and we're looking for a fugitive. We have reason to believe that she is here, in your hotel."

"How have you been able to determine that, Detective?"

"Cell phone triangulation." Eddie said.

Grace smiled. "Ain't technology grand?"

Dorny said, "That it is, and we're hoping that with your technology, you can help us track down our perp."

"I can certainly try. Let's start with a name and see if she's a registered guest. Follow me." Dorny handed Grace the arrest warrant. Grace looked at it and led them through the casino.

He ushered them through a door, up a set of stairs and into a large open area filled with computers, screens, video feeds and one-way mirrors that looked down into the pit areas of the casino. He walked briskly to a keyboard, looked at the warrant again, punched a few keys and then entered the name Candace Lansiquot into the system.

"Here we go. She *is* staying at the hotel. Room 803. Let's see if she's being rated."

Eddie asked, "What does that mean?"

Grace said, "When someone looks to get rated, they need to get a card from the casino, and they show it to the host while they are gambling. Now, depending on how long they play, how much they spend, how much they win or lose, they receive a rating. The rating would entitle them to perks, such as free meals, a complimentary room, maybe a spa treatment, things of that nature. If she's got a card, and she's playing now, we can track her movements in the casino." He fingered the keyboard again. "We're in luck, she's out on the floor playing blackjack. Do you have a picture of her?"

Dorny dug his hand into his breast pocket, pulled out a copy of Lansiquot's driver's license and handed it to Grace. A few more clicks of the keyboard and an overhead shot of a semicircular blackjack table populated by three men and three women came up on the screen.

Dorny and Eddie leaned over to the screen and scanned the women. Grace pointed to a woman sitting in the anchor seat—the last seat on the left, next to the dealer. "That could be her." Dorny nodded and Eddie agreed.

"Okay gentlemen, since this is my casino, we need to play this my way. I don't want to create a scene down there, so you need to let me escort her off the floor, then you can apprehend her."

Dorny said, "What will you say to her to get her to leave quietly?"

"I'll tell her that there's a problem with her room, and we need to move her to a different one. That way you can arrest her in her room."

"Okay, sounds good," said Dorny, "that will also allow us to search her room before you bring her up."

Grace had another security officer take Dorny and Eddie up to Lansiquot's room, while he went to retrieve her from the casino.

Once inside, the detectives searched the room and her suitcase but found nothing. The safe was locked, so they would have to wait for Lansiquot to open it.

Not long after they finished going through the room, Grace appeared with Lansiquot and opened the door. Dorny was sitting on the bed and Eddie sat in the chair by the desk.

Alarmed, Lansiquot strode in and demanded, "What are you two doing in my room?"

Dorny rose, held up the warrant and said, "We have a warrant for your arrest, Miss Lansiquot."

"This is ridiculous. I've done nothing wrong. I have a lawyer. You can't do this to me."

Eddie pulled out his handcuffs and walked over to Lansiquot. "The warrant says we *can* do this, so I need you to place your hands behind your back so I can cuff you."

Lansiquot turned and looked at Grace; he shrugged his shoulders as if to say "This is not my jurisdiction. They have a warrant."

Dorny said, "Wait Eddie, before you cuff her, Miss Lansiquot, would you be so kind as to open the safe?"

"Screw you!"

"Look, if you don't, I am sure that Mr. Grace will be able to override it and open it anyway. It will just waste time. And I'm sure you're going to want to speak with your attorney soon, so try and be cooperative."

"Fine, but at least let me tell my girlfriend who was gambling with me that I won't be back."

Grace said, "I can take care of that. She was the one you spoke to when we left the table?"

"Yes." Lansiquot went to the safe, punched in the code and opened it. The only things inside were some jewelry, her cell phone, and a purse.

The detectives allowed her to pack up her bags and Grace had a bellhop follow them down with her luggage. They agreed not to cuff her until she was in the car to avoid an unpleasant scene on the way out.

Once in the car and underway, Dorny said, "Perhaps now is the time to tell us what went down at the Bingham estate."

Lansiquot said, "I don't have a clue what you're talking about. I told you already, the only time I was there was at the fundraiser."

Eddie said, "Yeah, and you also told us that your fingerprints got on the headboard when you admired it. We now know that you and Doug were admiring it together. The two of you had sex in the bed that night."

"That's not true, where did you get that story?"

"A very reliable source," said Eddie.

"Well, it's a lie."

Dorny said, "Look, Candace . . . lying to us will only make things worse. Doug has already admitted to having sex with you that night, and we've checked your phone records. It seems you've been talking back and forth for a few months now. Sounds like the affair has been heating up."

"I don't believe you, and I'm not saying another word. I want my attorney."

Eddie said, "Suit yourself. Just keep in mind that you'll have a short window to make a deal with us, because we will be offering Doug Bingham the same deal. If he is willing to testify that you committed the crime, then he gets the deal and you get the maximum sentence, and vice versa."

"You're both out of your minds. I didn't do anything, so just get me Xander Van Buren."

Chapter 16

⌐━❊━⌐

WHILE HE WAS WAITING to be called to file papers at the St. Petersburg Courthouse, Xander Van Buren's cell phone rang. It was Stu Saxon. He told him he had urgent information and that they needed to meet in person. He wouldn't talk about it over the phone, so they arranged to meet at Van Buren's office a few blocks away. Unfortunately, he had to leave the court clerk's office before he could file the *pro bono* papers on another case he was working on and walked back to his office. By the time he arrived, Stu was waiting for him in the conference room. He had a very serious look on his face.

"Xan, check this out. Remember the algorithms I was telling you about?"

"Yeah."

"Well, my guys in tech came up with some scenarios that started to make sense. Then we received information from the Centers for Disease Control and the World Health Organization. It seems that China is having a health crisis. Some sort of super virus has been infecting people in Beijing, and it's starting to spread outside the country, to Europe and the Middle East. Apparently, it's also showing up in the United States. Looks like it's coming in through major airport hubs. People are actually dying from this virus, and the Chinese have been covering it up for at least the last month or so. Even worse, our government has been downplaying it, but now it looks like it is getting out of control."

"How bad is this, Stu?"

"Hard to say, but my sources tell me this may not be an accident. And with the info you gave me on Bingham, this guy definitely knows something. The FBI must get involved here—I can't keep this quiet."

"I understand. So, what's your game plan?"

"We're waiting for him to return from New York. Our intel has him scheduled to fly back today, on his private jet. We'll meet him at the airport and take him in for questioning."

"So, what about this super virus? Is there a vaccine?"

"It's all too new, we don't have much information, other than it appears that ground zero was Beijing. The FBI is now working with the CDC, WHO, and the counterpart agencies of other countries to figure this thing out. China has started quarantining the areas where it's been affecting their people. The best we can do to get ahead of this ourselves is to cut off travel from China, and any other country where this virus is showing up."

Van Buren was floored and had to readjust. "I need to be there when you question him."

"That would be impossible. But I'll keep you informed as best I can. I need to get back to the office now and get an update on when to expect Bingham. I want to be there at the airport to apprehend him."

Van Buren barely had time to walk Stu to the elevator when he was called back into his office to field a phone call from Dorny. He advised Van Buren that they had Candace Lansiquot in custody and that she was asking for him. A very busy day to say the least, but he preferred that. It sure beat sitting in the clerk's office waiting to file papers in a civil matter he had no business handling. It wasn't his area of expertise, foreclosure litigation, but a friend of a friend was having financial problems and he had agreed to help. He just hoped that his *pro bono* efforts wouldn't come back to bite him. In any event, he wouldn't be able to return to file the papers today, so it would have to wait until tomorrow.

He headed over to the police station to meet with Candace and decided to drive, because the heat of the day was oppressive. The trip took all of ten minutes. Upon arrival, he was greeted by Joe Healy, the same disinterested desk cop who always seemed to be in a state of annoyance. Van Buren wondered if he would have preferred to be out on the street, but something told him that if Healy were out on the street, he'd be just as annoyed.

"How goes it, Joe?" Van Buren said, smiling. "Can you ring Dorny for me?"

He looked up from the paper he was reading, took off his glasses and pursed his lips. "It goes, and keeps on going, but it never gets there." He picked up the phone and punched in an extension.

Van Buren supposed Healy thought that was a clever response, but he didn't get the joke. He also imagined Healy had been practicing that line for some time. Apparently, the job of a desk cop could really suck the life out of you.

Dorny appeared and motioned Van Buren to follow him in. He asked, "Where'd you find her?"

Dorny laughed, "Believe it or not, she was at a blackjack table at the Hard Rock."

"Really? Was she winning?"

"Doubtful, but no idea. She's been booked and I've got her in a room for you. Talk to her, and if she's ready to deal, and give up Bingham, we can discuss terms."

"Look Dorny, I'm about as sure as I have ever been that she had nothing to do with this, but let me talk to her and I'll get back to you."

121

"Up to you Counselor. If not her, we'll make the deal with Bingham, and she'll be the one rotting in prison for twenty-five to life."

Van Buren wasn't able to tell Dorny what he already knew about Doug Bingham from Agent Saxon, which made him pretty sure Candace was innocent, but things had a way of unraveling, so he figured he'd take this one step at a time. He also remembered that he had not told Stu about the thumb drive and wondered if he should have. Again, one step at a time. The life of a lawyer was all about the secrets.

Dorny opened the door and let Van Buren in to speak with Candace alone. He said to Dorny, "Make sure the mic is off and no one is watching from the other side of the mirror."

"I know the rules Counselor, you've got your privacy." He closed the door behind him.

Candace jumped up from her chair and rushed over, a little too close. "I can't believe this is happening to me! I had nothing to do with all this! You have to get me out of here!"

Van Buren gripped her lightly by the shoulders, "Candace, please calm down. Have a seat and we can talk." Tears welled up in her eyes. She sat back down, and he took the seat across the table from her.

Van Buren said, "I want you to tell me what happened when you were arrested. Did you say anything to them?"

She covered her mouth with her right hand and squeezed for a moment, then released. "I don't remember exactly what I said, but they told me that Doug has admitted that we had sex in his bed the night of the fundraiser, and they think we've been having an ongoing affair. They also said they have my phone records and that there were numerous calls between us over the last few months."

"Well Candace, you told me when we last spoke that you had only just met Doug, and he simply showed you his home. Is that not true?"

She hesitated and shook her head. "I didn't think it would matter, and I didn't want you to think badly of me, but yes, it's true, we were having an affair."

"For how long?"

More tears. "Around five months, I think."

"Have you spoken to him since all this has happened? And I need to know the truth, because they will know just by looking at your phone records."

"No, I haven't."

"Is there anything else you want to tell me about the relationship?"

"It really wasn't a relationship; we were each getting out of it what we wanted. I wanted business and contacts, he just wanted sex. So, it worked for both of us."

"Anything else?"

"As a matter of fact, yes. The night Layni was murdered, I couldn't have done it. I was with him, in Texas."

"Is there any way to prove that? Did anyone see you there? Did you fly on a plane?"

"Yes, I'm sure I could find a copy of the ticket . . . and couldn't we check with the airlines to prove I was on the plane each way?"

"We can. So why didn't you say so in the first place?"

"Because I promised Doug to keep it a secret."

"Where did you stay?"

"He had a hotel room at the Ritz-Carlton in Dallas. We were there for two days. He took his jet back and I took a regular flight from Dallas to Tampa."

"Okay, well this helps me a lot. And with this information, I think I can get you out of this. I wish you had just told me at our first meeting."

"I'm sorry. I just didn't want to ruin it with Doug. I really didn't think they could possibly believe I would kill someone."

"I get it, and I'll fix this. Just tell me what flights you took, the airlines, dates times, etc."

"I should still have the tickets in my phone, but they took it from me."

"All right, I'll talk to them. Just sit tight."

Van Buren went to the door and knocked. Dorny opened it and let him out. He looked at Dorny and smiled.

"Why the grin, Counselor?"

"Well, Dorny, this may be the easiest case I've had in quite some time. I believe that if you can give me my client's cell phone, there will be an indisputable alibi right in there, and you'll have to release her right away."

Bemused, Dorny said, "Really, so what's in her phone that's gonna cut her loose?"

"Turns out she was not even in Florida the night Layni Bingham was murdered."

"And so how will her phone prove that?"

"She's got plane tickets to and from Dallas. She was with Doug Bingham, and while he flew back on his private jet, she took a commercial flight and didn't arrive in St. Pete until later that day."

"Interesting. So why didn't she say so in the first place?"

"She promised Doug she would keep the affair a secret and really didn't think you could possibly believe she would kill someone."

"If you say so, Counselor, but tickets only prove she purchased them. We'll still need to check with the airlines to make sure she used them. We also must look into whether she flew back and forth in between the flights on her phone. In fact, I also would like to check out the hotel where she allegedly stayed to see if she was actually there. But, if what you're saying turns out to be true, we will certainly release her. In the meantime, we'll keep her here and hold off on the arraignment."

Chapter 17

MARIA CHEN AND DARRYL Yao were following Bingham's Land Rover on the Northern State Parkway as it traveled towards Republic Airport in Farmingdale. They planned to get close enough so that Chen could shoot out one of the tires and force them to stop on the roadside. They had been following two cars behind for at least a half hour, until traffic finally slowed down to less than 30 miles per hour, which provided a good opportunity to take the shot. They changed lanes and eventually made their way back in and behind the Land Rover. Chen kept the gun hidden until she was ready to shoot. Yao brought her in close enough and in one smooth motion, Chen opened the passenger side window and took the shot. Direct hit on the passenger side rear tire.

The Land Rover jumped and skidded, forcing Bingham to pull over. As he maneuvered off the road and on to a grassy median near the woods, Ashley shouted, "What was that dad?"

"I think we had a blowout. I'll check it out. You stay inside. And just to be safe, take one of my pistols. They're in the glove compartment. And give me the other one."

Ashley handed him a pistol. He slid the mechanism to load a cartridge and got out. He circled around to the rear and saw the blown-out tire. He continued around to the front passenger window and Ashley opened it.

Bingham said, "Yeah, the rear tire is flat, I'm going to have to fix it. Pop the trunk for me." Ashley reached over, hit the trunk release, and the rear hatch opened. Behind them, Chen and Yao had pulled over and were making their way forward to Bingham along the woods, but Ashley wasn't paying attention—she was watching her father through the side view mirror as he began setting up the jack.

As the two closed in on the Rover, Ashley finally saw them in the mirror. She screamed and pointed, "Dad, look out, by the trees!"

Bingham dropped the jack handle, grabbed his pistol from the ground, fired and missed. Chen and Yao returned fire, hitting the rear quarter panel of the Rover. He shouted to Ashley, "Get down," and circled to the driver's side of the Rover and opened the door. He beckoned to Ashley and she slid across the seat and got out. They moved around towards the front and Bingham peered around. Chen and Yao had made their way closer to the rear of the Rover and were coming at them. Bingham fired, Chen got off another shot and hit the Rover again.

Ashley and Bingham were hunched down behind the left front tire. Bingham said, "We need to get over to the woods and away from here. Do you remember how to shoot?"

"Yes, but I'm scared. That's the girl who attacked me, and Darryl is with her."

"Yeah, I see, he must have been the one who killed Layni. I had no idea he was a traitor. Mother fucker! Look, try to stay calm, I know this area. If we can make it to the woods, there's a road on the other side less than a half mile from here, and there's a shopping center directly across the street." He pointed through the woods. "Once we get to the shopping center, they won't dare follow us."

"Okay, but how do we get over to the woods?"

"You get in the back seat of the Rover. I'll take the driver's seat, I'll get it over to the woods, and then we'll jump out and run. Once we get into the woods, we can get behind the trees and fire at them as we move. We'll make our way through quickly. Just stay low."

"Are you sure we can do this?"

"Yes, let's go."

They slid back into the vehicle and Bingham accelerated towards the woods. Ashley grabbed her cell phone and slid it in her pocket. Chen and Yao began firing at the Rover. When they reached the woods, father and daughter jumped out and began to run. Chen and Yao gave chase, but Yao couldn't keep up—he was limping and trying to run but lagged further and further behind as they got deeper into the woods. Bingham and Ashley stopped behind a large tree and fired back at them.

Chen continued moving closer, darting between the trees, and firing as she advanced. The two moved slowly, scouting for larger trees to hide behind. As they went deeper into the woods, the foliage thickened, and it became more difficult to run. They tried zigzagging in the direction Bingham had pointed out, but the density of the brush prevented them from heading where they needed to go. They had to circle around a marshy area, which slowed their progress even more. All the while Chen kept firing.

Ashley whispered, "Dad, we can't go this way, the ground is getting soggy." She pointed. "And I see a pond ahead, we can't go that way."

"I see it. Just follow me, and hold your fire. We don't have another clip of cartridges. We can't waste our shots, or we'll run out of ammo." He grabbed her arm and pulled her along as they circled around the pond and ducked behind another set of trees.

Yao also circled wide as Chen took a more direct approach, fired, and changed clips as she moved.

Ashley was in better shape and Bingham started losing ground. She turned around and Bingham motioned her forward and said, "Keep going, I'll catch up. Don't worry about me. I'll slow them down. You get to the shopping center."

Breathing heavily, she said, "No, Dad, I'm not going to leave you here."

More shots rang out. Bingham was propelled forward and hit the ground face down. A direct hit to his back. The bullet went directly through him. Blood welled up in his mouth, he coughed, his eyes blinked rapidly and closed. He was gone.

"Dad, Dad, are you okay?" No response. Ashley screamed as more shots rang out. She looked back once more, saw that Bingham had not moved and took off, running faster than she had ever run before. She leapt over low brush, darting between the trees as if her life depended on it—and it did. Up ahead she could see daylight and heard cars traveling over the roadway. She was getting closer but couldn't get the picture of her father lying motionless on the ground out of her head. It didn't seem real to her. Ashley's chest heaving as she ran, Chen got off a few more shots and bullets whizzed past her. The bullets came so close, she could hear them zip as they went by. She kept running, reached the edge of the forest, burst through to the roadside, and crossed over between the cars. The parking lot to the shopping center was just ahead, and as she reached it an eerie calm came over her. She ducked behind a row of cars in the lot and turned and looked back. She couldn't tell if she was still being chased, so she crouched and ran between the cars until she came to the entrance to a furniture store. She slid the pistol into the waistband of her pants and entered the store. Once inside, she had a moment to breathe and the reality of what had just happened set in. She began to cry, and a showroom employee came over to her.

He said, "Miss, are you okay? What's wrong?"

She looked up at him. Red faced, blank stare, heavy breathing. Shaking, she said, "I was being chased. We need to call the police. They shot my father."

Chapter 18

BINGHAM'S JET ARRIVED IN St. Petersburg carrying only Ashley Bingham. Doug Bingham's body had not been found, but Ashley knew he was dead. She suspected that the two spies had taken his body to cover up the murder.

Special Agent Stu Saxon and Xander Van Buren were there to meet her. They had already been informed about Doug Bingham's death, so Saxon no longer had to deal with the red tape of an arrest; he felt it appropriate to have Van Buren tag along and find out what went down in New York. She exited the plane and walked down the stairs. They met her on the tarmac.

Van Buren said, "Ashley, you probably don't know me, but I was Layni's friend. I was also her attorney, and I knew your father. I am very sorry for your loss."

She looked at him, nodded. "Thank you."

Saxon said, "I'm Special Agent Stu Saxon, FBI. I know you must be going through a difficult time right now, but I need to ask you some questions."

Ashley said, "Can't this wait, I've just been through a hellish experience, and I need to get home and figure out what to do next."

Hard swallow. "My father is dead, there's so much I need to do, and I just don't even know where to begin."

"We understand," Van Buren said, "But there are some serious things going on, and we need to find out what you know, and what your father may have told you."

Saxon cut in. "Yes, we suspect that whoever killed him is involved in a much larger conspiracy. One that will affect the lives of people all over the world. Your life is still in danger, so you need to tell us everything your father told you."

Ashley shifted uncomfortably, the color drained from her face, and she lost her balance. Van Buren caught her as she passed out. They carried her inside the tiny airport and placed her on a couch. Momentarily she came to. Opening her eyes, she whispered, "What happened?"

Saxon said, "You fainted. Just relax. We'll get you some water and when you feel up to it, we can take you to the hospital for an evaluation."

"No, I'll be okay. I just want to get home. I haven't eaten anything since yesterday. They had a doctor examine me in New York. I just need to eat something and get some rest."

Van Buren looked at Agent Saxon. "Why don't we take her home and get her comfortable? Then we can follow up with some questions."

Saxon said, "Ashley, would that be okay? We can't leave you alone, you're still in danger. So, we're going to have some FBI agents stay with you for the time being." She nodded.

The three of them rode together in silence as Saxon drove them to the Bingham estate. Agents were already on the grounds outside, as well as inside the mansion. After getting her settled and fed, they sat down in the library to talk.

Saxon said, "Ashley, we need to know what happened in New York, what you said to the police, and what your father may have told you."

She sat on the couch staring at a picture of herself and Doug Bingham at her graduation, smiling, with their arms around each other's waists. She wore her graduation gown and a sash indicating she graduated with honors. She remembered how she felt that day, the promise of a bright future ahead of her. Van Buren said, "You must have loved him very much."

"I did. He was always there for me whenever I needed him, no matter how busy, no matter what was going on with him. That was Dad."

"I can see you two were very close."

"We were. As soon as he realized I was in danger, he flew to New York to get me. And if he hadn't warned me, I would have been abducted. But at least he would still be alive." She started to cry.

"You can't blame yourself. He did what any loving father would have done to save his daughter. I'm sure he would have much rather sacrificed his life than to see any harm come to you."

She wiped the tears from her cheeks, rubbed her eyes, and took a deep breath. "Okay, I'm going to get through this. I know what is going on is very serious. I didn't tell the police in New York anything, other than that dad believed I was going to be kidnapped, so he warned me and came to take me home. I told them how I was almost abducted in Manhattan, that the kidnappers must have followed us to Long Island, and that they chased us through the woods after we got a flat tire. I later found out that they had shot out the tire, but none of that matters now." She got up from the couch, walked over and picked up the picture from the desk, looked at it, touched her father's face, and smiled. "He was a great man, but sometimes he made mistakes."

"All of us do, Ashley. Just tell us what you know."

She put down the picture and moved away from it, over to the window. Her back was to them.

"I know who killed Layni. It was Darryl. He was with the woman who tried to abduct me. This is all part of a sick plot to unleash a super virus on the world."

Saxon said, "Yes, we have gathered some intel on that. Tell us what else you know."

She turned from the window, walked back to the couch, and sat next to Van Buren. Looking directly into his eyes, she said, "This wasn't Dad's fault, you know. He didn't realize he was getting in over his head. This was just supposed to be a business deal, something to do with the unfair trade balance between the U.S. and China."

Van Buren said, "Go on."

"Dad told me he arranged introductions between some U.S. politicians and Chinese oligarchs. The politicians wanted their help to oust the president. The oligarchs had a mutual interest, and both sides saw a way to capitalize on it by affecting international trade." She looked away from Van Buren and refocused on the picture. "Dad told me that it got out of control, and they cut him out of the loop after they decided on a plot to unleash the virus. But he was smart. He recorded the meetings, phone conversations, and took videos and pictures to protect himself. Apparently, they found out about it, and that's why they came after him."

Saxon said, "Do you know where the recordings are?"

"No, but he told me that everything was stored on a thumb drive he kept in his safe. And the safe was broken into the night Layni was killed."

As soon as Ashley said that Van Buren knew he had to tell them that he had the drive, and that Layni had given it to him the day she was murdered. He knew Stu would be angry with him for not telling him sooner, but he was just doing his job as an attorney. Van Buren stood up. "Hold on a second, Ashley, I need to say something." He looked at Stu. "Now don't be pissed, but I have the drive. Layni gave it to me, but she didn't tell me what was on it, and it is password protected."

"Xander, how could you withhold that from me? What were you thinking?"

"I know Stu, in hindsight I should have told you, but it wouldn't have changed anything. I don't have the password, so we couldn't have accessed it anyway."

Ashley interrupted, "Dad never had the chance to give me the password either."

Saxon said, "The FBI has some of the best cryptologists. We may be able to unlock the drive and find out who is behind all this. Xander, you need to get me that drive right now."

"It's in my office safe."

Chapter 19

MARIA CHEN AND DARRYL Yao had screwed up twice and ended up having to shoot Doug Bingham without recovering the drive. Their Chinese employers were not happy, nor were the U.S. politicians who were involved. All risked exposure and the U.S. politicians risked treason charges if the thumb drive went public. No one had a clue where it was or where they were, and the virus had started to spread uncontrollably. However, Chen still had the upper hand because she and Yao were the only ones who had been vaccinated, and she was in possession of the only existing formula for the vaccine.

Chen was born in North Korea and, after a troubled childhood, made her way to Hong Kong where she was further mistreated, but when she exhibited superior intellect and scientific abilities that impressed her handlers, she was groomed and promoted, thereby setting her up to be sent to the United States where she could be educated at one of the best universities in the field. She ended up studying at the University of California-Berkeley, where she honed her skills as a microbiologist and virologist, ultimately to be placed in the United States as a sleeper agent. The plan originally involved germ warfare, but as time went on, a wiser decision was made. They moved her to Beijing, where Chen was tasked with synthesizing the virus and creating the cure, so that her handlers would be fully protected. And while she was completely on board with anything that had to do with the demise of the Western world, because of what the U.S. had done to her father, she was also smart enough to realize that she was being used as a pawn by the Chinese. So, she took every precaution to protect herself and Yao, her life mate and strongest supporter. Being possessed of the only vaccine, she felt she was secure and hoped to become rich.

Yao was born in Hong Kong. His father was a chef who worked for a wealthy, high ranking government official. He was loyal to his country and served his employer well. Yao's mother was a spy. Along with his younger sister, they all lived together on his employer's estate. The young Yao was raised from childhood to be placed as a sleeper agent in the U.S. and, after a tragic accident in which both his parents were killed, Yao and his sister were adopted by the employer, and he was sent to the U.S. for schooling. He wound up at Berkeley where he met Chen, and the two fell in love. They both had a commonality of interest and similar backgrounds and when the time came for them to awaken, they were more than ready to serve their country.

Now they would have to cover their tracks. They purchased another vehicle from a used car lot, using Maria Chen's identity. Yao's car was abandoned in an area of East New York known to be gang territory. The car wouldn't last long there, especially with the keys inside.

They knew they couldn't return to China. It wouldn't be safe for them. So, they resolved to remain in Chinatown, in Chen's apartment in lower Manhattan.

Chapter 20

⌐━✳━⌐

AGENT SAXON MADE ASHLEY understand how critical it was to keep everything confidential and not to speak to the media. He also needed to brief his superiors and ultimately the president of the United States, so that a course of action could be decided upon. He and Van Buren drove to Van Buren's office, where he gave Saxon the thumb drive. The men then headed over to police headquarters to talk to Dorny and get Candace released.

Once more, good old Joe, the ever-disinterested desk cop, rang Dorny for Van Buren. Dorny appeared at the door, looking more tired than usual. "What is it now, Counselor? We still haven't confirmed your client's alibi. And who's your buddy?"

"I'm Special Agent Stu Saxon, FBI. We need to talk in private."

Dorny scratched his head behind his ear and took them inside to his office, closed the door, and sat down behind his desk.

"Okay, let's hear it."

Saxon said, "First you need to understand that what I am about to tell you must remain confidential."

Dorny agreed. Saxon continued, "This may have serious consequences, well beyond the scope of your murder investigation."

"Understood."

They settled into chairs. Van Buren took a deep breath, held it, and exhaled. "First of all, Doug Bingham is dead."

"What? When did this happen?"

"Yesterday, in New York. He was shot fleeing from two individuals who were chasing him and his daughter, Ashley. And we are almost certain that they were responsible for Layni Bingham's murder."

"How can you be so sure?"

"One of them is Darryl Yao, the Bingham's butler. Ashley recognized him as she fled. The other assailant was a woman, but we don't know anything about her, other than the hazy description Ashley gave. That's why the FBI is now involved."

"I don't understand. Why is this considered confidential?"

Saxon explained the situation to Dorny and advised him about the super virus. Van Buren told him about the thumb drive, after which he rose from his chair, closed the blinds that separated his glass wall from the pit area of the station house, and leaned back against the front of his desk. He folded his arms and shook his head.

"Sounds like a real mess, fellas. What can I do to help?" He hesitated, "Wait a minute, I have some info on Yao. We were looking into tracking him down to question him about Doug Bingham. He's got a car registered in Florida at Bingham's estate, as well as a driver's license, but we also found an address in New York City."

Saxon said, "That's a start."

"A few days ago, we put out a BOLO for his car locally, but I hadn't yet gotten around to contacting the New York police, because he wasn't a suspect."

"Well now the FBI is on it. Just give me what you've got."

Van Buren said, "You can trust Special Agent Saxon. He's a longtime friend of mine . . . and would you please release my client?"

"Give me an hour and I'll get that done, but the bigger question is what about this super virus?"

Saxon said, "I have already been speaking with the CDC, and the president will be briefed shortly. Then it will be up to the government as to how this is handled. But at this juncture it's still speculation. It would be imprudent to announce to the world that this contagion was released intentionally. We have to walk on eggshells with the Chinese. We can't let them know how much we already know, as it would undermine the investigation and create international turmoil. And not only do we have to be concerned about the Chinese, but this also involves U.S. government officials, so we must keep it quiet and allow the FBI to do its job unhampered by political scandal."

"That, gentlemen, will be your biggest problem. You know how bad the leaks are in this administration, and once the media gets wind of this, it will go viral."

"Apropos choice of words," Van Buren said, "but not funny."

"Just making a point," Dorny said, as he walked back behind his desk and began flipping through a file. "How long do you really think this can stay under wraps?"

"Hard to say, but we need to do our best here and not alert the media."

Dorny pulled a few pages from the file and handed them to Agent Saxon. "Here's what we've got on Darryl Yao. I'd appreciate it if you could keep me in the loop, and I'll do what I can locally to keep things calm, but you know a storm is brewing."

"No doubt. Just bring me Candace Lansiquot. I need to tell her about Doug Bingham. As to her release, you can simply inform her that you confirmed her alibi, nothing more."

Chapter 21

◦─✳─◦

NEWSFLASH - AP Wire

The contagion is spreading in the United States and people around the country are becoming very sick. Many are dying. The CDC has taken the initial steps to try to isolate where the virus originated. Armed with the information provided by the FBI, the CDC is reaching out to its counterparts in China. It is clear that the virus is also spreading there, and the Chinese government is attempting to downplay it. The only information China has provided, indicates that the disease came from bats in a wet market in Beijing. China has assured the U.S. government that it was an isolated incident and that there is no cause for alarm. The CDC is refuting this and has advised the White House that this is a serious situation, and that further action must be taken.

In the past week, the death toll in the U.S. has climbed to alarming levels, and the president has just shut down all travel to and from China. The progressive administration has left the country ill-equipped to handle the rapidly spreading virus. The far-left policies adopted over the previous three years have put the country in a weakened position, with little border control, a poorly funded military, and a lack of funds to help the American people in a time of need. Far too much has been spent on environmental change, and the systematic elimination of fossil fuels has taken a serious toll on the economy. Added to that is the increased tax burden that has drained the middle class of savings. President Bradshaw is being called an incompetent fool and a weakling by a large portion of the media as well as the opposition party. The president's failure to cut off travel quickly enough signals that he is incapable of running the country. Moreover, his inadequate handling of foreign policy and allowing China to continue to lie, cheat, and steal from the U.S. is beginning to cause serious civil unrest. Many other news outlets have lambasted the White House for not being transparent enough, and for generally not protecting the American people from an overseas contagion. The conservative wing of Congress is demanding that the president halt any further travel between the United States, Europe, and the Middle East and further insisting that the U.S. borders to the north and south be closed. Right wing conspiracy theorists are likewise demanding that America quickly isolate itself from the rest of the world. Many State and local governments are now ordering people to quarantine at home as they issue directives that restaurants, gyms, sporting events, nonessential businesses, and offices around the country be shut down as well. Everyone is being advised to wear masks and a new term of art has emerged, "social distancing," which requires people to stay at least 6 feet away from each other, if out in public. Groups of more than ten people are no longer permitted. The public beaches and parks are being closed. An atmosphere akin to martial law has come into effect. The Bill of Rights is disintegrating right before our eyes as the freedoms guaranteed by the U.S. Constitution are further restricted. Meanwhile, hospitals are overwhelmed with patients who have contracted the super virus, and health care professionals throughout the country are becoming infected. The country is not prepared for any of this.

The actions of all agencies of the government are being criticized. The population is starting to rebel as people all over the country are being laid off. The economy is tanking and the stock market is crashing. In a matter of a few short weeks, the country has been brought to its knees. In large cities, an eerie quiet set off by empty streets is creating more social unrest. Fear of another civil war is descending upon the population. The super virus is fast becoming the worst pandemic of the modern era. All available resources are being marshaled towards finding a cure as quickly as possible. The United States is not alone in this, as similar problems are arising throughout the world. The entire globe is now engulfed in a pandemic. In many places it is beginning to feel like the end of the world, and some religious leaders are even suggesting that the end of days are upon the face of the earth.

Chapter 22

SENATOR DENNIE SINKFIELD ENTERTAINED a private meeting at his home in Virginia. He was a broad-shouldered man with sharp features, a deep voice, and thick, jet-black hair. The three other members of the "gang of four" sat in his backyard on an unseasonably warm Sunday afternoon. It was early May. The pool cover had not yet been removed, but the lawn furniture was set up for spring. The chairs had been placed in a circle, far apart from one another, in an effort to comply with social-distancing rules. All wore masks except CIA Director General William Coggins. Sinkfield took the floor and addressed the group.

"Gentlemen, I'll be blunt. The situation has clearly gotten out of hand. We were promised a vaccine by our overseas partners before this contagion became a pandemic. As you know, that has not happened, and the Chinese operative who developed it has disappeared. I don't know whether to believe our partners when they say that they too have been duped, but the reality is that this has gone too far. If word ever gets out about what we've done, we're finished. We could even face the death penalty for treason."

Senator Aaron Strauss, a thin, beady-eyed, balding man with a weak chin and a pencil neck, said, "Frankly, Dennie, I didn't want to do this from the outset. You assured me that we were fully protected and that this would be a short-lived situation. You promised me anonymity. I shouldn't have even shown up today. If anyone is watching, this meeting will look very suspicious. Times have changed since this pandemic has taken over our country."

Deputy Assistant FBI Director Joseph Cromley, a tall man with puffy, dark circles under his eyes, a protruding chin and steel blue eyes, stood and moved to the center of the circle. "I'm tracking this internally. The agent appointed by Director Falk is Stu Saxon, a very competent fellow who managed to land the spot because he brought in the first good evidence of what was transpiring. He's out of our Tampa office. He's been back and forth to DC over the past few weeks, and he's working with a group of clean-cut agents who are loyal to the administration. They are in possession of Bingham's thumb drive. It's encrypted, and they have not been able to crack the password yet. He's got a team of experts working on it though. I'm trying to figure out a way to get my hands on the drive, and if I do, our troubles will be over—at least as far as implicating us. As to a vaccine, that's a whole other universe. All we know is that the virologist spy who unleashed this thing has the cure, but, as Dennie said, she's gone missing. We are attempting to gain access to the computer system at the virology institute. That should help us track her movements. Apparently, she's teamed up with another spy, one Darryl Yao, who, it turns out, was the Bingham butler. The Chinese managed to place him there a year or so ago, as a sleeper agent, right after we started negotiations. He's the one Saxon's team is looking for. They're hoping he'll lead them to the virologist. They also believe he murdered both Doug and Layni Bingham. We're looking for him too. We are fairly certain neither of them left the country. The last place they were seen was in New York. I have a few loyal agents of my own who are out there looking for them as we speak."

Coggins sat silently, chewing on a Cohiba Behike, one of the finest Cuban cigars around. He liked to smoke and chew it. His teeth were yellowed from the habit. He was a large man with a gravelly voice. Formerly a four-star general, he could command a room, even without speaking. He waited for a time, let the silence set in until all three men were looking at him. Then he inhaled, held the smoke for a beat, exhaled, and examined his cigar.

"Now, you boys knew from the beginning that this was a precarious way to proceed, to achieve the desired result. Although we can't prove it, the top of the whole damn Communist Chinese government is involved, not just the oligarchs. They weren't simply interested in helping to reconfigure our leadership. They intended to let this pandemic take out a large segment of their elderly population, and then some. They've got too many friggin' people over there. This is their version of the final solution. Frankly, it's brilliant. I have to give them some credit for forward thinking."

Sinkfield stood up, "Well that's not what this country's all about. Not something I'd ever approve of. We've got to stop this monster in its tracks, Director, no matter what it takes."

"Look Senator, I'm not suggesting we would ever do that, but there are some benefits."

"What do you mean?"

"Think about it—our pussy progressive president and our socialist senate have overburdened our healthcare system with unaffordable entitlement programs, many of which could be alleviated by the death of the elderly population. Imagine what would happen if all of a sudden, a large number of seniors were no longer around to use Medicaid, Medicare, or collect Social Security?"

Strauss said, "That's crazy talk, Director. We aren't China and I'll have nothing to do with something like that."

"I didn't say we would ever intentionally engage in such actions; I'm simply saying that for China, it works. And, yes, I agree, this must be stopped. I'll leave it at this: I've got well-placed people working another angle, but that's under wraps."

Cromley said, "You really shouldn't be holding back on us, Director. We need to be kept in the loop."

"Sorry, Chief, need to know basis. For your own good."

Strauss said, "So where do we go from here?"

Coggins took another puff on his cigar, exhaled, and spit out a piece of tobacco. "We continue working our angles, we keep our mouths shut, and go about our daily business. This will all work itself out, trust me."

Chapter 23

DESPITE THE QUARANTINE ORDER issued by the governor, Xander Van Buren, Esquire kept his office open through the pandemic. Business was slow, so it gave him time to clear up paperwork on several outstanding matters. He hadn't heard from Ashley Bingham for a few weeks, so the call, and her request to meet with him, aroused his curiosity. She showed up on time, and looking quite well in a white sun dress, her hair in a ponytail. She had a rather large carry bag with her. They sat in the conference room across from one another. She placed the bag on the table.

Ashley said, "I brought a mask, but prefer not to wear it." She held it up. "Do you mind?"

"Not at all, I don't usually wear one either. Do *you* mind?"

"No, this whole super virus thing is driving me crazy. I can't stand it anymore."

"Agreed, so what can I do for you?"

She reached into the bag and pulled out a sheaf of papers. "First, I have my father's will. I would like you to handle the probate, if that's all right."

"My brother, Griff, would be the one to take that on. I generally handle criminal matters. But I oversee everything in the office."

"That would be fine, as long as you oversee it."

"Absolutely. Is that all?"

"No, in fact, I would like you to get back involved with the murder investigations. It seems that Detective Dornhuber isn't involved anymore. Your friend, the FBI agent, has taken over the case, both here and in New York." She took a breath. "I also decided to go through Darryl's quarters, to clear them out, and I found something that may help locate him." She handed him an envelope with a letter inside. "I really don't have a clue what it says. If you open it, you'll see it is written in Chinese, but maybe the address on the letter will help. Perhaps you could get this translated?"

Van Buren took the letter out of the envelope and examined it. "Where did you find this?"

"I was taking out the drawers to have them sanitized, and I found it in the back of the dresser."

"This looks interesting, the address appears to be in Beijing. I'll get this translated and see what it's all about—and to answer your question, I would be happy to get back involved in this matter. Thank you for asking me."

"That would be great. I really want to get to the bottom of all this, and I feel awful that in some way my father actually may have caused this mess. I'm still trying to come to terms with everything that has happened in the last few weeks."

"I sympathize with you and promise to help in any way I can."

"That's why I came to you. And just so you know, I had you checked out before I decided to hire you. It seems you have quite a reputation in St. Pete."

Van Buren smiled. "Reputations can be good and bad. It really depends on which side of the 'versus' you're on."

Ashley laughed, stood up, handed him a check and a business card, took her bag, and spun out of the room. "Ciao."

He looked at the check; it was for twenty thousand dollars. They hadn't even discussed the fee. *Why couldn't all clients be so forthcoming?*

He looked at the letter again, took it and the envelope to the scanner, and scanned it into his computer. He headed back to his office, sat down, and called an old attorney friend and former client who had relocated from China, and who would be able to translate the letter. "Qin, it's Xander. I need your assistance with something."

"Anything for you, Xander. What can I do for you?"

"I'm going to email a letter to you. It's written in Chinese. I need to know what it says. I also need you to keep this confidential."

Qin laughed, "It's always confidential with you. Send it to me and I'll take a look. No charge."

Van Buren laughed, "It's okay, you can charge me, that way it's attorney–client privileged."

"Fine. I'll email you later when I have the translation."

He said thank you and goodbye, hung up the phone, opened his computer, and sent the email to Qin.

✳ ✳ ✳

Two hours later, Qin's reply arrived. The first attachment was an invoice for translation services for one hundred dollars with a big smiley face emoji on it. The second attachment was a translated letter which read as follows:

Dear Darryl:

I've been missing you these past months being stuck here in Beijing, but what I am working on is very important to the cause and will also be very lucrative. We will both be able to settle down wherever we choose, and we will never have to worry about money again. I have to be careful though because my handler can't be trusted. I believe he is trying to get me to return there once my mission is complete. He's telling me it will be the only safe place in the world, but I think he is more interested in me and keeping me locked away there. Anyway, I will never return to China, but I must see this mission through and then we will be together again forever. I know you have your job to do as well. We will coordinate everything so that we can meet in New York once our missions are complete. Then we can figure out where we want to live. I love you always. Love, Mai

Van Buren made a call to Agent Saxon. He picked up on the third ring. "What's up Xan?"

"Hey Stu, I think I've got something that will help your case."

"I'm all ears buddy, lay it on me."

"It's a letter I just had translated from Chinese to English. Ashley found it in Darryl's quarters. It's from the woman spy who was with him when they shot Bingham. I'm emailing it to you now."

"I'll get on it right away."

"Great, but now you need to do me a favor and bring me up to date on progress you've made with this nightmare."

"Sure thing, Xan. On the Darryl Yao front, all I can tell you is that everywhere we've looked is a dead end. This guy's a ghost. The address in New York is no longer his—it was a rented apartment that is now occupied by an elderly couple who are isolated there, with no outside contact due to the lockdown in New York. It's really bad up there, many more deaths than in Florida, or most other states for that matter. As to the virus, we have traced ground zero to a virology institute in Beijing—"

"Beijing! That's where the letter came from. It has to be the same woman. She must be the one who started this whole thing. Check your email and pull up the letter."

"Okay, gimme a sec."

He could hear Saxon clicking away on his keyboard. "Got it, I'm reading it now."

"So, what do you think? It sounds to me like China hatched this plot."

Saxon said, "Yeah, we've got some separate intel, and coupled with this, I think that North Korea may have played a role here too. They benefit from friction between China and the U.S." He took a pause. "You know what? I think they're trying to instigate a war."

"Sounds crazy, but it makes sense, Stu."

"Yes, it does, and not only that, but we also have intel that there isn't a single case of the super virus in North Korea. So, I'm willing to bet they have the cure, or a preventative vaccine."

"The thing I don't get here Stu, is, why would anyone in our government want to have any part in this? Politics can't have deteriorated to that extent."

"I've got some theories, but we have to be careful. I've got a feeling that we've got a few really bad guys on the inside. I'm fairly certain I'm being watched, so I'm going to need your help. There are only a few agents working with me who I can trust, so I'd like you to do an independent investigation, which we'll keep just between us. I'll feed you intel as it comes to me, and you run with it. When you uncover something, we'll talk in person."

"You know I'm always here for you, buddy. Together we'll get to the bottom of this."

"Great, give me a little time and I'll see what I can dig up for you regarding this so-called 'love letter.' In the meantime, I'm headed to DC to brief the president."

Chapter 24

A FEW HOURS LATER, Agent Saxon arrived at the White House. He arranged the meeting with the president, on the down low, so he could speak with him privately. It was highly improper, but under the current administration, sometimes protocol had to be avoided. Leaks were rampant and the president had a lot of enemies. He was ushered into the Oval Office, where the president was seated behind his desk. The door closed behind him, and he was alone with the most powerful man on the planet.

President Bradshaw said, "Good afternoon, Agent Saxon, please have a seat." He pointed to the opposing couches located in front of his desk, stood, walked out from behind and sat down on the couch across from Agent Saxon. "So, tell me, why all the secrecy? What's going on?"

"Mr. President, with all due respect, the last few times we met there were several other people in the briefing room, and confidential discussions were leaked. I realize that you're aware of some of this, but I don't want it to jeopardize my investigation any longer. Frankly, I suspect that we've got some bad actors in powerful positions within our government. Individuals who don't want me and my team uncovering who is responsible for this pandemic."

"These are very serious accusations. Can you name names?"

"No sir, I don't have that as of yet, but what I can tell you is that I've come across some new information, which suggests that this was a coordinated effort among North Korea, China, and a group of DC insiders in our midst."

"I've had my suspicions as well, Stu, the 'deep state' is still active . . . but without more, there's little I can do."

"I realize that sir, and I'm working on it. I also wanted you to know that we suspect that North Korea may have been trying to spark a war between the U.S. and China."

"I've suspected that too, but that isn't something we can tell the American people, at least not at this juncture. Once we have more, perhaps then I'll be able to have a press conference. In the meantime, if I go public without more, the press will have a field day."

"Yes sir, I get it. I guess what I'm really trying to say is that we both need to watch our backs."

President Bradshaw laughed. "I've been doing that for most of my life, Stu. I certainly have no intention of stopping now."

Chapter 25

SAXON AND VAN BUREN met the next day at their favorite spot, the St. Pete high school basketball court, for an afternoon workout. Van Buren brought the ball, the water, and the beer. Saxon brought new intel on the woman spy. They shot around for a while, played a quick one-on-one game, and Saxon finally beat Van Buren.

Breathing heavily, Saxon said, "Chalk that one up to pure hustle, Xander."

"Every dog has his day; I'll get you next time." He tossed Saxon a water bottle. "Take a drink of this, then I'll let you have a beer."

"Ever prepared, Xan, that's what I like about you."

"As are you—so tell me, what have you got for me? I'm looking forward to sinking my teeth back into this case."

They sat down on a bench. Saxon pulled out a small blue folder and handed it to Van Buren. "Inside you'll find contact information for Dr. Daniel Xinghuan. He was one of the first to contract the super virus, and he brought it into the country. Thankfully, he survived. He worked at the Institute for Virology in China and should have info on the spy. He's now at the Rocky Mountain Laboratories in Montana, working on a cure."

"Montana? Traveling under present conditions may be problematic."

"That leaves you two choices. You can drive, or you can ask Ashley Bingham for her jet. After all, aren't you on her payroll now?"

"Well, driving is out of the question, especially to Montana, so I suppose I could ask her." Van Buren smiled, "Wouldn't be the worst way to travel . . . guess I'll give her a call." They each downed a bottle of Corona, and Van Buren rushed off to reach out to Ashley.

The call took less than two minutes. She was more than happy to fly him to Montana, provided she could tag along. Having little choice, but also looking forward to the company, he agreed. They coordinated to leave the following morning, giving her the time, she needed to make the necessary arrangements with her pilot.

Van Buren pulled up to his house sweaty and looking forward to a dip in the pool to cool off. Greeted at the front door by his two Newfs wagging their tales, a sense of calm came over him. He had been oddly stressed over the past few weeks, unsure if it was related to the spread of the super virus, or if it was because he had so little control over the events and people who caused it. But his dogs always managed to refocus him to what was most important. They were unaware of any of the changes to everyday life and looked to him to feed, love, and play with them. Happy to oblige, he prepared their dinner, brought them out back, and took a swim while they ate. It wouldn't take long for them to wolf down dinner, and then they'd be nudging him for a walk. He looked forward to that, because it gave him time to think while they traversed the trails just a few blocks from his home. Beyond that, his four-legged pals helped keep the loneliness out of his life. Ever since his wife had died, he hadn't been able to look ahead more than a day at a time. She was his world, and even though more than a year had gone by, he still missed her smile, her laugh, and the way she made him feel, just by being with him. It seemed that tragic events always managed to follow him around, to the point where all he could do was to plug along day by day, waiting and wondering when he'd come out of the tailspin. The seclusion brought on by the pandemic just added fuel to the fire, so it was good that he had a new and important mission to look forward to.

✳ ✳ ✳

After a restless sleep, Van Buren rolled out of bed, walked the dogs, and fed them, called his brother, and asked him to look after them. Then he headed to the airport to meet Ashley.

She was already waiting on the tarmac, looking radiant. How she could do that at 8:00 A.M. was remarkable. While she managed to put her father's death behind her and move forward, she still felt empty inside. But she put on a good front.

She smiled. "Good morning Mr. Van Buren."

"Please, call me Xander."

"Okay, *Xander,* I'm looking forward to our adventure. Let's get moving; I'd like to hear your plan."

They climbed the stairs into the Gulfstream G400, a very comfortable and sexy plane, that jetted him into a world he had never experienced. He took a window seat. Ashley sat opposite. The hatch closed quickly, and they were taxiing in a matter of minutes. This was nothing like a commercial flight, and he had to admit, it felt special. Once airborne, and at level altitude, a flight attendant appeared from the rear of the plane and asked them for breakfast orders. Ashley chose a fruit bowl with yogurt. Van Buren followed her lead. This all seemed routine to her.

She said, "Relax, Xander. This is a very safe plane."

"I wasn't worried about that. I'm just not accustomed to this sort of . . . treatment."

"Well perhaps you need to try to get used to it."

He smiled, "I doubt that I can, but I'll enjoy it anyway."

"Good idea. So, tell me, what's your game plan? I want to be a full part of this."

Without telling her where he obtained his information, he explained that they were going to interview the doctor who first contracted the virus, and who unwittingly brought it into the country. It was his hope he could give more details, and possibly identify the female operative who worked at the institute while he was there.

After briefing her, they sat in silence as the jet hummed along above the clouds. Periodically, Van Buren looked out the window, and when the clouds cleared out, he could see farmland and housing developments peppered along the countryside below. Ashley seemed at peace with the world while reading *Allure* magazine. Van Buren must have fallen asleep, and when they hit some turbulence, he awoke with a start. She giggled.

"Still uptight, huh Counselor? Do you have a fear of flying?"

"No not at all."

"It's okay, you do feel the air a bit more in a smaller plane. I remember when I was a kid, Dad would take me up in a little Cessna propeller plane he flew, and we would really get bounced around quite a bit in the wind. Dad would tell me it was a ride, just like a roller coaster, and it was meant to be fun. Ever since then, if I ever hit turbulence, I'd get a thrill. I love when my stomach jumps into my throat."

"Well, I was in the Marines, and we flew quite a bit, but in large, cargo planes. I parachuted regularly during that time, so I'm used to the stomach jump. Though I can't say I enjoyed it."

Ashley's eyes danced, "Marines, hmm that sounds interesting. Were you ever involved in anything dangerous, like fighting in a war zone?"

"I was lucky enough to avoid war zones, but I was engaged in some special ops overseas in what we would call 'urban combat,' where we went after terrorists. Unfortunately, I've had friends who have been killed on missions with me. But thankfully, I was never wounded."

"Terrorists, that must have been scary!"

"Yes, it could be very scary at times, but we were well trained soldiers, and the guys I fought with always had each other's backs."

Ashley sat silent for a minute before she said, "Dad taught me how to shoot a handgun."

"Really, what made him want to do that?"

"I don't remember. It was a long time ago, but I think Dad just wanted me to be able to defend myself. He even had me take martial arts lessons for many years. I got to be pretty good, you know."

Van Buren smiled. "I'll bet . . . well, at least I know I'm in good hands in case we get attacked."

Ashley laughed, "I've got your back, soldier."

"So, what do you do in New York?"

"I work in interior design. People hire me to help them decorate their homes. I deal with mostly wealthy clientele who have too much money and don't know what to do with it. Believe it or not, some of my clients will redecorate their apartments every few years, just because they can."

"Some people are never satisfied. How about you? Are you one of those never satisfied types?"

"Me? Ahh no. I'm sure you think that just because I grew up wealthy that I'm a spoiled brat, but I'm not. And while Dad always made sure I was well taken care of, when I went off to school, I decided that I had to do things on my own. My friends thought I was crazy, but I wanted to be like everyone else, so I took a job on campus and worked for my money. I got a scholarship because of my grades, so Dad didn't have to pay for my tuition either. I haven't asked him for money in years, but *he* always asked *me* if I needed any."

"That's very commendable. So, what else do you do to occupy your time?"

"I keep pretty busy. I enjoy the arts, so I go to museums and art exhibits, I train at a gym, I even volunteer at a senior center in Manhattan." She giggled. "Oh, and I love to shop. I'm always looking for new clothes, that's my Achilles heel."

Van Buren laughed, "If that's your worst trait, I think you'll survive." She had an easy manner and made him feel comfortable. He found himself drawn to her, despite an almost twenty-year age difference. For the first time since Tara died, something inside of him had reawakened. But the age difference weighed heavily on his mind. This wasn't something he should be thinking about, so he pushed it out of his head. "So, have you thought about what you're going to do looking ahead? Griff told me he took a quick look at your father's will. Apparently, he left everything to you since Layni died before he did."

"I really hadn't thought much about it. I totally love New York City, but there's a lot to be said for living in St. Petersburg, so I may have to maintain dual residence and fly back and forth as needed. And frankly, right now, with the super virus lockdown, I probably won't be going back to New York for quite some time." She sat quiet for a bit, and then out of the blue said, "So tell me, is there a woman in your life?"

Van Buren hesitated and looked out the window for a beat. "There used to be. I was married, but Tara passed away over a year ago."

"Oh, I'm sorry, I didn't mean to bring up something like that."

"No, it's okay, I've moved on, sort of. We had a great marriage, and I still miss her, but I keep busy and try not to think about the past."

"I can relate."

"Of course you can, and your wound is still fresh."

"Yeah, I do miss Dad, but my last day with him, he came to my rescue and saved my life. So as much as it hurts, I'm left with a memory that will stay with me forever."

They continued talking for most of the remaining flight. The conversation just flowed, and he sensed that she might have more than a business interest in him, although it could simply be wishful thinking on his part.

※ ※ ※

After a smooth landing, they departed the plane. Ever prepared, Ashley had arranged for an SUV rental. A black Lexus NX 300 was waiting for them when they arrived. She set the GPS, and Van Buren drove to the lab. As they got close, they could see the complex in the distance. It was an impressive set of structures with the main building just up ahead. A row of ten brick columns stood bold and silent sentry over an all-glass facade.

They entered. It was cold and antiseptic. They presented their identification at the reception counter and were advised to wait for someone to take them inside. As Van Buren gazed around, it was clear that there was exceptional security throughout the building. Cameras were ever present, and so were armed security guards.

A few minutes later, they were approached by a man in a lab coat who ushered them into a conference room, where Dr. Daniel Xinghuan was waiting. They introduced themselves and sat down at one end of the table.

Dr. Xinghuan said, "I understand you wanted to talk to me about my time at the Beijing lab."

"Yes, doctor. I'm aware that you contracted the super virus there, and so did several your colleagues, some of whom perished as a result."

"That is correct."

"Were you ever able to determine how the virus was transmitted?"

"Initially we believed it was accidental, but after further investigation we suspected it was intentional, though we had no way of proving it."

"Can you provide me with the names of your colleagues who contracted the virus?"

"That won't be a problem."

"Thank you, and let me get right to the point. Did you have occasion to work with a lab technician named Mai?"

"Yes, sure, Mai Ling. She disappeared about the same time the virus started to spread."

"Interesting, so tell me, would you have access to any of her records, perhaps employment info, a photograph of her, something which we could use to try to locate her?"

"I still have some friends over in Beijing that work at the lab. I could make a call and see."

"That would be great. And is there anything you can tell us about Ms. Ling?"

"May I ask why are you so interested in her? She was a first-year lab tech but did show some promise."

"Let's just say that she is a person of interest and that anything we discuss here should be held in the strictest of confidence."

"Understood. She kept to herself, took direction well, and didn't cause any trouble that I'm aware of."

"Do you recall when exactly she disappeared?"

"Well, I recall that I was at the end of my tenure there, and she didn't show up for work for about three days before I left, and then within a few days of my arrival back in the states, I became very sick, so I assume that I contracted the virus while at the lab and brought it back with me. I really didn't put her disappearance together with anything at the time."

"Do you know what her duties were, what she worked on while at the lab?"

"My recollection was that she assisted a few of us doing research and testing. She was entry level, so ordinarily she wouldn't have been working independently on anything."

"So how would she have been monitored?"

"Reports are filed on a regular basis, and each doctor would have documented whom he or she worked with and on what subject matter, but it wasn't rigid. The most important thing everyone was concerned about was safety. We were all diligent in making sure that we worked in a sterile environment and that there was no chance that any contagion could leak or be removed from the lab. We were all required to strip down naked and go through a screening shower every day at the end of our shifts."

"So, you must have been infected inside the lab somewhere."

"Yes, it would have had to have been a leak or an intentional act by someone."

"Do you recall if anyone was working with this particular super virus during that time?"

"I wasn't aware of everything that the other doctors and scientists were working on, but there would be a record of that as well. Again, the problem will be that we are dealing with China, and secrecy policies will prevent me from obtaining that information easily. I have one good friend there who I will attempt to get all this information from and let you know."

"Thank you, and keep in mind that anything you can find regarding Mai Ling is extremely important."

"I understand. I will get on it right away."

"Much appreciated, and on another and equally important note, can you tell me how soon we can expect a vaccine for the virus?"

"We are working very diligently, and so are labs all over the country, and the world for that matter. But what we do here is quite complicated, and testing is so very important. We do animal trials first, mice, then monkeys generally. Our science moves slowly. I wish I could give you a better answer, but at this stage we are months, if not years away from a vaccine. My best recommendations are to get tested, to maintain social distance, and to wear masks when in public places where people congregate."

Ashley said, "The new normal."

"Unfortunately," the doctor said, nodding.

※ ※ ※

The two stayed overnight at a local hotel, in separate rooms. By morning, Dr. Xinghuan called, and they returned to the lab. They met in the same conference room, and he provided them with an employee record containing all of Mai Ling's personal information, age, height, weight, schools attended, degrees earned, last known address, and photo. He advised them that his contact had to be very discreet, and that more information would be forthcoming in a few days, but he had to get it out slowly. Van Buren thanked him, and they headed off to the airport. He texted Saxon with the vital stats and a photo of Mai Ling, and Saxon said he would run her name through the federal database and check with Customs and Homeland Security to see if they could match up a passport with her name and picture. Van Buren hoped that by the time they returned to St. Petersburg he would have some more information.

Chapter 26

DEPUTY ASSISTANT FBI DIRECTOR Cromley met privately with CIA Director Coggins on a rainy night in a parking lot on the outskirts of Langley, Virginia. Cromley entered the lot first, and moments later, Coggins pulled up next to him. Rain drenched Cromley as he bolted from his car and got into Coggins' SUV. The stench of cigar smoke nauseated Cromley, but he sucked it up, hoping the meeting would be quick.

Coggins said, "I don't think we can trust Senator Strauss. He's too weak. He needs to disappear."

"Agreed, but that's a tall order. Strauss is protected. He's no fool, he's always got a security detail with him."

"True, except when we call a meeting. He's extremely paranoid about letting anyone know when we get together. You saw how he was at our last meeting. The guy is shitting a brick right now, thinking we're going to be exposed."

"So how do you want to accomplish this?"

"You're the only one I can trust, Joe, which is why I didn't mention it at the meeting. But at this point I need to bring you up to speed." He chewed his Cohiba, opened the window and spit.

"I've been working with a double agent. Someone we turned a while back, before this project was conceived."

Squinting, Cromley turned up his head and said, "Really, who would that be?"

"That would be Darryl Yao."

"You mean Bingham's butler, the spy the FBI is looking for? He's a double agent?"

"He is."

"And you know where he is right now?"

"No, I don't know where he is at the present time, but I do know how to contact him."

"What about the other one? Is she also a double agent?"

Coggins smiled. "No, she is loyal to her country and doesn't know about Yao's allegiance."

"You never cease to amaze me, General. Someday you'll have to tell me how you pulled that one off."

"Someday, Joe, if we live long enough."

"Okay, so even with Strauss out of the way, we still haven't solved our problem."

"Correct, you still need to get the thumb drive. In the meantime, I'm working an angle to pin this all on Strauss. And with him out of the way, our boys will have someone to blame, and a dead-end trail."

"Sounds good to me, but can you rely on Yao?"

"He'll get the job done, and then I'll make him, and the girl disappear."

"Covering all the angles, huh, just let me know what you need from me."

"Appreciate that, I'm glad I can count on you. So, what is the status on the thumb drive?"

"So far, no one's been able to crack the code. Bingham must have used a very high-end cryptographer to lock it up. That's good for us, but I think I've figured a way to get access to the drive. Right now, they've got it in a restricted area that I don't have access to. My plan is to go up the chain of command and suggest to the director that he let my people try to break the code. Once we have it, I've got an agent I can trust, who is one of the best hackers in the business. He's assured me he can wipe it clean without anyone knowing about it, so even if it ultimately can be unlocked, the data will be gone."

Coggins took a long draw on his cigar, exhaled, and smiled. "I like your style, Joe. When this is all over, and I get in the White House, I'll make you the new FBI Director."

"Looking forward to it, General. Something must be done about this nightmare of a president, and I believe you're the man to do it."

"The coalition is growing. A few more months of lockdown and his entire administration will collapse. Then we come in with the vaccine and nothing can stop us."

"What makes you so sure we'll have a vaccine?"

"That's the beauty of my plan. We kill two birds with one stone. When Yao comes to take out Strauss, he's going to bring the girl. We grab them, and once they are under our control, we have ways of making them talk. Worst case, we take their blood and let the scientists synthesize something from their immune systems."

Chapter 27

NEWSFLASH - AP Wire

The number of daily deaths from the super virus has been rising steadily and scientists warn that this may be only the beginning. People need to take this pandemic more seriously. President Bradshaw has stated that stronger steps must be taken by everyone to help slow the spread of the virus. "We have to change the way we live until we have a vaccine," said President Bradshaw at his latest briefing. "Wear a mask. Stay home. Wash your hands."

Congressional lawmakers are in a pathetic standoff regarding the amount of financial aid that should be given to the countless millions of people suffering during the pandemic. Foolish members of Congress on both sides of the aisle seem more concerned with politics and making the other side look bad, rather than helping the American people through this crisis.

The vast number of people seeking medical attention are being told to convalesce at home rather than risk the spread of the super virus at local hospitals. The logic behind this is flawed and seems to violate the Hippocratic Oath. "You can't see a doctor unless you aren't ill and can prove it," said Jonathan Reichman, professor of health metrics sciences at Stonybrook University in New York. "It's an absurd irony that doctors are unwilling to care for the sick and those who need treatment. The government must step in and force a change to this policy."

Additionally, over one million people are losing their jobs every week due to the restrictions on travel, dining, and canceled sporting events. The Labor Department announced the other day that 1.5 million people had filed for unemployment in the last week of April alone.

The illness, coupled with the rate of growth of unemployment is crippling the American people and if the President doesn't step in now and show real leadership, calls for his resignation will justifiably be right around the corner.

Chapter 28

AFTER A SMOOTH RETURN flight, Van Buren and Ashley Bingham arrived in St. Pete, disembarked and walked to the parking lot of the small airport. Ashley asked him to keep her informed, then she kissed him on the cheek, smiled and, as she drove off, she waved. He waved back awkwardly, still pondering the kiss. As he drove to the office, Van Buren called Agent Saxon to see if he had come up with anything useful from the intel he'd sent him.

"You back in St. Pete, Xan?"

"Just landed. Tell me you've got some good news."

"Check your email. We've got some leads. Looks like our perp has assumed a new identity. Homeland Security has facial recognition capabilities and with the picture you sent me we found that she used a new passport to leave China a couple of months ago. She landed at Kennedy Airport in New York and went through Customs there. This was before the borders were closed. You'll see she's changed her appearance, but the facial recognition technology keys in on bone structure, positioning of the eyes, ears, and mouth, as well as the nose, so hair length and color don't register."

"Wow, that's great technology. Is there anything else?"

"She bought and registered a car in her new name, so we have an address too. Looks like you'll be heading to New York to locate and verify."

"Locate and verify? You don't want me to bring her in?"

"No, too dangerous and you don't have the authority. Once you confirm you've found her, I'll fly with my agents, and we'll take her into custody. I just don't want to tip my hand and alert anyone on the inside who may be watching me, and who could interfere, before I know exactly where she is. So, if you find her, keep her in your sights, but keep your distance."

"You realize you're sending me right into the lion's den. New York has more super virus cases and deaths than any other state."

"I don't expect you to fly commercial, so call Ashley Bingham again and get her to fly you to New York. Once you're there, make sure to wear a mask."

"I always knew you cared, Stu."

After he hung up with Saxon, he placed a call to Ashley, who was more than happy to fly him to New York . . . provided of course that she could tag along. She pointed out that she would be able to help out because she lives in Manhattan, and knew the city very well. They arranged the trip for the following day and planned to meet at the airport at 8:00 A.M.

Chapter 29

CIA DIRECTOR COGGINS HAD already arranged for damaging evidence to be hidden in Strauss's office in the Capitol Building, as well as in his computer. His close network of talented and trusted agents had an easy time planting photographs and documents that made it appear as if Strauss was colluding with the Chinese for financial gain. Strauss's office had also been bugged, so Coggins knew every move Strauss made, and recorded every conversation he had.

The General, as he preferred to be referred to, had made a lot of friends over the years, both in politics and in the military, and over the past eight years, in the CIA. He fashioned himself a modern-day J. Edgar Hoover, and brought in the people he trusted from his time in the service, while aligning himself with like-minded congressmen and senators who were convinced that Coggins would help to bring about a major change in U.S. domestic and foreign policy. He was not afraid of war, nor was he afraid of collateral damage, even if it were on U.S. soil. In fact, he had secretly hoped that the pandemic would spark a confrontation with China and a war with North Korea. He'd had enough of China's theft of U.S. technology and felt it was time to put the Communists in their place and show the world the true military might of the United States. He also knew he had support for his plan at the highest levels of the military. Coggins had set his sights on the White House as well. He felt that if Eisenhower could do it, so could he. And, as far as he was concerned, the plan was working perfectly, despite what the group of four had said. He dreamed of the day when the drain from government entitlement programs was brought under control by a mass reduction in seniors applying for benefits. It pleased him to no end that the super virus was exponentially more deadly to those over age sixty-five.

Coggins used his burner phone and texted a code number to Yao. Yao texted back that he would return the call when he could talk. First, he had to distance himself from Chen, so he could speak freely. He waited a few minutes, then told Chen he was going to take a walk and pick up some wine for dinner. Once outside, he put his mask on and walked to an alley to call Coggins. He really didn't need the mask, he was immune. But with the mask on he could walk around freely, without fear of being identified. Thankfully, the leg wound he suffered from Bingham's bullet had almost healed, so he wasn't limping anymore.

"I thought we weren't supposed to have any contact, General. What's going on?"

"I'm reactivating you for one last mission."

"Hold on. You told me that I was finished after the last one. I'm hiding in a safe house waiting for this lockdown to pass, and I have no ability to travel discreetly."

"Look kid, you can handle this one. I'll even help set it up, it'll be easy. Just bring the girl with you and tell her the order comes from China. She'll believe it when she hears who the subject is."

"Yeah, who is it?"

"Senator Aaron Strauss."

"Whoa, a Senator? That doesn't sound easy. If I even decide to take this on, it'll cost you double my usual rate."

"I'm not concerned about the price. The most important thing is timing. It has to be done quickly, and I'll coordinate it so that you'll barely have to break a sweat. I'll make sure there's no security detail, and that he's in a location where you can get at him with no witnesses."

"So where is this supposed to go down?"

"It'll be in Virginia, but not in public. In fact, he'll be there expecting to meet with me, so he won't suspect a thing."

"Virginia? How am I supposed to travel there under current conditions? I can't take a plane; the airports are deserted. And I'm a wanted man. I know the FBI is looking for me, they know what I look like, I'll get picked up in no time."

"Don't sell yourself short, kid, you'll think of something."

"I'm not liking this from the get-go."

"You don't have to like it. Do I have to remind you of what I did for you and your baby sister? If it weren't for me, she'd be dead, and you'd be in a Russian prison."

"That debt was already paid."

"Not as far as I'm concerned."

"When is this going to end?"

"This will be your final mission, I promise."

"That's what you said the last time."

"You'll just have to believe me, and as a bonus, I'll also help you to disappear so that the feds stop looking for you."

"I guess you're giving me no choice. So how do I proceed?"

"First, figure a way to get down here, and when you arrive, contact me in the usual way and I will lay it out for you—and don't take too long. I'd like to coordinate this within the next two days."

"I'm going to have to drive."

"Just be quick about it—and make sure to bring the girl to help you."

✳ ✳ ✳

Yao needed more than a bottle of wine after that conversation. He adjusted his mask and made his way to the liquor store. He didn't like the General and he didn't trust him, but he had little choice in the matter. In any event, this would be his last mission. After that he would disappear, with or without the General's help. He would have enough money to get to Hawaii, where he intended to live for the rest of his life.

He returned to the apartment with two bottles of Chardonnay and a large bottle of Grey Goose vodka. Chen was cooking dinner and the odor of garlic and sesame oil made his mouth water. Even better, Chen was dressed in a tight pair of black jeans and a matching black top that left her stomach fully exposed. She looked sexy and his mind started to wander. After putting the wine in the fridge, he opened the Grey Goose, dropped a few cubes in a glass and poured a generous amount of vodka over the ice. Chen smiled at him, and he smiled back.

She said, "Is that for me?"

He took a sip, walked over to Chen, kissed her, and handed her the glass. "For you baby."

She took a sip, handed it back to Yao and said, "How about a splash of cranberry juice?"

"Very demanding today, aren't you?"

Chen extended her arms, turned her thumbs, and pointed to herself, "If you want a piece of this . . ."

"I do."

Broad smile. "Then a little cranberry juice is not too much to ask."

Yao took out the cranberry juice and poured some into the glass. "We need to talk."

"I'm listening."

"I've been given a new mission, and we need to move on it quickly."

"You can't be serious. This is not a good time for us to be out in public. The streets are empty because of the lockdown."

"I know, but this can't be helped. The orders came from high up. But I was promised it would be the last one."

"Promises, promises, I don't believe that for a minute, but tell me, what's the job?"

"A senator, in Virginia. He must be taken out."

"Come on, that's crazy. We can't do that and expect to get away with it. We're wanted, the police are everywhere, and people are quarantined at home. How do you expect to accomplish this?"

"We've got someone on the inside that is going to set him up. He will be alone and without any security detail. We just need to drive to Virginia in the next day or so."

"I don't like this. I won't go. You can do this yourself and I'll wait for you here."

"I need you with me, and I don't want to leave you alone . . . please."

"This one sounds too risky, why don't we just leave now and disappear, they won't be able to find us. Let's just get in the car and drive to California. We can hide there for a time, until things cool down."

"Look, I don't have a choice this time. At least come with me and I'll do the job myself, then we can leave from there to California."

"I'll have to think about it."

Chapter 30

XANDER VAN BUREN ARRIVED at Albert Whitted airport with mixed emotions. On the one hand, he looked forward to seeing Ashley again . . . on the other, he was concerned about the mission, and bringing Ashley with him into a potentially dangerous situation. After all, the people they were looking for had already tried to kidnap and kill her and had already killed her father and stepmother. Protecting her was paramount.

As he reached the tarmac, Ashley was standing outside the plane waving at him. When he got close, she smiled and said, "Like my outfit?"

Once again, she looked great and had even dressed for the occasion. She wore a dark green beret, dark jeans and a dark green top that resembled military fatigues. "Impressive. Did you go out shopping for that?"

"No silly," she said, sarcastically, "I just happened to have all this at home."

"Well, when it comes to you, I couldn't be sure. You did tell me that your worst vice was shopping."

"That I did. I see you pay attention."

"Always."

They boarded the plane, settled in, and took off for New York. As they taxied on the runway, Ashley said, "So we're really going after those two spies?"

"Well . . . I am. I'd prefer you to stay with the plane."

"That's not happening. I'm going with you wherever you go. I can help. I can guide you around Manhattan, and I can help identify both of them."

"Yes, but this is dangerous. They tried to kill you once—they won't have any problem trying to do it again."

"I can take care of myself."

"I'm sure you can, I'm just worried that you're getting involved in something over your head. These two are trained killers."

"Look, as far as I'm concerned, I have to make up for anything that Dad did to cause all this, so whatever it takes, I'm there one hundred percent. I already told you, I have some skills and I can protect myself. Besides, you need some back up, you're just a lawyer." She laughed.

"Very funny. You know I'm a former marine sergeant."

She reached out and touched his hand. "I'm only kidding, I know you're a big boy and can handle yourself."

"Yes, I can. And if you want to come along, you must do as I say. We aren't to approach them, just locate and verify. Those are my instructions. And we must stay out of sight, they'll recognize you."

She saluted, "Yes sir, Sergeant."

They sat in silence for a while and as the weather changed, the plane started to bounce around a bit. The pilot came on the speaker and advised them to expect some heavy turbulence. Moments later, the plane took a big drop, leaving Xander's stomach in his throat. The lights in the cabin went off and the air conditioning stopped. The pilot came back on the speaker and said that he was going to pull up above the storm and advised them that once they were at level flight again, Ashley would need to access the computer in the cabin to get the lights and air conditioning back.

It took a few minutes more before the plane climbed above the storm and levelled off. Ashley unbuckled and walked over to the flat screen, took the mouse and keyboard out of the drawer, and accessed the computer. The screen lit up and she scrolled a list of prompts, clicked on "Salon" and continued scrolling. Another list of prompts appeared on screen, A/C, Computer, Heat, Lighting, Movies, Music, TV, Video Recording and WIFI. She clicked on A/C first and restarted the system, then she clicked on Lighting and turned the lights back on.

Xander said, "That's an impressive system, what is video recording?"

"I'm not sure. I don't remember seeing that prompt before." She clicked on the prompt. Three date links appeared, 12/31/19, 6/19/19, and 1/14/19. She clicked on 12/31/19 and a video appeared on the flat screen. It was a recording of Doug and Layni with another couple apparently celebrating New Year's Eve on the plane. The four were drinking champagne and partying. There was no sound. Ashley said, "Look how happy Dad looks, they're all laughing and having fun celebrating New Year's. I don't know why there's no sound though. Let me see if I can fix that."

She tapped the keyboard and tried a few different commands but couldn't get the sound on. "I'll try another video, maybe it's just a problem with that one." She tapped the keyboard again, returned to the date prompts and clicked on 6/19/19 and another video appeared on screen. It quickly went to white static and appeared not to be working properly. She then went back and clicked on the 1/14/19. This time the screen loaded, and Doug Bingham was seen sitting in the cabin with four other men. Still no sound, but as he looked closely at the other men, he began to realize who they were.

Ashley looked at Xander, "Do you know these men?"

"Yes, I do. From left to right that is CIA Director William Coggins—they call him the General—Deputy Assistant FBI Director Joseph Cromley, Florida Senator Aaron Strauss, and Virginia Senator Dennie Sinkfield."

"What would they be doing on the plane with Dad?"

"I don't know for sure, but my thinking is, based on the date, that these are the government insiders that Stu Saxon is worried about. I'll bet these are the guys that are involved in the super virus conspiracy." Xander stood up and walked over to the screen trying to make out what they were saying, but it was impossible. "This is big, Ashley. I must get this intel to Stu right away, he needs to know about this. We may have just uncovered the biggest political corruption conspiracy this country has ever seen."

"You mean these guys are responsible for the super virus?"

"I can't be positive, but it sure looks like it. I know that all of them are diametrically opposed to the current administration's policies. To put it mildly, they despise progressives."

"So much so that they would get involved in unleashing a pandemic in our country?"

"It appears that way. What other explanation would there be for a meeting like this?"

"Well, what do we do? Can they be arrested? I mean they are very high up in the government. How does that work? Who would be able to arrest them?"

"There are procedures that must be followed, and this video alone, without more, is probably not enough to arrest them, especially without sound. But at least Stu will know who the enemy is, and maybe he can initiate a covert investigation?"

"We have WIFI. Do you want to send him an email?"

"No, too dangerous. I wouldn't want to put this in writing. I need to call him."

"I'm not sure if your cell phone will work at this altitude, but give it a try."

Xander took out his phone and looked. "No signal."

"Let me buzz Captain Carl." She pushed the intercom button, "Carl, we need to make a phone call but there's no signal right now. Is there anything you can do?"

"I think we're too high up right now. When the weather clears, we can reduce altitude and maybe you'll be able to get a signal."

"Okay, thank you." She looked at Xander, "I guess we have to wait . . . but this is insane. People with all this power, and they're actually involved in something so evil. I can't believe what my dad got himself into."

Chapter 31

CHEN WOKE UP IN a foul mood. She didn't get much sleep because she couldn't get Yao's new mission out of her head. She did not want to accompany him, in fact, she did not want him to even take on the mission, but she didn't want to leave him out in the cold with no back up either. She knew there was no way she could talk him out of the job . . . he would go with or without her . . . so she had a difficult choice to make.

She got out of bed and made a pot of coffee while Yao was in the other room packing for the mission. It was times like this that got him charged up. He enjoyed the prep before the mission. Sifting through his hardware and checking his guns and ammo breathed life back into him. Being cooped up for such an extended period was getting to him. And though it was part of the job, this time was different, because the super virus quarantine kept him even more isolated. As much as he loved Chen, he knew that at some point he'd have to tell her who he was really working for, and he didn't know how she would respond. He knew she loved him, but was her love strong enough? He was prepared to kill her if she took it the wrong way, but inside, he truly hoped she'd get past it, and that they could make their way to Hawaii together. He had no intention of telling her anything though, until after the mission was completed.

Chen came into the room and leaned against the doorpost with a cup of steaming coffee in her hand. She watched Yao in silence as he cleaned his pistol and reassembled it. Once done, he slid the mechanism back and forth a couple of times to check the action. Pleased, he set it down and began loading the magazine with hollow point 40 caliber cartridges. The clip was tight and as he inserted more cartridges, he needed to use his magazine speed loader to insert the last few.

Chen said, "So you're really going to do this?"

"I have to, but I swear, it will be the last job. Then we can disappear."

"I'm really worried this time; something just doesn't feel right. I mean, why now? Right in the middle of this pandemic?"

"You know it isn't our place to ask why. We just do as we're told, that's the job."

"I know, but sometimes we need to think outside the box."

"Look, Maria, I'd rather not get into it, but if you insist, then first tell me what made you do what you did? I mean, this virus is affecting the whole world, and all because of you. Shouldn't you have questioned that when you took on the assignment?"

"That's not fair. You knew the pressure I was under, and the only way to free myself from China and get back to the United States was to comply. Besides, do you really think I give a shit about the rest of the world?"

"That's pretty cold."

"Yeah, well you know about the horrors I endured growing up. From what the U.S. government did to my father, to being raped and abused as a child, I don't feel I owe anything to anyone. Nobody protected me, I had to do it all myself, but I'm still standing, and finally free."

"I know, but I thought you got past all that, and as you said, now you're free. I want to be as well . . . which is why I have to do this one last job."

"Sorry, I don't like bringing up my past, it just makes me angry. But don't get me wrong. I totally understand where you're coming from too, and I want to help. It's just we have to do this right. We made some mistakes with Bingham. It was sloppy, and now they know who we are, so we must take more precautions."

"Agreed. So does that mean you'll come with me?"

"Sort of. We'll prep for the mission together, I'll go with you, but when it comes time to execute, I'll stay back and monitor from afar. That way, in case anything goes wrong, I'll be in a better position to assist."

"I'm sure we can make that work." Yao pulled a duffle bag out of the closet, sifted through it and removed a pair of stealth communicator throat mics. Showing them to Chen, he said, "We can use these. We wear them around our necks, insert the earpieces in our ears, and we can whisper to each other. No one will hear us."

"What's the range?"

"About a half mile."

"Okay, that should suffice. Now we need to know the location so we can prescreen it."

"Once we get down there, I'll make contact with my counterpart and set it up."

"Fine, but we have to clear out of here completely first."

"Yes, that would be best."

"I'll need a few hours to pack, but I can be ready by one."

Chapter 32

⸺✳⸺

As XANDER AND ASHLEY got past the storm, the pilot brought the plane down to a lower altitude and Xander's cell phone signal returned. He called Agent Saxon.

"What's up Xan? You in New York yet?"

"Not yet, Stu, still on the plane, but something's come up and you're not going to believe it."

"Try me."

"So, Ashley was working with the onboard computer and she came across a video taken with a hidden camera. It's a video from more than a year ago of a meeting Doug Bingham had on the plane. Get this, the participants were CIA Director Coggins, Deputy Assistant FBI Director Cromley, and Senators Sinkfield and Strauss."

"What were they talking about?"

"Unfortunately, there's no sound. We aren't sure if it's broken and there is no sound recording or that there is simply something wrong with the playback."

"Well, either way, knowing that crew and what Bingham was involved with, it seems pretty clear what they were meeting about. I knew there was something going on inside the FBI. I just didn't realize how high up. Cromley's a prick to begin with, and I know he's been monitoring my investigation. Now this is beginning to make sense. I'm not sure who I can trust. Cromley has a lot of friends and supporters inside, so we must be very cautious until I find a way to catch him . . . I need you to get me that video."

"For now, I'll replay it and record it with my phone. That will preserve it, and I can text you that so you'll have it right away."

"Good idea. And once you send it to me, I'm going to get the president involved. At least I know I can trust him to do the right thing and bring in the attorney general. This is big, Xander. We really need to be extremely careful. Coggins is a very powerful and dangerous man too."

"Understood. I'll keep you posted on our progress after we arrive in New York."

After they disconnected, he replayed the video, recorded it with his phone, and sent it to Agent Saxon. Then he examined the system as best he could and realized that the only way to preserve the recording would be to remove the computer from the plane and have it analyzed. They would have to wait for the return flight to St. Petersburg to do that.

Xander sat on the plane looking out the window as the ramifications of what they had seen in the video continued to play across his mind. To even suspect that members of the U.S. government had plotted what appeared to be an overthrow of the current administration by causing a pandemic that was killing people just didn't seem real. Yet, from all accounts, that is exactly what was happening. Life had effectively been put on hold for most Americans. Commerce had all but ceased, the unemployment rate was close to fifteen percent, and the hospitals were filled with people suffering and dying from the super virus. Civil unrest was at an all-time high, the population no longer trusted the government to protect them, and riots were popping up all over the country.

Ashley cleared her throat, "Xander, are you okay? You haven't said a word in almost half an hour."

"Sorry, but I'm still trying to wrap my head around what we just saw. Some of the country's most powerful men are pure evil, and the people gave them the power to do this to us. And we're the only ones who actually know what's going on. This is a huge burden to carry on our shoulders. We need to stop this and expose it for what it is."

"Yes, I know, and to think Dad was part of all this is the most difficult and horrible thing I have ever experienced in my life."

"I knew him back in high school. He was a few years older than me, but we played on the same sports team when he was a senior. He always had an attitude about him, like he was better than the rest of us, but I never would have suspected he was capable of this."

"Well, to me he was the best dad in the world. He was always attentive, made sure to be at all my dances and games. He took me everywhere, and we had a great relationship all my life. I can't even recall that he ever raised his voice at me. What I've seen since he was killed is a completely different man than the one I grew up admiring. It's just awful."

"I'm sorry you had to see all this. I can't imagine what you're going through now with this realization."

"I still love him though. Is that wrong?"

"No, it's understandable. He was your father, and until recently I guess he was your hero. That's hard to get out of your mind, let alone your heart."

"As long as you don't think me a bad person for still having feelings for him."

"Believe me, I don't. Just being here and doing what you're doing to try to make up for it tells me the kind of person you are deep down. And to me, that's all that matters."

"Thank you Xander, that means a lot to me."

The plane started its initial decent and they sat in silence until they landed. After taxiing on the runway, they stopped, and the hatch was opened. Each grabbed their small suitcases and rolled them to a waiting SUV. The airport was small and appeared only to service private planes. There were no commercial jets and no security station. Ashley lifted her suitcase into the back of the SUV, unzipped it, and pulled out a pistol and two magazines.

"Whoa, what do you think you're doing with that thing?"

"It's for protection. Just in case. And thankfully I had this with me when they attacked me and Dad, or I wouldn't be here today. Don't tell me you didn't bring a weapon?"

"I did, but that's different. I've been trained."

"Well, I've been too."

"It's not the same, Ashley. I was in the military."

"I know, you've told me that a few times already. Don't worry, I know how to use this pistol and I will only use it in self-defense. But it *is* coming with me."

"Fine, just keep the safety on and keep it out of sight. The gun laws in New York are not as lax as they are in Florida."

They left Republic Airport on Long Island at 11:30 A.M. and drove to Manhattan on the Long Island Expressway. The trip to the city took over an hour, but with almost no traffic they arrived in downtown New York City relatively quickly. Taking the Brooklyn Bridge across, they made their way to Greenwich Street. Xander drove as Ashley looked at the numbers on the buildings.

She said, "We're getting close, do you want to park and walk, or should we stay in the vehicle?"

"There aren't many people on the street, so just put your mask on. We'll get as close as we can and see if there's a safe spot to observe from. We may be here for quite some time."

"Well, why can't we just go inside the building?"

"It's too dangerous, and I am only authorized to locate and verify. Then we call in the FBI."

"So, we're going to just sit and wait for someone to come out of the building?"

"For the time being, yes. Let's just hope they have to do some food shopping sooner rather than later."

"Okay, slow down, it's coming up on the left. And look up ahead on the right, there's a parking space, pull in."

Xander parallel parked in the space very close to the apartment building.

Ashley said, "It's eerie how empty the streets are down here. You don't know New York City like I do, but I can tell you this, I have never seen it so quiet. Even at two in the morning there are usually people on the streets around here."

"Scary, isn't it? And to think, in this day and age the global solution to the pandemic is to quarantine the world."

"Do you think it will ever go back to normal, Xander?"

"I don't know, but I suspect this will be the new normal for some time, until and unless a cure is found."

"What a nightmare." Ashley turned as a car approached the building. She pointed, "Hey look, that car just stopped in front of the building."

"I see."

Ashley grabbed his arm, "Holy shit, it's him! It's Darryl, he's got a mask on, but I can tell it's definitely him."

Yao opened the trunk and walked toward the entrance to the building. Maria Chen walked out carrying a backpack and wheeling a duffel bag. Yao went inside and brought out two suitcases while Chen placed everything in the trunk.

Xander said, "Looks like they're going someplace. They've packed a lot of stuff."

"What do we do?"

"We have to follow them and see where they're headed. I'll let Stu know." He took out his phone and called him. "Stu, it's Xander. We're just outside of the apartment building, and the two of them are loading up a car. It looks like they're moving out."

Stu said, "Okay, follow them but be careful, and keep me posted."

"Will do."

Minutes later they got in the car and drove off. Xander pulled out slowly and stayed far enough behind so as not to be noticed. They made their way on to the Brooklyn Bridge. Xander continued trailing them as they followed the exit ramp into Brooklyn and got on to the Brooklyn Queens Expressway heading south. With so few cars on the road, they had to maintain a greater distance to avoid detection. But once they reached the Verrazano Bridge leading to Staten Island, Xander suspected they were in for a long trip. He even wondered if they intended to drive all the way down to Florida, though that would have been foolish, since Yao and Chen had to know that the FBI was looking for them. So why return to the scene of the crime?

After a couple of hours, the monotony of the drive lulled Ashley to sleep. Her head resting on the window, she looked peaceful, as if she didn't have a care in the world. A sharp contrast to the way Xander would have expected her to feel, but she continued to surprise him with her level of maturity and understanding. He turned the radio to a smooth jazz station and pressed on, ever conscious of keeping back, but not losing sight of their car.

They had already traveled through most of New Jersey when they pulled into a full-service rest stop off of I-95. There was a gas station and various fast-food restaurants along with a souvenir shop. Surprisingly, everything was open, but Xander didn't dare come close or exit the vehicle. He took the opportunity to fill up on gas while his quarry went inside, presumably to get something to eat.

Xander called Agent Saxon. He picked up on the first ring, "What's up Xander?"

"I'm trying to figure that out. We've been tailing them on the highway for about three hours, they're headed south on I-95. We're still in New Jersey, and I'm wondering where in the world they're going."

"That is strange, but just keep following and keep me posted."

"Will do. Have you made any progress on the video I sent you?"

"I'm working on something. I've got a few agents that I trust who are doing a covert on all four creeps. Without a warrant it's all I can do, but I have a few tricks up my sleeve and I'm trying to find a way to access Cromley's internal email. Not much I can do about Coggins since he's CIA. As to the two senators, I've got to be careful. I don't want to blow my chances on arrests by violating their rights. If we could only get access to the thumb drive, I'm willing to bet there is more than enough in there to fry all of them."

"Amen. So where are you with that?"

"Still locked up tight, but I've got my best guys working on it, and hopefully soon we'll crack it. Then the fun will really begin."

"Okay, gotta go, they're on the move."

Chapter 33

AGENT SAXON PLACED A direct call through to President Bradshaw on a private line they had set up to keep prying eyes and ears out of the loop.

"Mr. President, I have some serious and troubling news that I need to give you over the phone, and then I must come see you with the proof. We will need to get the attorney general involved as well. I assume you can trust him?"

"Yes Stu, he is a man of integrity, and I trust him. So, what is it you've found?"

"I have a copy of a video tape of a meeting between Doug Bingham and four high level government officials who are probably responsible for the pandemic."

"Who are they?"

"CIA Director Coggins, Deputy Assistant FBI Director Joseph Cromley, Senator Dennie Sinkfield, and Senator Aaron Strauss. They had a meeting on Bingham's jet over a year ago and the only thing that makes sense, based upon the intel we already have from Ashley Bingham about what her father told her before he was killed, is that these men orchestrated this conspiracy to bring down your administration."

"Well, what do they say on the video?"

"That's the problem, the sound is corrupted, there is no volume. We don't know if it's fixable, but the meeting itself, coupled with everything else we've gathered, is very damning."

"Yes, but it's all circumstantial."

"True, but what other explanation could there be?"

"I don't know but we will need to see it and run it past AG Hammer. When can you get up here?"

"I've got a flight out of MacDill AFB in a half hour."

"Ok, just speak to no one, we need to be extra vigilant."

"Copy that, Sir."

"I'll have a copter waiting for you at Joint Base Andrews."

Next, Saxon met with his tech guru and had him substitute a fake thumb drive, fully encrypted and password protected, and he took the real drive with him. Knowing that both the FBI and the CIA were compromised, he could no longer take a chance of having it stolen or destroyed. It was the only real evidence he had that could bury the traitors, and he wasn't going to let it out of his sight. He also instructed him to set up a video feed in the room and intentionally leave it unattended for a time, just to see if someone would try to steal it. Saxon needed to stay at least two steps ahead of his adversaries, and he felt he had it under control.

Three hours later, Agent Saxon met in the Oval Office with President Bradshaw and Attorney General Terrence Hammer. AG Hammer was a career prosecutor who originally hailed from Texas and had graduated from Harvard Law School. He was a stocky man with a thick white moustache that ran across his cheeks and encircled the outside of his chin. He spoke with a heavy southern drawl. He never let politics get in the way of his office. A very fair man, he was well respected by those on both sides of the aisle and had no problem being confirmed for his position. Stu played the video and reminded both the president and the AG about what Ashley

Bingham told them about what her father had done. Bingham had been meeting with members of the U.S. government, along with Chinese oligarchs initially in an attempt to affect international trade, but that the conversation deteriorated into a more dramatic and evil plot to unleash germ warfare, and ultimately the pandemic. He further explained that Bingham was cut out of the loop when he voiced his opposition to the plan and that must have been when they decided he had to be eliminated. However, since he was in possession of incriminating evidence of the conspiracy, they needed to secure it before it got in the wrong hands. Of course, as the situation degenerated and they could not locate the thumb drive, they did the next best thing and killed his wife, and then him.

AG Hammer listened intently as he continued to replay the video, trying to read the lips of the men at the meeting. The problem was that they weren't always facing the camera, and it was very hard to see anything in the degraded phone video version. Saxon said he would procure the better copy from the plane when he could get access, but that it was in New York at the present time. AG Hammer also suggested enlisting the services of a lip reader.

Saxon said, "So what do you think? Is there enough here to bring these guys in?"

AG Hammer said, "Too circumstantial, but I think I can bring this to the FISA Court and get a short window for surveillance warrants on all these men. But it must be done on the down low. If anyone gets wind of this, it will blow sky high. The fact that they were meeting with Chinese operatives gives me the in I need to try to sell the court on it, and with the pandemic as part of this conspiracy, I think I can get a judge to sign off. However, there are a few things I am going to need. First, can you get me an affidavit from Ashley Bingham detailing what you've told me? Second, can you get the Bingham plane down to Joint Base Andrews so we can access the computer system?"

"I can't get a written affidavit yet because Bingham is in transit and cannot stop, but I can certainly get her to send a video file of herself testifying to what she has told me. And, as to the plane, I will speak to her and get that done as well."

"That will work."

President Bradshaw interjected, "This is an attempted coup here, Terry. We've got to stop this and fry these men and make an example. We also don't know how deep this goes. I've known for quite some time, as have you, that the far right has just gone off the deep end. They lost the election and still can't figure out how to recover. So instead of trying to serve the people, they're trying to undermine the legitimate government and destroy the people. This pandemic has been killing our country, and it must stop now. Please get on this right away."

"I'm on it Mr. President, I'll have this in front of the court by the end of the day."

Agent Saxon said, "Excuse me, sir, but there's more."

"More?" President Bradshaw asked. "What do you mean?"

"As we speak, I have a trusted operative who is following the two spies down I-95 to an unknown destination. These are the spies that killed Doug and Layni Bingham, and the woman spy is the one we believe created the virus. We intend to intercept but need to see where they are headed. We suspect that they may be on another mission and want to catch them in the act. With everything we've just uncovered, it is my belief that one or both are operating at the direction of these four men."

President Bradshaw said, "Okay keep me in the loop." He turned to AG Hammer, "And as soon as you get those warrants, please let me know."

"Will do, sir. I'll just need the video testimony from Bingham."

"Copy that, Sir," Stu said. "I'll make the call now."

Agent Saxon left the Oval Office, took out his cell, and called Xander. He explained what was needed, and Ashley immediately called her pilot and advised him to head to Joint Base Andrews. Then she made a video on Xander's phone detailing everything she knew and was told by her father. He sent it to Agent Saxon. Agent Saxon then put together an entire summary and background on everything he knew from Darryl Yao to Mai Ling/Maria Chen to the Institute of Virology in China so that AG Hammer would have all the ammunition he needed when he went to court.

Chapter 34

—✳—

AG TERRENCE HAMMER SAT across from Judge Lucille Faber of the FISA Court in her chambers. A diminutive Black woman with a strong, solid, gravelly voice, she wore her robe with distinction, and took her role on the court very seriously. She could command a courtroom with just a cold stare.

"So, tell me, Mr. Hammer, to what do I owe the pleasure of your visit today? Over the phone you said it was a matter of national security, and that piqued my interest."

"Well, Your Honor, to begin with, this conversation must remain solely between us for the time being. I have a story to tell and an application for FISA warrants I will be seeking, but I need to know that this will not leave your chambers. I don't even want a clerk or stenographer to hear this."

"That's a tall order, Mr. Attorney General, from the get-go this entire meeting is patently improper. I think you know that. I can't recall ever having the attorney general of the United States making an application for a FISA warrant. I don't even know if it is proper protocol. This has never been done in all the years that FISA has been around."

"I know that Your Honor, but this is a very special circumstance."

"I guess you'll have to convince me, but we must have a record of this application, so without a stenographer, I'm going to have to record this on my cell phone, and you may do the same. That way we each have a record and if this goes sideways, I'm covered and so are you."

"Very well, Judge."

"Okay, so what is this all about?"

"First, I'll start with the big picture and then circle back to it as I proceed."

"Go ahead."

"The matter centers around the super virus pandemic. It began with what appeared to be an unrelated double homicide where a very wealthy international trade financier's wife and friend were murdered. His name was Doug Bingham, and he resided in St. Petersburg, Florida. As the investigation progressed it was learned that a year and a half ago, he made introductions and brokered a deal between high-ranking U.S. government officials and the Chinese. Their initial intent was to upset international trade with a view towards undermining the current administration and our economy. At some point the discussions turned into a plan to develop a virus that would affect the world and destroy the U.S. economy. All this to oust the president and seize control of the government. A coup if you will. Mr. Bingham became concerned about the new developments and voiced his opposition. He had been protecting himself by recording conversations and allegedly securing documents that would implicate these men. He stored it all on a thumb drive and secreted it. The men got wind of this, and that is what led to the first homicides, but they did not find the drive. Subsequently, they attempted to kidnap his daughter and use her as leverage to get the drive. Bingham saved his daughter, and he then told her what was going on. He did not, however, give the names of the individuals at that time. When he rescued his daughter, they were chased by two spies, one was Darryl Yao, who turned out to be Bingham's own butler and the one who murdered Mrs. Bingham and her friend. The other, Mai Ling, now going by the name Maria Chen, was the spy who infiltrated the Virology Institute of China, synthesized the virus, and unleashed it. They managed to kill Doug Bingham, but his daughter Ashley survived and escaped. I will now play a video of Ashley Bingham, where she relays the information her father told her about this plot before he was killed." AG Hammer played the video for Judge Faber. "As you can see, it is very detailed and shows the disturbing nature of this conspiracy."

"I see that, but I hope you have more."

"Yes, Judge. This morning we received another video, this one taken on Doug Bingham's plane over a year ago showing a meeting with Bingham and the four men against whom I am seeking the FISA warrants."

He cued up the second video for the Judge, who looked on intently—as she realized who the men in the video were, she sat up and took notice.

"That's General Coggins and Deputy Assistant FBI Director Cromley with the senators. Are you telling me these men are plotting against our country? Do you have sound for this video?"

"These are the men, Your Honor, and as to audio, right now, no, we are trying to secure the original video from the plane and will have our tech people try to pull the audio from it if available."

"Mr. Hammer, if what you're saying here is true, this is a scandal to end all scandals. The problem I have here, though, is this is all circumstantial. We have no sound, and this could just be an innocuous meeting."

"Perhaps without the other supporting evidence I have presented, but with Ashley Bingham's detailing of her father's business dealings and the current state of our country, there is something highly suspect, and it needs to be investigated. All I am asking for are surveillance warrants against the men, so we can uncover the truth.

"That's a tall order with only this evidence, Mr. Hammer."

"Judge, you see what we're up against here. If we don't do something fast, this could all blow up even more. For all we don't know, these men could hold the key to curing the virus. They are evil men plotting against our nation. This is national security at its most delicate."

"Well, I'd be sticking my neck out right onto the chopping block if this goes any other way, but seeing as this pandemic is killing our nation, I'll have to use some judicial discretion and sign off on the warrants. But I'm only going to give you 72 hours to do this in. If you don't come up with anything in that time, you'll have to come back and reconvince me."

"Will that be 72 hours from signing or from getting the surveillance initiated?"

"That will be 72 hours starting at 9:00 A.M. tomorrow morning, so get your boys into action and do it fast."

"Thank you, Judge."

"Good luck, for all our sakes."

After AG Hammer left the judge's chambers, he called the president and advised him that the warrants had been secured. He then placed a call to Special Agent Saxon and relayed the news as well. Saxon had remained in DC and quickly called a meeting with his local operatives in a private conference area at FBI headquarters.

Including Saxon, there were nine agents. He called the meeting to order. "Ladies and gentlemen, we've got a highly classified mission we are about to engage in. This will require the utmost in secrecy, there must be no leaks, no outside communications. The only person you are to report to is me, until further notice. Anyone breaking protocol will be charged with a high crime, so before I begin, is there anyone in here now who is unable to comply with my demands?" After five seconds of silence, Saxon proceeded. "Good. Now we have just been given FISA surveillance warrants against four high ranking government officials who will need to be tapped, traced, and followed. These men are powerful and well protected. Getting access is not going to be easy, but we can do it. We need their cars, their homes, and their offices bugged and monitored, as well as surveillance on them directly. They can't be in all places at the same time, so when they leave home, go in, when they leave their car, go in, when they leave their office, go in. This isn't surveillance 101 here. All of you know exactly what needs to be done. Accessing their phones and computers shouldn't be too difficult—as long as they are using government-issued devices, we have easy access, and I'll handle and arrange that from right here."

Agent Jill Stanley asked, "So who are we after?"

"I'm getting to that. Our targets are CIA Director General William Coggins, Deputy Assistant FBI Director Joseph Cromley, Senator Dennie Sinkfield, and Senator Aaron Strauss."

Agent Davis Cooper said, "You've got to be kidding me. We're going after top brass? What did they do?"

Saxon said, "These men are directly involved in an attempted government coup. We believe they are responsible for the super virus pandemic, and we are all going to help to prove it. Now you see why this is at the top of our national security agenda and must be kept in the strictest of confidence. If this gets out, we lose our window. They can't see us coming."

Agent Ray Olderman interjected, "So how do we play this?"

"There are eight of you, so I'm going to team you two to a squad, and each squad will go after one man and secure the surveillance. This will be twenty-four seventy-two, meaning for the next seventy-two hours, this is all you will do. That is our FISA warrant window. We need to come up with something during that time. I have your assignments on this sheet with detailed info on their homes and vehicles, everything you need to track them. I'll read your assignments out loud, the rest you can digest on your own. Then gather your gear and get going. Agents Stanley and Olderman, you're on Strauss. Agent Cooper, you team up with Agent Stacey Maxwell, you're on Sinkfield. Agents Paul Cash and Zeke Culpepper, you've got the General. Now I'm sure you understand, he's going to be the toughest fish to fry. He's the head of the CIA and is probably paranoid to a fault, so take it slow and easy. If you can't get at him one way, don't push it. Better not to alarm or alert him. Lastly, Agents Rick Hobley and Miles Melis, you've got our FBI buddy Cromley. He too is a sneaky piece of work, so be careful, but please, let's get these guys. They need to hang for what they've done to our country. Everyone synchronize and make sure to report to me every few hours with updates. Dismissed."

Special Agent Stu Saxon had finally come into his own. He was now in command of a major task force involving a global pandemic and possibly about to take down four high level government officials. He stood there alone looking intently at, and admiring, his new command post. A full wall of separate screens in front of him flickered static that would soon turn to communications from his elite staff of operatives. He smiled. His career had been moving in the right direction, and he had been near the top of the food chain, but still chomping at the bit to get a big assignment, and this one had fallen right into his lap because of his good buddy Xander Van Buren. Had Xander not asked for Saxon's help at the very beginning, he would have never had this opportunity. *Sometimes dumb luck just puts you in places you would have never conjured in your wildest dreams.*

Chapter 35

⸻ ✳ ⸻

A FTER A NIGHT OF setting up surveillance at Sinkfield's office, Cooper and Maxwell broke for breakfast at the local Denny's. They ate quickly and once back on the road, Cooper drove, and Maxwell logged onto the onboard computer as they headed over to Senator Sinkfield's home. A plot survey and building plans, compliments of the local building department, made it easy to determine the lay of the land, a five-acre complex in a secluded and wooded area. The plans didn't show any special security details, and hacks into the local ADT and other private security companies showed no active accounts. In fact, the home had been constructed some forty-five years before and had barely been remodeled or updated. It had been Sinkfield's parents, and as an only child, he took it over after they died.

Sinkfield had already been spotted on his way to the office so his home was the perfect starting point. Divorced, he lived alone, and his son was quarantined at school in his off-campus apartment at Yale University. Still cautious, they parked on a road near the rear of the home and climbed a stone wall to access the property. With their high-tech gear, they determined there were no cameras filming and edged their way towards the rear entrance. Picking the lock on the door was easy, and as suspected there was no alarm. Sinkfield was either a moron, or he believed he was untouchable—which meant he was a moron, because no one was untouchable. They quickly scurried through the house, placing mini-mics in various rooms and by the phones. They were in and out in less than ten minutes. They left more mini mics out by the pool area and put a few video camera feeds in the trees in the backyard.

Satisfied, they headed to DC to see if Sinkfield had settled into his office, so they could bug his car and GPS track it, and then head over to listen in on his office chatter.

※ ※ ※

Cash and Culpepper were having a much more difficult time. The General's house was locked up tight. Security cameras were at every corner post both on the front and rear property lines and on the house. There was no way they were intruding without being seen, so tapping the house was not happening. The best they could hope for would be with a sound dish, but that was only good to a certain distance and the audio was not that reliable. They'd need to try and get his SUV when he went to work. Cash's sister, Ava Lovelle, worked at CIA headquarters as a secretary on the same floor as the General, so he enlisted her to help get a bug into Coggin's office. She agreed to handle it discreetly. She didn't much care for Coggins and had had her suspicions about his allegiance for some time. She had a high-level security clearance and had been working there well before Coggins had come on board, so she knew the lay of the land and could get in and out of his office relatively quickly. Cash gave her two high tech bugs, which she managed to place by the General's desk and in his phone before he came to the office that morning.

At 8:30 A.M. Coggins garage door opened, and he pulled his SUV out and headed to his office. Culpepper drove as they maintained a safe distance through the suburban streets of Langley, Virginia. Coggins's home was a short fifteen-minute ride to headquarters. He stopped off at a Starbucks along the way, boldly walked in with no mask, and picked up a coffee and croissant, brought it back to his vehicle and proceeded on his way. When he reached headquarters, he didn't need to show his badge. He was ushered through by the security guard and proceeded to park on level 3. Culpepper waited for a few more cars to clear through, pulled in and showed his FBI badge, and was ushered through on that basis. The men cruised the lot on each floor until they located Coggins SUV and got to work. Getting inside the vehicle was not a problem; they installed a bug under the dash and a GPS tracker beneath the vehicle and were on their way in five minutes.

※ ※ ※

Cromley's home was in a townhouse in Washington, DC. He had a government-issued security guard standing directly outside the home, so interior access wasn't happening there. Agents Hobley and Melis circled around the back where there was a rear attached garage but again, no access and two security cameras sat in plain sight crisscrossing the entire back portion of the gate and driveway. No luck there either. The up-to-date intel on Cromley told them he had flown to Tampa, apparently to check on Special Agent Saxon's progress with the investigation. He must have known that Saxon was in DC, so he used the opportunity to head to Tampa. Saxon surmised that Cromley would try to make his move and secure the thumb drive, but he was way ahead of him. It was safely in his possession where Cromley could never get at it. Hobley and Melis drove to Joint Base Andrews, located Cromley's vehicle, bugged it, and attached a GPS tracker before heading to FBI Headquarters to bug the office.

❋ ❋ ❋

Agents Stanley and Olderman made their way to Strauss's home. He lived on a quiet street of well-appointed private homes on a quarter acre lot in a DC suburb. It was not a lavish home, simply a modest rental. His primary residence was in Florida, not too far from Florida State University in Tallahassee, but he hadn't been there in some time and wouldn't be returning until the July recess. He too lived alone, while his wife stayed in and maintained the Tallahassee home. She was a shy homebody and remained as far from the political limelight as she could get, only socializing on the most necessary of occasions when she needed to be seen to help her husband appear to have a strong, happy marriage. There was none of that though; it was all for the cameras. She had fallen out of love with her husband years before. There had even been rumors that Aaron Strauss was gay, but those rumors never got full sunlight and the media simply chose to ignore it. It had no bearing on his ability to lead, and the mood in the country about such things had tapered off. No one really cared.

The agents found an ADT sign out front as well as a Sentrex Systems sign. They hacked into ADT and found no account, but when they hacked into Sentrex Systems they found an existing account.

Stanley said, "I've got a Sentrex, I know exactly how it works. I can get into that thing in less than one minute and disable it. The signal isn't sent to the station for sixty seconds, giving the homeowner enough time to enter the home and punch in the code. However, aside from the silent alarm to the station, the only other caveat is it is also hooked up directly to a motion sensor camera feed." She pointed to a dark cylindrical glass protruding from above the front door. "And until the system can be disabled, any movement and that camera clicks on and starts recording. So, the recording will go on before I can disable."

Olderman said, "Why can't we just shoot it out with a rifle?"

"Risky, we leave a trail. He comes home, sees the broken glass, knows he's been infiltrated and becomes suspicious."

"There's got to be a way."

"There is. How about we go to Sentrex, get another lens so we can shoot it out, and then simply replace it and clean up the mess. That's a standard lens. He'll never know the camera is broken inside the housing lens."

"Tough to do in broad daylight."

"Perhaps, but I've got a plan. Sentrex sells logo shirts, so we simply pose as a repair crew fixing the lens. It will only take a minute—the lens screws right back into the housing. I had to replace mine after it fell while I was cleaning it. Trust me I know this system. There's a Sentrex store right downtown. Let's go for it."

"Copy that."

※ ※ ※

Cooper and Maxwell checked in with Saxon first. Cooper said, "We're up and running boss. Sinkfield's home was a breeze. Huge property, no security whatsoever, we've got mics and cameras inside and out. We just finished placing the GPS tracker and bug in his car, but he's in his office so that's off limits for now. We'll stay close to Capitol Hill and keep our eyes open."

Saxon said, "Thanks for checking in. Keep me posted." He closed his phone and then got back with Jason Turlough who was an FBI agent techno wunderkind out of the DC office on loan to him to help access the devices of all four men. The FBI had a very sophisticated system for tracking and accessing the computers and phones provided to all government staff, from the lowest secretary all the way up to, but not including, the president and vice president of the United States—the only two who still had full secrecy. NSA made sure that even the highest-ranking members of government were not fully cognizant that their phones and computers could be accessed, viewed, and compromised. Emails and texts could be accessed even if erased, and phone numbers logged both incoming and outgoing. They could also hear conversations in real time and replay recorded phone messages. Within an hour, the big screens on the far wall of the operations center began scrolling phone numbers emails and text messages.

Saxon said, "Jason, can you associate names with the phone numbers on the logs?"

Jason punched a few keys on the keyboard and the data realigned with names of the parties associated with the phone numbers.

"Can you organize them by number and name, so we have a list of each caller, date and time, and length of call?"

"Sure thing, boss." He punched another set of commands into the keyboard and the data realigned again.

Saxon walked over closely to the screen and wrote some notes on a pad. "It looks like there's some phone chatter between all four of these men. No conference calls but see the pattern here. Looks like Coggins initiates a call to Cromley, who then calls Sinkfield, who relays to Strauss. They're discreet, the calls are few and far between, but they are consistent. Short, all less than one minute, but they must have a purpose. Let's check these dates and see if we can spot any unusual events or activities around the times after these calls were made."

"Roger that, boss."

* * *

Agents Stanley and Olderman returned from Sentrex, parked diagonally across from Strauss's home. Olderman took the rifle shot, one for the lens, a second for the camera inside. He was a former sniper, and the shots were a piece of cake. No sounds from the rifle, no nosey neighbors outside, mostly everyone keeping to themselves in the midst of the quarantine. With Sentrex shirts on their backs and a ladder and a tool kit, they managed to replace the lens in thirty seconds, clean the debris, and enter the house right after. Stanley got to work on the keypad and, true to her word, the system was disabled in twenty-five seconds. They raced through the home, bugged the office, the kitchen, the living room, and Strauss's bedroom, as well as the phone. In and out, five minutes. They headed to Capitol Hill to locate his car.

✳ ✳ ✳

Agents Hobley and Melis checked in with Saxon and brought him up to speed.

Hobley said, "Cromley's house was inaccessible, boss—too much security, so we couldn't take a chance. We're over at Joint Base Andrews. Just located Cromley's vehicle; it's in the lot."

Saxon said, "Yeah, he's on his way to Tampa. He knows I'm up here, so I think he's going to make a play for the thumb drive. If we can get him on camera doing that, we'll be that much closer to nailing that son of a bitch."

Melis said, "Once we're done here. We'll be back at headquarters, and we'll get his office bugged. Then we wait."

"Copy that. I've got my boys down in Tampa keeping a quiet watch there."

✳ ✳ ✳

Cash and Culpepper checked in with Saxon next. Cash said, "No good at Coggins home, too much security. We can't get within a hundred yards without being spotted. His set up is top notch, but we had to figure that. CIA, former general. He won't take any chances. We've got his SUV bugged and tracked though, and my insider at the CIA bugged his office, so we're good with that. I don't think he suspects that he can be tapped inside his CIA office."

"Good job, I'm working the computers and already have access to all their emails, texts, and phone logs. There's been some chatter between all of them over time, not a lot, they're cautious, but we've got a timeline and we're checking external events that may have occurred around the times of the calls. The emails are short and cryptic, but we'll figure it out. Stay in touch and if you hear anything give me a ring."

"Will do, boss."

Agent Saxon sat down at the far end of the conference table, still scribbling notes as the screens scrolled text messages and phone calls. He zeroed in on a date only ten days before where Sinkfield texted Cromley:

Sinkfield: Set up meet with all, urgent.
Cromley: When?
Sinkfield: Sunday 1 p.m.
Cromley: Where?
Sinkfield: My place.
Cromley: Okay.

Shortly thereafter Cromley called Coggins. The call lasted 45 seconds, then Sinkfield called Strauss, another 30 second call. Saxon made a note of it. "You see that, Jason? The four of them had a meeting on Sunday, May 17th at Dennie Sinkfield's place."

"That's right."

"So, these guys are still in bed together plotting something. Any significant current events after that date?"

"Other than Memorial Day on Monday, sir, nothing eventful other than the usual twenty-four-hour nasty news cycle, which may or may not have any bearing whatsoever. Many of the states were starting to open with phase one and two of reversing the lockdowns and letting Memorial Day play itself out, hoping the virus wouldn't spike."

"CDC should have data on that pretty soon, and I don't think it bodes well for any of us. This thing ain't going away so fast if you ask me."

"Sad but true, I think."

Chapter 36

GENERAL COGGINS RODE THE elevator to his office carrying his Starbucks bag in one hand and a briefcase in the other. An unlit cigar hung from the corner of his mouth. He nodded as he passed the secretarial pool along the corridor to his office. Ava Lovelle passed by him walking in the other direction and gave him a smile. Coggins raised his chin and kept walking. He entered his office, tossed the briefcase on his side chair, sat down and opened the Starbucks bag. He placed his cigar in the ash tray, tore the lid off the coffee, and began drinking as he clicked on his keyboard and scanned his email list. Nothing noted of interest, he took out his burner phone and texted Yao.

> Coggins: Where are you?
> Yao: Will be in Virginia later this afternoon. Game plan?
> Coggins: Sunday 7 P.M.
> Yao: Where?
> Coggins: Will advise.
> Yao: Roger, but I need to scout, must have advance notice.
> Coggins: You'll know in an hour.

Coggins switched phones and called Cromley. "We're on. The horses need to be brought to the stable."

Cromley said, "Where and when?"

"Same locale as last time, Sunday 7:00 P.M."

"Acknowledged."

* * *

Culpepper called in to Saxon, "Just intercepted a phone conversation with Coggins and Cromley. Looks like they're setting up a meeting Sunday evening at the same location of a prior meet."

Saxon said, "That would be Sinkfield's place. They met there ten days ago. I'll let Cooper and Maxwell know. They're watching Sinkfield and have already staked out his house."

Chapter 37

⌒—✳—⌒

Xander and Ashley slept in the SUV and kept a close watch on Yao and Chen, who spent the night in a cheap motel in Virginia. By 9:00 a.m., they were on their way. They followed the two spies well into Virginia, exited the highway, and drove through a semi-rural area with huge homes on large parcels of land.

Xander called in to Stu Saxon. "Stu, we're moving through a rural area of Virginia. How do you want us to handle this? I'm thinking these two are on a mission and getting ready for something significant."

"I think you're right Xander. We've got some chatter in DC, as well. AG Hammer was able to secure FISA warrants on the gang of four, and we've been listening in. It appears they're setting up a meeting at Senator Sinkfield's home in Langley tonight. I'm willing to bet those two are headed there. I'm thinking that at this point you should back off and come in from the field. I have agents that I'm going to be stationing over there, so you don't need to stay in harm's way."

"That's not happening Stu. We're seeing this through. We'll stay out of sight, but we've come too far to walk away now.

"Look, just stay clear for now. I'll text you Sinkfield's address, so you don't have to trail them any longer. Give it a few hours—my men should be in place by 3:00 p.m. Then you can make your way over, but stay clear and out of sight."

"Copy that."

Chapter 38

❦

YAO HAD ALREADY REVIEWED the boundary survey Coggins sent him, along with a Google Earth search to get the full lay of the land. Sinkfield's home was on a secluded five acres with a preserve in back. The surrounding neighbors also had large multiacre parcels, so it was quiet and easy access. He entered from the rear, where there was a scalable eight-foot stone wall. The woods were thick at that end of the property, and he could easily hide and make his way to a clear vantage point up in a tree that gave him a visually direct and clear path to a semicircular row of outdoor furniture set up around a large round granite table. Coggins assured him that his target would be highly visible and easily identified. Yao was fully prepared and had already found many pictures of Senator Strauss online.

Yao set up a perch in the trees and scouted around with his binoculars. He also carried a set of night goggles and an infrared scope for the evening events, but for now, the daylight binoculars allowed him to see all around the property. No one was home, so he took the bold step and wandered through the woods and got close to the house. He measured the distance with his rifle scope as well, and as he made his way to the edge of the clearing, about seventy-five feet from the pool area, he swept slowly back and forth along the entire perimeter of the property and checked the grounds and the trees using his multifunction Delta X-100-4 countersurveillance sweeping system. The Delta was a high-tech gadget that easily identified electronic devices using spectrum analysis software, various handheld RF probes, and broadband RF antennas to assess the entire five-acre environment. A perfect countermeasure device for Yao's needs. It helped him to locate a video camera set up high in a tree on the south side of the property. He climbed up and blacked out the lens on the camera just to be sure, then circled to the north side, where the Delta detected another camera. He disabled that one with black paint as well.

His last move before retreating from the property was to place a bug underneath the granite table where the men would be sitting that evening. He wanted to be able to hear the conversation. Fully confident and prepared, he returned the way he came, retreated over the stone wall and back to Maria Chen, who had been parked and hiding in the woods a half mile from the property.

Chen said, "How'd it go? Were you able to gain access?"

"It was easy. The yard is peppered with trees and the entire perimeter is lined with heavy woods as well. No one can see in from the outside, and the positioning of the trees allowed me to set up a perch high in the trees near the rear. The Delta identified a couple of security cameras, which I blacked out, and the line I have from the tree I scouted gets me a clear shot from about 250 feet away. With a shot like that, and night goggles, I won't miss."

"Sounds like a plan, but to play it safe, we need to get you back here well before dark and set up. Better that you're here way before anyone shows up. That way, if anything changes, you'll be prepared."

"Agreed. The meeting starts at 7:00 P.M. so we'll get back here around 3:00 P.M. Now let's find a quiet place to rest until later. We need to stay out of sight."

Chapter 39

GENERAL COGGINS COORDINATED HIS two most loyal agents, Kirk Fenton, and Tyler Santry, to set up in the rear yard behind the stone walls of Dennie Sinkfield's home. The men weren't taking any chances and made sure they set up vantage points, one high and away in the trees and the other on the ground and ready to move at a moment's notice. They needed to be in place well before Yao and Chen returned for the evening festivities. It was imperative that the two spies feel fully confident that they were alone and free to take out Senator Strauss with no resistance.

There was an abundance of places where Fenton and Santry could hide without fear of being seen. Fenton took the south corner of the yard and Santry took the north corner. A massive pine tree formed the perfect cover. Fenton scaled the tree carrying a backpack strapped across his shoulders. It contained a rifle and scope, binoculars, night vision goggles, ammo, and a communications device, along with food and water. His pistol was clipped to his belt. He assembled the rifle in short order, screwed the scope on, and scanned the area. The branches of the tree were well positioned, and he was able to rest the rifle directly across a thick branch firmly in a V-shaped groove. He chewed on a beef jerky as he watched

Santry make his way across the ground from the north corner to a stone outcropping halfway towards the house, where he dug in near a deteriorated part of the stone wall. Santry positioned himself behind the wall while still maintaining a clear view of the yard and pool area. He set up on the ground and covered himself with loose brush and leaves that allowed him to blend seamlessly into the landscape. He assembled his rifle, checked his scope, range, and distance, then checked his pistol, sliding the mechanism back and forth to confirm the action.

In the quiet of the early afternoon, all that could be heard were birds chirping and a soft wind whistling through the trees.

Santry checked in over the audio feed. "I'm in position, Fent. I can't see you, just give me an idea where you're at."

Fenton said, "Follow the line of trees running on the south side near the back edge of the property. There's a thick pine, I'm about 30 feet up, and I've got a clear line directly to that round table in the back yard. Where are you?"

Santry said, "I see the tree, but not you. I think you're hidden well enough. You won't be noticed."

Fenton said, "I watched you moving along the stone wall and then lost you. I've run the scope back and forth three times and you're also out of sight. Now we just wait. Radio silence until the party starts."

"Copy that."

Chapter 40

IT WAS GETTING BREEZIER towards the afternoon, but still a pleasant spring day when Agents Cooper and Maxwell returned to Sinkfield's home to set up surveillance. They came in through the rear and crept along the tree line until they reached the stone wall. Fenton spotted them first as they climbed over the wall and landed on the other side. Having no choice, he broke the radio silence and called Santry.

"We've got a problem. There are two operatives who've just entered the zone. Not sure if they're hostile, but they're certainly not with us. No discernable logos or badges, but they do look FBI to me."

Santry said, "So how do we play this?"

"Our instructions are to complete the mission at all costs. The spies have to be allowed to get Senator Strauss, then we take them out. Anything in the way of that must be eliminated. We have no choice—we take out these two and hide the bodies."

"You're sure about this? I wasn't planning on killing FBI agents when I woke up this morning."

"Look, we were chosen for this mission because of our elite status. Our country is depending on us. You know the importance of this cause. The General has our backs. Remember, there's a bigger picture here than just two lives. I need your help, so man up. I've got a shot at one of them, an easy line. The other one is moving towards you, along the stone wall. We need to get them at the same time—my gun, your knife."

"Copy that. I'm on it. I see him. He's about seven seconds away. Time your shot, six, five, four, three, two, one."

An almost silent pop came from the rifle and hit Maxwell in the back of the head. She went down without a sound.

Agent Cooper stopped in his tracks when he heard a thud from the rear. Before he could turn, Santry was on him from behind. With his knife, he sliced across Cooper's throat. Cooper reacted more quickly than Santry expected, and the cut only broke the surface of his neck. Blood gurgled from the wound, but Cooper was still able to turn and face Santry. For a split second they caught each other's eyes, and the two made recognition. They'd met before, but in the microsecond of the moment, neither could place where. The men grabbed at each other and began tumbling on the ground, wrestling for the knife as Fenton looked on from above. Santry rolled over and elbowed Cooper across the nose, splitting it wide open. Cooper grabbed the knife and sliced Santry's shoulder, cutting into the thick of his deltoid. The two men rose and squared off. Cooper kept moving forward, swiping the knife across his body as he backed Santry up against the stone wall. Santry charged, hitting Cooper at the waist, and taking him to the ground. Santry grabbed Cooper's head and brought his knee up into his left cheek. The bones in his face splintered and Cooper was out. Santry reached for his pistol and pointed it at Cooper's forehead. For a split second he thought about pulling the trigger, but then he realized that sound was not an option, so he took the knife from Cooper's hand and cut the FBI agent's throat. Blood sprayed back onto Santry. He spit, wiped his eyes with his sleeve, wiped the blood from his blade, and holstered it.

Chapter 41

COGGINS HAD TO GET out of the office. He was anxious despite all the preparation. He needed to take a ride and clear his mind. With much still to be done, he needed reassurance from his agents but could not run the risk of contacting them. His best course of action was to take a long drive and enjoy a good cigar. He did, however, need to reach out to Cromley and confirm that he had accomplished his mission in Tampa and would be back well in advance of the gang of four meeting a few hours from then.

* * *

Cromley flew into MacDill AFB and drove to FBI headquarters in Tampa. Once inside he located Agent Saxon's deputy assistant, who had been working on the encrypted thumb drive. Agent Bolles was expecting him but didn't let on that he knew.

Cromley said, "Good day, Agent Bolles. We've had a change of plans about the drive. The director has asked me to bring it to DC for further analysis. You boys have had more than enough time with it and can't seem to decrypt. We're taking over from here."

Bolles said, "This is highly improper, sir. I was instructed not to let this drive out of my sight. I've been working on the encryption for weeks now."

Cromley said, "And you've come up with nothing, which is why I am taking over. It's been far too long with no progress. Time to let the big boys handle this."

"I don't know sir; I was given strict instructions. I'm going to need to make a call."

"Agent Bolles, are you seriously questioning my authority here? Need I remind you who I am?"

"No sir, I uh . . . it's just that I have my orders."

"And I am overriding your orders. Now hand me the drive."

Bolles reached over and removed the drive from the computer and handed it to Cromley. "I'll need to let Special Agent Saxon know about this. As you know, he's the lead investigator, and he has asked me to keep him apprised of everything as relates to the drive."

"He should already be aware that I am taking over this aspect of the investigation. Your whole team is incompetent, which is why I've had to come down here in person to assume responsibility. I'll have this drive decrypted in no time."

Chapter 42

XANDER AND ASHLEY WAITED until after 4:00 P.M. and made their way to the dirt road through a preserve that bordered the rear yard of Sinkfield's property. Xander suspected that would be where Yao and Chen would go; it was the most vulnerable access point. They pulled over, drove into the woods, and covered the SUV with branches, proceeded on foot, and found their way to a heavily wooded area inside the preserve that separated a small number of very private, very large, and very expensive homes situated on many acres of secluded land.

Continuing closer to Sinkfield's land, they came to an even denser grouping of trees and saw the SUV they had been trailing, also partially hidden in the brush. Minutes later, Yao exited the vehicle wearing a backpack. He disappeared deeper into the woods while Chen remained behind. Kneeling behind a tree and peering around, Ashley whispered, "Why don't we get her now? She's all alone. We can surprise her and take her down."

"We're not authorized, and it's too dangerous. And taking her down will make a lot of noise. Besides, we don't know what level of communication she has with Yao, and we need to get them both.

Stu assured me that there will be agents on the premises, and once we know what Yao is up to, we can figure out our next move."

"Copy that, Sergeant." Ashley said, smiling. "So, what do *you* think they are up to?"

"My thinking is that these two spies are planning to take out one or more of the four traitors that were on the plane with your father."

"Wait, isn't that a good thing?"

"Not necessarily. We don't know who ordered the hit and what they may be trying to hide. We, and I'm not talking about you and I, but rather Stu Saxon and the FBI, need to make sure no one gets killed. After all, if Chen has a vaccine for the virus, she is a primary target and must be taken alive."

"Got it. Let's just hope she has a vaccine."

Chapter 43

IT WAS 6:30 P.M. and Dennie Sinkfield was on edge. He wasn't thrilled about having another meeting at his house with the gang of four. With every meeting they ran the risk of being exposed. Each had to dismiss their respective security detail, and that too was suspicious. Moreover, the virus was still spreading at an alarming rate. More and more people were becoming infected, and many were dying. Senator Strauss showed up first, a half hour early. As Sinkfield led him through the door, he could see the pained expression on the man's face. Perspiration had gathered across his forehead and his beady eyes blinked rapidly as he adjusted his mask. "Where's your mask, Dennie?"

Sinkfield shifted his gaze down and reached for his neck. "Give me a sec. I think I left it in the bathroom."

Strauss made his way into the expansive den, found the bar, and fixed a vodka on the rocks. He pushed the ice around with a stirrer, lowered his mask, took a long sip, and emptied the glass of its contents. He reached for the bottle again as Sinkfield entered the room. Strauss quickly pulled up his mask then poured himself another round.

Sinkfield said, "Mix one for me . . . make it a double."

Strauss said, "Under the circumstances, I think it might be safer if you poured your own, don't you think?"

Sinkfield huffed, "Whatever. Don't you think you're taking this a little too far? You're not sick." He walked behind the bar and fixed his own drink.

"We must take all precautions, Dennie. The pandemic is no joke. It seems every day, it's getting worse."

"Yes, but we've been isolated for some time now," Sinkfield said, "so we should be safe."

"Frankly, I don't want to take any chances," Strauss said, as he downed his second drink. "So do you have any idea why the General called this meeting?"

Sinkfield placed his finger in his glass, poked at the ice, pulled his mask down and took a sip. "Not exactly, but I suspect he wants to bring us up to date on a plan he's been working on. And I believe that Cromley may have secured the thumb drive."

"Well that sounds like good news for a change. But I came here early because there's something I wanted to discuss with you, so let's go outside. I'm not comfortable talking indoors, Dennie."

"Ever the cautious one, aren't you?"

"Someone has to be." Strauss poured himself another round and added more ice.

"You better go easy there, Aaron. You were never much of a drinker and the party hasn't even started yet." Sinkfield finished his drink and poured another. Glasses in hand, the two men walked out into the yard.

As they reached the pool area, Strauss began feeling the effects of the vodka. He placed his glass on the table and sat down.

Sinkfield sat across the table from Strauss and sipped his drink. "So, what did you want to discuss?"

Strauss said, "It's about Coggins. He seems to be enjoying all this. I mean, I appreciate how much he's done for the cause, and the end result will make it all worthwhile. We will get our power back and crush those progressive fools. It's just that I get the feeling that this is like a combat mission to the General. He's treating this like a war game—perhaps 'game' is a poor choice of words."

"It certainly isn't a game, but I understand where you're coming from. Coggins was in the military for almost forty years. He runs everything in his life that way. Everything is a mission to him. That's why the CIA has been so effective under his watch."

"Still, with his sights on the presidency, I'm concerned about the way he'll govern. Once this is over, we should think more seriously about a different candidate, but that's just between us. If Cromley ever found out about this, he would go straight to Coggins."

"You're right, we don't need any dissension right now. We're all in this together, and we must see it through to the end. Now let's get back inside. They should be here any minute."

Chapter 44

YAO HEARD THE ENTIRE conversation. He had returned to the property three hours earlier under the watchful eyes of Agents Fenton and Santry. They had him pegged since he scaled the stone wall and watched him as he climbed a tree not too far from where Fenton had set up his perch. They maintained radio silence, but both were concerned that the woman spy was nowhere to be seen. Either she had slipped by unnoticed, or she had stayed behind as backup. Either way, this posed a problem, but they would have to deal with it later. They were stuck in position and had to let things play out as planned.

Yao also noted that his target was one of the two men who had been talking in the yard, but he was instructed by Coggins not to make the hit until all four men were together, so he had to wait. The shot would have been easy, but he remained patient and followed his orders. That was how he always operated, and it had served him well. He leaned back against the trunk of the tree limb he was sitting on and went into meditation mode. He began by placing the tips of the fingers of both hands against each other as if making a steeple, then he slowly rolled his left thumb over, around, and down his right thumb, he did the same with his pointer finger and each one thereafter, finishing with his pinky. Then he started over, this time rolling his right pinky over his left and so on. He quickened the pace, moving all fingers simultaneously, continuing repeatedly, going faster and faster until, satisfied with the level of coordination, he stopped. Mind and body were aligned, and he was ready.

Chapter 45

C OGGINS AND CROMLEY ARRIVED within five minutes of each other. The gang of four now all in the den, Sinkfield went behind the bar to take drink orders. Coggins took a double scotch, neat, Cromley drank a club soda, and the two senators refilled their vodka.

Strauss said, "General, aren't you going to wear a mask?"

"Sorry to disappoint, Senator, but I don't carry one."

"I have spares."

"You don't get it Aaron. I don't believe in masks, haven't worn one, and don't intend to. They make you look weak and stupid. If the virus gets me, so be it, I'll take my lumps, but no one is going to make me put on one of those things, so if you're uncomfortable, just keep your distance."

Strauss looked over at Sinkfield for support. Sinkfield looked away, pulled down his mask, and took a long sip of his drink.

Coggins removed a cigar from his shirt pocket, placed it in his mouth, and reached into his pants pocket for a lighter. Sinkfield was visibly disturbed; he despised the odor of cigars and cigarettes and never let anyone smoke in his home, but his expression of displeasure went unnoticed under his mask.

Sinkfield said, "Gentlemen, let's move this party out back where we can talk."

"Good idea," Coggins said as he lit the cigar, blew out, and started chewing. Then he lifted the bottle of scotch from the bar and headed towards the back door. Cromley followed with the two senators close behind.

Coggins took a seat giving himself a view towards the rear of the property, knowing that Strauss would not want to sit close by and had to take a seat across the table from him, thus putting his back to the rear of the property. A perfect angle for a head shot from Yao. He didn't know exactly where Yao or his agents were positioned, but his seasoned guess was they were at the rear of the property up in the trees. Nevertheless, he was prepared, and carried a .22 strapped to his calf.

Cromley finally spoke up. "Gentlemen, I have some good news. I have the thumb drive in my possession." He reached inside his breast pocket and pulled out a small plastic bag that contained the drive.

Sinkfield said, "Have you been able to decrypt it?"

"Not yet. I only returned from Tampa with it this afternoon and came right over here. Tomorrow, I intend to have my boys look at it, and then it will be destroyed."

"Why not simply destroy it now?" asked Strauss. "Why risk any further exposure?"

"I'd like to see what it contains, and I also need to cover my tracks. Agent Saxon probably already knows I have this, and if I don't try to decrypt it, that, in and of itself, will be suspicious. So, I have to try, and whether I succeed or not, I will find a way to wipe it clean."

Chapter 46

$\smile\hspace{-0.5em}\bowtie\hspace{-0.5em}\smile$

V AN BUREN'S CELL VIBRATED. It was Stu Saxon.

"Xander, I think we may have a problem. I haven't been able to reach either of my two agents who should be on Sinkfield's premises. They were supposed to check in hours ago and have not responded to my calls."

"That doesn't sound good, Stu. We're situated about a half mile from the Sinkfield property in a preserve at the rear. Yao has been gone for well over three hours, and Chen is sitting in her vehicle hidden in the woods. We've got an eye on her. How do you want this handled?"

"Are you able to make your way to the home?"

"I should be able to, the woods are thick where I am. I'll just have to circle around so Chen can't see me."

"Okay, be careful. If my agents are down, that means there's a serious threat. I'm going to send a few more agents, but it may take some time."

"Copy that." Xander looked at Ashley. "You're going to have to stay here and out of sight. It's far too dangerous for you to come with me."

Ashley said, "I get it. I'll wait here and keep an eye on Chen. Just text me when you know what's going on."

"Will do."

Xander set off through the trees, redirecting his angle of approach to come in from the neighbor's property. There were still deep woods in the preserve and the sun was going down, so he felt comfortable that he could get close without being detected.

Chapter 47

THE AUTOMATIC LIGHTS CLICKED on outside as the sun set in the backyard of Sinkfield's home. The gang of four sat around the table by the pool area. Yao had the cross hairs of his rifle scope focused on Strauss, as he contacted Chen using his throat mic.

"Any activity on your end, Maria? I'm about ready to take out the target, just waiting for it to turn dark, probably another twenty minutes."

"All quiet here, just get it done and get out of there. I'll be waiting for you."

❋ ❋ ❋

CIA Agent Fenton could still see Yao through the trees and had his rifle pointed directly at him. He could see that Yao had his sights set in the direction of the men sitting at the table and planned to take him down as soon as Strauss was killed. Agent Santry had already relocated his position to a spot between Yao and the exit to the preserve by the dirt road, just in case Fenton missed the target. Still no sign of Chen, Santry surmised that she must be waiting nearby to assist but had sensed absolutely no movement for the past two hours. He lay in wait on the ground, covered in brush, his shoulder aching from the knife wound he had sustained in his scuffle earlier in the day with FBI Agent Cooper. The wound wasn't too deep, and he had managed to stop the bleeding, but it throbbed and hurt. He was no stranger to pain; he'd been wounded in Afghanistan years ago, before he joined the CIA. Then it registered with him; he remembered where he knew Cooper from. His team had joined forces with a team of new recruits before the urban assault where he was shot, and Cooper was part of that new team. He felt even worse now, knowing that he had killed a fellow soldier.

※ ※ ※

Coggins stood and pushed his chair away with the back of his thighs. He raised his glass, put down his cigar, and spit. "Time for a toast gentlemen. With the thumb drive now secured and chaos reining supreme throughout the country, President Bradshaw and the progressive pussies that are in control are finished. In the next few weeks, I intend to announce my run for the highest office in the land."

Cromley stood, emptied his club soda on the ground, and reached for the bottle of scotch that rested on the table near Coggins.

Coggins said, "It truly must be a special occasion for you to have a drink, Joe."

"That it is General." He raised his glass. "Here's to a new world order."

Sinkfield and Strauss stood and raised their glasses. In an instant Strauss collapsed, his glass falling to the ground and shattering on the bricks below.

Sinkfield raced over to Strauss, who lay on the ground with the front of his head missing and blood everywhere. He screamed, "Aaron, what the hell—Oh my God, he's been shot! He's—he's dead! Somebody do something!"

Coggins yelled, "Everyone move, get low and back to the house, there must be a sniper here!"

＊＊ ＊＊ ＊＊

Yao moved quickly after the shot hit its mark. When he stood to strap the rifle to his shoulder, he was grazed in the thigh with a bullet. Fenton had missed. He was aiming for a head shot, but Yao had moved too quickly. Yao lost his balance and fell, getting whipped by branches as he went down. When he landed, he twisted his ankle and broke his right arm. His face had been slashed as well, but his night vision goggles had protected his eyes. Luckily, the bullet had not gone deep into his thigh. He couldn't locate his rifle. He still had his throat communicator and called out to Chen. She didn't respond. He lay there for a time, not fully understanding what had just happened, until finally he was able to stand. Realizing he'd been shot; he pulled his pistol from the holster strapped to his hip. Limping, bleeding, and hurting all over, he made his way toward the stone wall.

＊＊ ＊＊ ＊＊

Ashley had already decided that she wasn't going to wait for Xander to return. She had her pistol and intended to surprise Chen and capture her on her own. Once darkness set in, she crept slowly through the woods and approached the vehicle from the rear. It was too dark to see inside, but she knew Chen was in the driver's seat, so she stayed low and slid along the ground, gun in hand. As she crawled past the driver-side rear tire, the driver-side passenger door opened suddenly and knocked Ashley to the ground, sending her pistol into the brush. Chen quickly leaped from the car and jumped on Ashley. The two grabbed at each other and Chen managed to land a blow to Ashley's side. Ashley reached up and clawed at Chen's face, scraping across her right eye and digging deep into her eye socket. Chen was momentarily blinded and lost her grip on Ashley, allowing her to roll away. She stood up just as Chen rose from the ground. The two faced off.

Chen shouted, "You again! I don't know what you're doing here, but you've just made your last mistake." She charged at Ashley, who raised her leg and pushed out a hard front kick maneuver she had learned and practiced years ago while taking her kickboxing lessons. She landed the blow directly to Chen's lower chest. It took the wind from her. Ashley stepped forward and rolled out a rear leg round kick to Chen's head. Chen blocked it, recovered her breath quickly and punched Ashley on the side of her head. Ashley fell back but remained on her feet. Chen moved forward and threw another wild punch. Ashley ducked under it and stepped forward, connecting with a right uppercut to Chen's jaw. Ashley was surprised at how much the blow hurt her hand, forgetting that she had always worn boxing gloves when she practiced, so she wasn't prepared, but neither was Chen. The blow hit its mark and broke a few of Chen's teeth. She spit them out. Enraged she swung wildly at Ashley.

Ashley stepped back and felt the gun beneath her foot. She quickly dropped down and reached for it, but Chen was on her before she could grab it. The two began to wrestle on the ground. Chen was now on top throwing punches wildly as Ashley kept deflecting them with her arms. She used her hips and thighs and grabbed Chen's shoulder and managed to roll her off and onto her side. Ashley pulled away, stood, and tried to kick Chen, but Chen deflected it with her forearm as she rose from the ground. The two stood face to face again, each waiting for the other to make a move.

※ ※ ※

Xander heard the commotion by the pool and saw the men ducking for cover at about the same time he heard sounds of something crashing through the trees towards the rear of the property. It was almost completely dark, but the moon was out, and it gave him some light through the trees. He moved slowly towards the sounds in the direction of the preserve along a partially standing stone wall that bordered the property. He stopped in his tracks when he saw a figure climbing down from a pine tree. Xander watched as the figure raced in the direction of the sounds he had heard. It was clear there were multiple operatives on the property, and any movement by him could alert them. He took out his pistol and stayed in position for a time before moving again.

Agent Fenton came down from the tree and ran towards Yao to finish him off. He knew that Agent Santry would be nearby, but they couldn't let Yao escape alive. He put on his night vision goggles, which made it much easier to traverse the brush. As he got closer to Yao's position, he could see the man limping toward the stone wall at the back of the property. He then saw Santry racing towards Yao from the other direction. Yao saw him too, raised his pistol and fired off two shots. Santry returned fire but was hit and went down.

Shots rang out up ahead of Xander. As he got closer, more shots went off. He held his position and began to worry about Ashley, and whether she would stay in hiding after hearing the shots fired. He took out his phone and texted Stu Saxon.

Xander: I'm in a hot zone, multiple shots fired. I've seen
3 men so far. Are your agents on the premises?
Saxon: No, they're still 30 minutes out. Stay out of sight,
you can't go up against those odds.
Xander: Copy that. Also commotion at house, I heard
some yelling, someone maybe shot and killed.
Saxon: Ok, just stay where you are and wait for my
agents.
Xander: I can't do that, I left Ashley behind. I have to
make sure she's OK.

❋ ❋ ❋

Yao managed to locate a break along the stone wall and squeezed
his way through. Santry had been shot in the chest and lay on the
ground. Fenton ran over to assess his condition, and when he saw
the wound, he knew there was no hope. He left him and gave chase
to Yao, following him through the broken area of the stone wall
and into the preserve. With his night-vision goggles, he could see
Yao up ahead, but with the density of the woods, he didn't have a
clear shot. Yao limped, weaving his way through the preserve as
Fenton gained on him. Yao stopped behind a large tree, called out
to Chen on the throat mic and fired off multiple shots from his
pistol. Fenton returned fire.

❋ ❋ ❋

Ashley and Chen circled one another, each looking for an opening to
attack. Shots rang out, startling both. Chen charged. Ashley jabbed
with her right hand and threw a left cross. Chen was unprepared
for a left-handed response and took a blow to her nose, breaking it.

She went down and Ashley grabbed the gun from the ground and shouted, "Don't move, or I'll shoot you dead right here!"

Still groggy, Chen reached up, felt her nose, and looked at the blood on her hand. "I underestimated you, but this is not over yet."

Ashley said, "It looks over to me, I'm the one standing here with the gun."

⁕ ⁕ ⁕

Yao stayed low and continued moving from tree to tree while looking back and searching for movement in the woods behind him. Clouds settled above the forest and the moon disappeared. Within seconds, the sky opened, unleashing torrential rains. Lightning flashed and thunder followed, drowning out the silence.

Fenton had already moved more directly towards the dirt road, figuring he could circle around from the north, rather than chasing blindly towards Yao, who not only had night vision goggles, but who also appeared very adept at combat in the woods. He wasn't going to make the same mistake as Santry did and get himself killed.

Limping, Yao continued zigzagging on an indirect route through the preserve, inching his way closer to the road, but Fenton was much faster and exited the woods before him. He crossed the road, reentered the woods on the other side and eased his way along, masked by the sounds of the pouring rain. When he found a good vantage point, he dropped to the ground, propped his rifle on an outcropping of rocks, and waited.

⁕ ⁕ ⁕

Xander scaled the fence and cut through the neighbor's property to the south and into the clearing in the backyard. The storm clouds had covered the moon, so it was easy for him to make it through quickly.

And with the two men focusing on each other, he had no trouble getting through the preserve behind the neighbor's land. The only thing on his mind was getting to Ashley before it was too late. Within minutes he was soaked, but he was much further along than the other men and getting close to the dirt road. He knew that once he reached the road, he would have to be extra cautious, because Chen would have heard the gunfire and could be headed back in the direction of the sounds. He just hoped Ashley stayed in position behind the trees.

* * *

Drenched, Yao made it through the preserve, dragging his leg as he headed towards Chen. Fenton spotted him up ahead and lined him up in the cross hairs of his scope. He had a clear shot, but a flash of lightning lit the sky, momentarily blinding him. The night-vision goggles absorbed too much light and he lost his target. He waited, readjusted, caught another glimpse of Yao working his way further down the road, sited him and fired. Yao was propelled forward and hit the ground face down. Fenton sidled across the road, approaching the fallen man cautiously, but Yao was dead.

* * *

Xander was within 50 feet of where one man had been shot and watched as the other man approached him. Not knowing which, if either, was on his side, he held his position and waited, watching as Fenton checked the downed man. Confirming he was dead, Fenton moved on and Xander followed him as he continued slowly along the tree line in the direction of where Xander had left Ashley, Chen, and their SUV.

* * *

Ashley had located a rope and duct tape in the back of Chen's SUV, lashed her to a tree, and taped her mouth after placing a sock in it. She had been waiting out of sight for fifteen minutes. She had heard the gunfire and did not know whether Xander or Yao would show up. She was soaked, shivering from the cold, and scared.

Fenton crept along the edge of the forest panning back and forth with his night-vision goggles. As he came closer to Chen's SUV, he was able to make out the muffled sounds coming from Chen as she tried to holler through the tape.

He edged his way through the woods and came up to the SUV. A few feet away he found Chen tied to the tree. Ashley remained hiding in the distance.

Fenton smiled and said, "Well, well, looks like someone did my work for me. Now all I have to do is finish the job." He pulled his pistol from his hip and pointed it at Chen's head. "But before you die, I want you to know that your partner is dead. I killed him after he finished his job. He outlived his usefulness and now it's your turn." He tore the duct tape from her mouth. "Any last words?"

Chen spit out the sock. "You won't kill me, I'm the only one who has the vaccine for the virus."

Ashley stepped out from where she was hiding. "She's right, we don't want to kill her. We need the vaccine."

Fenton turned and pointed his pistol at her. "Whoa, and who might you be?"

"I'm on your side, so put down the pistol. You don't need to kill her. Se's too valuable—we need her alive."

Fenton lowered his weapon and took on an apologetic tone. "Look Miss, you apparently have no idea who you're dealing with. There is no *we* here. I have a job to do, and I can't leave any witnesses, so I'm sorry to say, but you're not leaving here alive either." As Fenton raised his pistol, Ashley jumped behind the tree.

Ashley shouted, "I'm working with the FBI. Why are you doing this?"

* * *

Xander heard Ashley shout and saw Fenton up ahead. He charged Fenton and hit him in his lower back. Fenton dropped the pistol but was quick to respond and very strong. He rolled Xander off and reached for a knife that was attached to his belt. As Fenton raised it up above his head to stab Xander, a shot rang out. He collapsed and Ashley stepped out from behind the tree. Wounded, Fenton tried to roll over and reach for the pistol that lay beside him. Ashley shot him again, killing him.

Xander said, "Ashley, are you okay?"

"I'm fine. What's going on here?"

"I'm not sure, but Stu Saxon sent more agents. They should be here any minute." Xander looked up at Chen tied to the tree. "How'd you manage to pull that off?"

Ashley smiled. "I told you I had some skills."

"Impressive."

* * *

Coggins, Cromley, and Sinkfield were back in the house. They had heard additional gunfire coming from the rear of Sinkfield's yard.

Panicked, Sinkfield said. "Aaron is dead. We've been breached. That could have been any one of us lying dead outside."

Coggins removed his pistol from his calf holster. "Just relax, Dennie, it's all under control. I've got a couple of my men out there, and they'll track down the shooter."

Sinkfield said, "Men? You have agents in my backyard? Our meetings were supposed to be secret! No security detail, remember?"

Coggins said, "We received some intel that the spy who killed Bingham and his wife would be coming after us, so I took extra precautions. My agents are loyal to the core and support our cause. This was the best way to smoke him out and get the girl spy as well. It's unfortunate that we lost Strauss, but it's a small price to pay to capture the spies. I suspect that very soon my men will have apprehended them and that will solidify my bid for the presidency."

Sinkfield took on a challenging tone. "You planned this from the get-go, didn't you Bill? Using us as human targets? How could you be so sure that you wouldn't be the one to get shot and killed?"

Coggins spread a flat smile, "I'm the best at what I do, haven't you realized that yet Dennie?"

"I don't doubt that for a minute, but this is way too coincidental." Looking at Cromley accusingly, Sinkfield said, "What about you Joe? What was your role in all of this?"

Cromley said, "What are you suggesting here? I don't have a clue about any of this."

"Please, you're the assistant to the head of the FBI, you can't expect me to believe you weren't in on this. The two of you have always been in lock step." His eyes darted back and forth between Coggins and Cromley. "I'm no fool, you two concocted this whole thing. You wanted Strauss out of the picture. Somehow you knew he was unsure about supporting your bid for the presidency." Looking at Coggins he said, "Am I next? Are you going to eliminate me?"

"Calm down, Dennie. You're imagining things. Trust me, this will all work out. Joe's got the thumb drive and soon we'll have captured the virologist spy that created the virus. A vaccine won't be too far off." Coggins took out a cigar, bit off the end, chewed and swallowed it. He made his way to the bar, put his pistol on the bar top, removed another bottle of scotch from within and poured himself a drink. "Are you men going to join me?" He lit the cigar. "Time for a celebratory toast."

Cromley walked over to the bar. "I'll take a scotch, Bill."

Senator Sinkfield sat down on the couch shaking his head. "This is a bit too much for me. Aaron is lying dead on the ground from a bullet to the head and you two men are toasting. There's something wrong with this picture."

Coggins poured a scotch for Cromley. The two men clicked glasses and drank.

✳ ✳ ✳

Special Agent Stu Saxon had heard the entire conversation from the bugs placed by Agents Maxwell and Cooper. He was also in possession of evidence collected at the office of Senator Strauss along with a recorded conversation between Cromley and Coggins obtained from the bugs in both of their vehicles. The most damaging evidence, though, came from the computer taken out of Bingham's jet. Saxon's team had been able to fix the audio issues with the recording, and that meeting, along with the other evidence, was more than sufficient to obtain arrest warrants.

✳ ✳ ✳

Agents Cash and Culpepper were three minutes from the Sinkfield residence when Agent Saxon's phone rang.

"Xander, I've been worried about you. What's going on over there?

"We've got everything under control. Yao is dead, along with a couple of rogue CIA agents. But we've got the girl, and she's very much alive."

"Well, that's good news. Any info on my two agents that were on premises?"

"I never saw them, but I suspect they're dead. There was a lot of gunfire, but all is quiet now. When are your other agents going to get here?"

"They should arrive any minute. I've got them going to the house to secure it."

"Okay, we'll drive around to the front and meet them there with the girl."

"No, hold off on that until my agents secure the house. We were able to get the audio from Bingham's jet, and it was enough to obtain arrest warrants. Attorney General Hammer is in the loop, and one of his men has already been to Judge Faber's home. The warrants have been signed, and I'll have them in a few minutes. Then I'll email them to my agents, so they can make the arrests. Until then my agents will be waiting outside. I don't want the traitors trying to leave before the warrants come through. Coggins is a dangerous guy and Cromley's a slime, so until they are secured you need to wait."

"Understood."

※ ※ ※

Agents Cash and Culpepper approached the Sinkfield residence with caution. Cash went around back and Culpepper waited in the bushes by the front door. Both had their guns drawn. Cash moved into position in the rear yard and located a spot where he was able to see in through a window. Coggins stood by the bar and Cash could see the pistol on the bar top within Coggins' reach. He radioed to Culpepper.

"Z, I see the three men in the den. Coggins is standing at the bar with Cromley, and he's got a pistol nearby. Sinkfield is sitting on the couch. I've checked the back door and it's unlocked, so as soon as we get the warrants, you can ring the bell. I'll enter from here."

"Copy that."

Minutes later the warrants came through. Culpepper signaled Cash and rang the doorbell. Coggins said, "That must be my agents. Go answer the door, Dennie."

Sinkfield rose from the couch, walked down the hall to the front door and opened it. "Good evening, Senator, I'm FBI Special Agent Zeke Culpepper." He flashed his badge, pushed his way past Sinkfield and moved slowly towards the den.

As soon as Coggins heard "FBI" he grabbed his gun and pointed it towards the entrance to the den.

Cash spoke through his mouthpiece, "Z, Coggins has his gun in hand. He's looking towards the entrance to the den and has his back to me. I'm coming in from the rear."

Cash quietly opened the door and shouted, "FBI. Put down the gun, General."

Coggins spun around and pointed his pistol at Cash.

Culpepper entered the den pointing his gun. "You don't want to do that General. Drop the weapon. NOW!"

Coggins said, "Who are you two? You have no authority here. Let me see your warrant."

Cash was firm, "Once more General, put the weapon down."

Cromley said, "Agents, as Assistant Director of the FBI, I order you to stand down."

Cash moved towards Coggins. "I'm afraid we can't do that sir. We have warrants, and you're all under arrest."

Coggins placed his gun on the floor and Cash retrieved it.

Culpepper said, "All of you, down on the ground, put your hands behind your backs."

Cromley demanded, "Show me the warrants."

Culpepper said, "You'll see them once you've been cuffed. Now MOVE!"

The three men obliged and were handcuffed. Culpepper took out his phone and produced the digital copies of the warrants.

Cash called Saxon. "We've got them, sir. We're all secured here."

Saxon said, "I'm already on my way, along with more backup. This is going to be a long night. You can expect Xander Van Buren to show up shortly with the girl spy. Apparently, there are a number of dead bodies in the vicinity as well."

"Copy that."

Chapter 48

✦

NEWSFLASH - AP Wire:

Yesterday evening FBI agents arrested CIA Director William Coggins, along with FBI Assistant Director Joseph Cromley and Senator Dennie Sinkfield at the senator's home in rural Virginia. Senator Aaron Strauss was also found dead at the scene from a sniper shot to the head, in what authorities have described as a major undercover FBI operation that has exposed corruption at the highest levels of government. A source, who spoke on condition of anonymity because he has no authority to speak on behalf of the FBI, advised that the four men were involved in a plot to overthrow the government. The source stated that the men were working with the Chinese, who created the super virus that led to the current pandemic. Agents stormed the Sinkfield home after uncovering video evidence of the men conspiring to commit treason.

As the agents searched the surrounding premises, they discovered the bodies of two FBI agents, two CIA agents and a Chinese spy. In all, including Senator Strauss, six were pronounced dead at the scene and another spy was apprehended. She is alive and is suspected to be the mastermind behind the virus. Her name was not released, and the investigation is ongoing.

Chapter 49

MARIA CHEN WAS BEING held at FBI headquarters in Langley, Virginia. Initial attempts to get her to talk proved futile. She had demanded an attorney; however, as a noncitizen spy, she was not entitled to U.S. Constitutional protections. At least that's what Special Agent Stu Saxon and his team told her. They kept her hands cuffed behind her back in a holding cell for twelve hours before Saxon made one last attempt to get her to talk. She was then ushered into a large conference room with only Saxon present. He removed her handcuffs.

Saxon offered her a chair at the table, "Please sit down. Can I get you something to drink?"

Chen said, "Oh, so now you're going to play Mr. Nice Guy after treating me like a war criminal?"

"Standard operating procedure, Ms. Chen. You're a spy and a threat to my country, but I will give you one last chance to help yourself. We know you have the formula for the vaccine, and we're willing to offer you a deal if you provide it and information on who you work for."

"Apparently you don't know much about me or what I believe in. You are wasting your time."

Saxon remained standing on the other side of the table. He turned and looked at the mirror, then back to Chen. "If you go to trial on the crimes you are charged with, you'll get the death penalty. Plain and simple. Tell us what we want to know, make a deal, and I'll have that taken off the table. You'll get life in prison."

"That's your offer?" Chen chuckled. "To me that means nothing. Send me back to my country, and I will give them the vaccine. That is the only deal I will make."

"Look, Ms. Chen, you don't have much of a choice. We already have your blood and Yao's blood. Our scientists are examining it as we speak, and they will soon be able to synthesize a vaccine. It's only a matter of time."

"Yes, but time is a valuable commodity, and the virus is spreading as we speak. How many more dead are you and your country willing to accept?"

Saxon sat down, "You're mistaken if you think you have any bargaining power here. I assure you, this is your last chance. The only offer on the table is life in prison. There is no way that the FBI can justify to the American people that a spy who created a pandemic is simply being returned to her country—as if deportation would be considered some sort of punishment. This is far too public, and the American people want to see justice done. So, I'm going to give you one last chance. It's now or never. Make the deal or it's the death penalty."

Chen leaned back in her chair, thought for a moment then reached into the back of her mouth and pulled at her furthest left molar and twisted it out. Before Saxon realized what she was doing she bit into the false tooth, released the cyanide, and swallowed. In seconds, her mouth started to foam up, she began convulsing and fell out of her chair. Saxon raced around the table, but it was too late, Chen would be dead in minutes, and there was nothing he could do about it.

Chapter 50

AFTER TWO DAYS OF rest and reflection, Ashley Bingham arrived at the office of Xander Van Buren to meet with him and his brother, Griff. The meeting was called to go over Douglas Bingham's estate.

Xander led Ashley into the conference room and sat down next to her. Griff came in with a large file, placed it on the table and sat down across from them.

Griff smiled. "Well, I'm glad everything worked out. It looks like the good guys actually won this one."

Xander said, "Not entirely, bro. Don't get ahead of yourself. The pandemic is still out there, and Maria Chen managed to commit suicide before giving up the vaccine, so all the scientists are left with is samples of her blood."

"True, but thankfully you're both alive and the evil at the top levels of our government has been rooted out and will be punished accordingly."

"Agreed." Looking back at Ashley, Xander said. "And Stu also told me that when his technology team went through the computer from your jet, the video that was all static actually contained the password to the thumb drive. The FBI has been able to access it and all the evidence against the three men." Looking back at Griff, he said, "Now tell Ashley what you've found out about the Bingham estate."

Griff pulled some papers from the file. "Yes, well there's a lot going on here. First, since Layni died before your father, you are the sole beneficiary of everything in the estate. The physical assets like the mansion, the cars, the yacht, the airplane, they are all owned free and clear. You are now the majority shareholder of Bingham International Ltd., which is involved in international trade. It is a private company with an approximate value of over 400 million dollars. You are also the sole shareholder of Synergy Properties, LLC and Luxor Corp. Synergy and Luxor are basically investment vehicles."

"Meaning what?"

"Synergy is primarily a REIT, that is a real estate investment trust, which owns rental properties ranging from multifamily homes to apartment complexes and retail stores, strip malls, shopping centers and the like. Based upon the information your father's accountants provided, the value is somewhere in the neighborhood of 75 million dollars. There is a management company that handles all the properties."

"And what about Luxor?"

Griff rubbed his chin with his thumb and index finger and looked over to Xander.

Xander said, "I'll take it from here." He looked at Ashley. "Apparently, your father was working with an investment advisor friend of his named Grant Perkins. Perkins did all the investing in the financial markets for your dad through this company. It is an entity created in Switzerland that invests in stocks, commodities, and derivatives."

"Derivatives, what are they?"

Griff interjected, "In simple terms, derivatives are options, futures, and other types of secondary ways to play the market. They offer a lot more leverage than simply buying stock, but they are also a lot riskier."

Xander said, "Yes, and in this particular circumstance, it appears that the investments were made in contemplation of the pandemic."

"I don't understand."

"It's like this, your father knew that the virus was going to affect the world economy, so in anticipation of this, he and his advisor selected various derivative products, as well as stocks and commodities that would either go up or down, based upon the industry the company was in. They believed that the economy would tank and the stock in many companies would drop significantly, while in some sectors the company stock would go up."

"So, what does all this mean?"

Griff said, "In broad terms, the investments were very profitable, and this company is worth around 150 million dollars at present value."

Ashley stood and placed her palms on the table. Shaking her head she said, "Well, this is dirty money. I can't accept that. It's just wrong."

Xander said, "Ashley, the money is yours. What you choose to do with it is up to you."

"I can't believe my father would do something like this. It's now clear to me that he did this all for profit. This is terrible."

"I'm sorry you had to find out about it like this, but either way, the money is yours."

Deep in thought, Ashley began pacing.

Xander said, "Look, you don't have to make a quick decision about this. You're a very rich woman and you have many options. Give it some thought."

"No, this is something I have to do right now. That money is blood money! I can't accept it." She turned to Xander and looked him directly in the eyes. "What if you were to set up a charity of some kind, perhaps one that gives the money to the families of those who suffered and died from the virus?"

Xander said, "That is certainly an option."

"Yes, that's it then. I want all that money to go to charity, and I want you to handle it."

Xander said, "That's very commendable, but are you sure? You're talking about a huge amount of money."

"I haven't been surer of anything in my life. From everything else you've told me, I have more than enough to live on for the rest of my life, and at least by doing this I can hopefully try to get past what my father was a part of." She began to cry. "Just take care of it for me, I don't want to have anything to do with any of it."

Xander took her in his arms and held her tight as she sobbed. After a few seconds, Ashley gazed up into Xander's eyes and pulled him towards her, offering her lips to his. The two engaged in a long, passionate kiss. Xander pulled back, wiped a tear from Ashley's eye and they kissed again.

Epilogue

NEWSFLASH - AP Wire

CIA Director William Coggins aka "The General," was found dead of an apparent suicide in his cell at the Federal Detention Center in Washington, DC. The death is being reported as suspicious under the circumstances. Insiders are questioning how such a high-profile individual would be left alone in his cell long enough to hang himself with bed sheets. Jailhouse officials were asked why he wasn't put on a suicide watch from day one, but no one seems to have any answers. The Senate Judiciary Committee has opened a new investigation, and sources say they will be focusing on disgraced Senator Dennie Sinkfield, who has agreed to turn state's evidence and testify against FBI Assistant Director Joseph Cromley in exchange for leniency and a plea deal. Cromley continues to assert the position that he was operating undercover to root out the individuals involved in the plot to undermine the current administration. He has told reporters that he learned about the conspiracy between Coggins, the senators and Chinese oligarchs early on and was gathering evidence to use to indict Director Coggins but had to build his case with caution. He claims that the meeting where he was arrested was set up with the intent to secure tape recordings of Coggins implicating himself and that he understood two of his FBI agents were in position at the scene in order to secure the recordings. He further states that they were killed at the scene, murdered by rogue CIA agents that Coggins had stationed there.

In response to those claims, Senator Sinkfield is prepared to testify that Cromley was an integral part of the entire operation. Early evidence suggests that Sinkfield's claims are supported by the evidence. The FBI advises that they have video and audio evidence of the conspiracy but cannot release the tapes. Unnamed sources advise that the tapes are of conversations among the conspirators that clearly indicate that Cromley was a fully involved and willing partner who helped to orchestrate the treasonous plot. The FBI also stated that Cromley has tested positive for the super virus. As a precaution, he has been isolated and placed on a suicide watch in his cell.

On another important note, top medical scientists are confident that through analysis of the blood of the two Chinese spies, they may be able to synthesize an effective vaccine to the virus.

❈ ❈ ❈

Doug Bingham sat up in his lounge chair on the beach at the Myakoba Resort in Tulum, Mexico. His shoulder was still bandaged, and he winced in pain, but smiled at Candace Lansiquot who approached carrying a pair of tropical drinks clipped with slices of pineapple. She looked spectacular in a colorful sarong she had wrapped around her waist, her smile evident beneath oversized Gucci sunglasses.

Also available on Kindle, by Howard K. Pollack:

EVERYWHERE THAT TOMMY GOES

In a story inspired by actual events, a young man is accused of serial murder and to clear his name he must face the truth about his troubled childhood, a mysterious enemy, and a secret so dark it will make him question his own innocence.

An attractive young bartender goes missing from a popular New York City hot spot and the only evidence found at the scene points to Tommy Sullivan. Fearing arrest, he runs, and is secretly followed by his new friend Troyer Savage. When an even more horrific murder occurs and Troyer vanishes in its wake, Tommy is left in a stupor, bathed in the victim's blood.

As his blackouts and memory lapses multiply, Tommy becomes lost between nightmare and reality. Things only get worse for him when the police build a case that links him to bodies buried in shallow graves among the sand dunes at Gilgo Beach on Long Island.

With the police in hot pursuit and the psychological tension building by the minute, the action never lets up as Tommy pieces together parts of the puzzle from clues buried deep within his tragic childhood. However, the dark secrets from his past may belie the actual truth.

Howard Pollack, a practicing attorney in New York, is also the author of the well-reviewed mystery thriller, EVERYWHERE THAT TOMMY GOES, loosely based on the Gilgo Beach murders on Long Island.

Made in the USA
Middletown, DE
18 June 2022

67385578R00149